The Informer

'*The Informer* by Liam O'Flaherty must be accounted a little masterpiece of its kind ... his portrait of the brutish informer is so marvellously vivid, and his whole narrative, with its slowly increasing atmosphere of terror, so perfectly unfolded that the book must be ranked very high indeed ... easily its author's best work. It is a quite unforgettable story.'

Sunday Times

The Wilderness

'*The Wilderness* is essentially a simple story of unbridled passions, frustrated ambitions and hunger for land, but in the hands of O'Flaherty it becomes a *tour de force* that tears through the mind with the careless abandon of an Atlantic breaker.'

Sunday Press

The Black Soul

'Embodies an energy that is genius.'

W.B. Yeats

'An elemental book because the primitive passions run free.'

AE

Famine

'A major achievement — a masterpiece. The kind of truth only a major writer of fiction is capable of portraying.'

Anthony Burgess

'The author's skill as a storyteller is at times breathtaking. This is a most rewarding novel.'

Publishers Weekly

'A marvellously visual writer who prints his description on the retina.'

The Guardian

Skerrett

'One of the most powerful novels that this master-writer has ever produced.'

The Irish Times

'Liam O'Flaherty is a great, great writer whose work must be unique in any language, any culture. He has all the potential for becoming a matrix for the yearnings of another generation.'

Neil Jordan

'Powerful in language, majestic in scope, utterly honest.'

Sunday Press

LIAM O'FLAHERTY
The Informer

WOLFHOUND PRESS

This edition published in 1999 by
Wolfhound Press Ltd
68 Mountjoy Square
Dublin 1, Ireland
Tel: (353-1) 874 0354
Fax: (353-1) 872 0207

Published 1925, 1958, 1964, 1971, 1980
© This edition 1999 Liam O'Flaherty

 Wolfhound Press receives financial assistance from the Arts Council/An Chomhairle Ealaíon, Dublin.

British Library Cataloguing in Publication Data
A catalogue record for this book is available from the British Library.

ISBN 0-86327-677-6

10 9 8 7 6 5 4 3 2 1

To my beloved Margareteen

Cover Photograph: The Father Browne SJ Collection
Cover Design: Sally Mills-Westley
Typesetting: Wolfhound Press
Printed and bound by the Guernsey Press Co. Ltd, Guernsey, Channel Islands

LIAM O'FLAHERTY

Born in 1896 on Inishmore, the largest of the Aran Islands, Liam O'Flaherty grew up in a world of awesome beauty, echoes from his ancestors and the ancient pagan past. From his father, a Fenian, O'Flaherty inherited a rebellious streak; from his mother, a noted *seanchaí*, came the deep spirituality and love of nature that has enraptured readers through the decades.

In France in 1917, O'Flaherty was severely shell-shocked. After eight months' recuperation, he spent several restless years travelling the globe. In 1920 he supported the Republican cause against the Free State government. Influenced by the Industrial Workers of the World's programme of social revolution, O'Flaherty organised the seizure and occupation of the Rotunda Theatre at the top of Dublin's O'Connell Street in 1922. He hoisted the red flag of revolution, calling himself the 'Chairman of the Council of the Unemployed', but fled three days later to avoid bloodshed. Later that year he moved to London, where his writing skills came to the attention of critic Edward Garnett, who recommended to Jonathan Cape the publication of O'Flaherty's first novel. For the next two decades, O'Flaherty's creative output was astonishing. Writing in English and Irish, he produced novels, memoirs and short stories by the dozen. Remarkable for their literary value and entertainment, O'Flaherty's books are also crucial in their charting of the ways and beliefs of a peasant world before it was eclipsed by modernity.

Like the work of many authors of his time much of O'Flaherty's work was banned in Ireland. Liam O'Flaherty died in Dublin in 1984, aged eighty-eight years, having enriched forever Irish literature and culture.

Other books by LIAM O'FLAHERTY
available from WOLFHOUND PRESS

FICTION

Famine
Short Stories: The Pedlar's Revenge
The Wilderness
Skerrett
Insurrection
The Assassin
The Ecstasy of Angus
Thy Neighbour's Wife
The Black Soul
Return of the Brute
Mr Gilhooley

AUTOBIOGRAPHY

Shame the Devil

FOR CHILDREN

The Test of Courage
All Things Come of Age

OTHER

A Tourist's Guide to Ireland
The Letters of Liam O'Flaherty
(Edited by A.A. Kelly)

FORTHCOMING

The Collected Stories of Liam O'Flaherty

CHAPTER ONE

It was three minutes to six o'clock in the evening of 15 March 192—.

Francis Joseph McPhillip ran up the concrete steps leading to the glass-panelled swing door that acted as street entrance to the Dunboy Lodging House. The House, as it was called in Dublin, among criminal and pauperised circles, was a grey concrete building of four stories. It stood on the left-hand side of a wide wind-swept asphalt lane off B— Road on the south side of the city. A maze of slum streets surrounded it. An indefinable smell of human beings living in a congested area filled the air around it. From the building itself, a smell of food and of floors being scrubbed with soap and hot water emanated.

A drizzling rain was falling from a black bulging sky. Now and again a flock of hailstones, driven by a sudden gust of querulous wind, clattered down the lane, falling in little dancing groups on the hard, perspiring asphalt.

McPhillip ran up the four steps and peered into the hall hurriedly through the glass door. He put his face so close to the glass that his excited breath caused an immediate blur of vapour on the frozen pane. Then he turned about. He crouched against the angle of the doorway and peered around the corner of the wall, up the lane through which he had just come. He wanted to find out whether anybody was following him. He was a murderer.

He had killed the secretary of the local branch of the Farmers' Union during the farm-labourers' strike at M— in the previous October. Since then he had been hiding out in the mountains with a group of men who were evading arrest; brigands, criminals and political refugees. He had just come into Dublin half an hour previously on a goods train. The conductor of the train was a member of the Revolutionary Organisation, to which McPhillip himself had belonged when he shot the Farmers' Union secretary.

He saw nobody of account in the lane. An old woman crossed near the far end. She had a black shawl about her head and in her hand a milk-jug, with a corner of the shawl drawn across its mouth to keep out the rain. A man was singing forlornly, facing the kerb on the right-hand side, with his cap held out in front of him. He was begging, but nobody took any notice of him.

McPhillip's eyes darted about everywhere, with the speed and acuteness of one who has perfected his detective sensibilities by necessity and long practice. The street was quite safe. He sighed and turned about to survey the interior of the House.

He was a man of middle size and slightly built, but his shoulders were broad enough for a giant. His body narrowed down from the shoulders, so that the hips and waist were totally out of proportion to the upper part of the body. His right leg opened outwards in a curve below the knee and he placed the toe of the right foot on the ground before the heel when he walked, so that his walk had the crouching appearance of a wild animal stalking in a forest. His face was thin and sallow. His hair was black and cropped close. His eyebrows were black and bushy. His eyelashes were long and they continually drooped over his eyes. When his eyelashes drooped his eyes were blue, sharp and fierce. But when he raised his lashes for a moment to think of something distant and perhaps imaginary, his eyes were large, wistful and dreamy. They were soft and full of a sorrow that was unfathomable. His jaws were square, sharp and fleshless. His lips were thin and set tightly. This gave the lower part of his face a ferocious appearance. His nose was long and straight. His cheeks were hollow and on the cheekbones a bright flush appeared when he was seized with a fit of hard, dry coughing which he tried to suppress.

He was dressed in a shabby pair of wrinkled navy blue trousers and a fawn-coloured, shabby raincoat, buttoned up around his throat like a uniform. His boots were old and thin. They creaked with moisture soaked in through their torn soles. He wore a grey tweed cap. Under his left armpit he carried an automatic pistol in a leather holster. The pistol hung from a lanyard that was suspended from his neck.

As he stood looking in through the door, the fingers of his right hand were thrust in between the first and second buttons of his raincoat. The tips of the fingers rested on the cold butt of the automatic.

Within the hall three old men were waiting in a row outside the closed glass window of the office on the right-hand side. The nearest old man to the door wore a brown pauper's uniform. Both his eyes had cataracts and he seemed to be on the point of going into a faint. He was leaning on a stick and his head kept bobbing like a man that is in a drunken stupor and is on the point of falling asleep. The second old man wore a torn old dress suit. He looked like a waiter thrown out of employment through old age. He had a sharp lean face. The farthest old man was dressed in a medley of unspeakable rags and he shook his body continually trying to scratch himself on the insides of his clothes. The three of them stood in silence. Beyond them, four more concrete steps led to a long passage through the building. A corridor crossed the passage at the far end. Men passed along the corridor now and again in groups.

McPhillip was about to push through the door when the glass panel was pulled up with a screech and a man's head appeared at the window. The man cracked his thumb and forefinger and motioned the nearest old man to approach, the old man dressed in rags. The old man started and cried out in a weak, childish voice: 'Oh be Janey I'd forgotten.' Smiling weakly and muttering to himself, he began to rummage among his rags. The man at the window looked at him, pursed up his lips angrily and disappeared.

Presently he reappeared from around the corner of the office. He came up to the old man and stood in front of him with his hands on his hips and his legs spread wide apart. His neat blue trousers were perfectly creased. He was in his shirt-sleeves, so that his diamond sleeve-links and the large diamond in his tie flashed in the half-darkness. His hair was glued to his head with perfumed oil. Its odour pervaded the whole hallway. He looked at the old man with an expression of mixed contempt and anger. The two other old men began to snigger fawningly and tried to appear to have absolutely no connection with the ragged old man.

At last the ragged old man found a red handkerchief, and in his excitement he could not undo the knot that bound it together in a ball.

'Here,' he cried, holding out the handkerchief to the clerk, 'there are five pennies and four half-pennies there. Me fingers are all stiff with the rheumatism an' I can't untie it. Maybe ye'd do it for me for th' honour o' God?'

Then he looked up into the clerk's face with his mouth open. But the clerk, without taking any notice of the handkerchief, was looking at the old man's face as if he were going to strike him. The old man began to tremble.

'Get out of here,' yelled the clerk suddenly in a thunderous voice.

Then he became motionless again. The old man began to babble and shiver. He turned about and shuffled down the steps to the door, scratching his shoulder-blades against his clothes as he moved. He went down two steps and then paused uncertainly and looked behind him. Then he shuddered, took another step, lost his balance and slipped. He slithered to the door on his buttocks. The other two old men began to laugh and titter. The clerk scowled at them. 'What are ye laughing at?' he cried.

They stopped immediately. 'Hey you,' he continued, pointing his finger at the ragged old man, who had reached the street outside and was standing irresolutely on the kerb looking back over his shoulders. 'If I catch you here again, you old fool, I'll hand you over to the police. Go away now and get into the workhouse where you belong. Huh!'

The old man wrinkled up his monkey-like face into a grimace of surprise and misery. He cast a terrified look at the haggard face of McPhillip, that peered at him out of the angle of the wall to the left of the door. Then he mumbled something and set off down the lane at a broken trot. The other two old men in the hall began to whisper to one another as soon as the clerk turned his back and walked back into the office.

'Be the holy,' said one, 'he should be shot, wha'?'

'So he should,' whined the other old man, 'the dirty, rotten — to be goin' about like that.'

Then they shuffled up to the window for their bed tickets. The clerk swore at them and called them filthy names, but they kept apologising to him and sniggering.

While the two old men were getting their bed tickets at the window, McPhillip pushed through the door quietly and slipped along the hall. He turned to the right at the far end. He stopped there. He leaned up against the wall casually, took a cigarette from his pocket and lit it. He looked around examining the passage. It was a wide corridor with a concrete floor and walls of glazed brick. There were windows at regular intervals opening on a large yard at the rear of the building. In the alcoves formed by the windows seats were placed. By the opposite wall there were spittoons placed at equal distance of three yards or so. Men were strewn along the passage in groups, some sitting on the seats conversing in low voices, others walking up and down singly or in pairs, with their eyes on the ground and their hands muffed behind their backs in their coat-sleeves. They were all wretchedly dressed and melancholy. Some were quite young, but their faces had already assumed the dejected appearance that is usually found only in the faces of old men who have been disappointed in life.

Puffing at his cigarette slowly, McPhillip examined the hall and the men who passed, with the same quick, sharp cunning with which he had examined the street. Again he could see nobody that aroused his interest. Again he sighed gently and moved away to the right. He entered a large room through a swing door.

The room was crowded. It was furnished with long tables and wooden forms, like a café for the working class. There were newspapers on some tables. On others there were games of draughts and dominoes. Men sat at all the tables. Some read. Others played games. The majority, however, sat in silence, their eyes staring vacantly in front of them, contemplating the horror of their lives. Those who could find no seat stood about the tables, watching the progress of the games, with their hands in their pockets and their faces set in an expression of stolid and absent-minded indifference.

McPhillip walked about from one table to another, his cigarette in his left hand, the fingers of his right hand clutching the butt of his automatic, between the two top buttons of his raincoat. Nobody noticed him. The melancholy eyes, that were raised casually to look, saw only another shabby wreck like themselves. Even had his identity been suddenly disclosed by means of a loud trumpet to the men in that room, it is questionable whether the news would have occasioned excitement in more that a few breasts. Casual workers, casual criminals and broken old men, their connection with the ordered scheme of civilised life, with its moral laws and its horror of crime, was so thin and weak that they were unable to feel the interest that murder arouses in the tender breasts of our wives and sisters.

McPhillip examined the room carefully without discovering what he wanted. Then he walked out into the corridor again. He entered another room that was used by the occupants of the lodging-house for the purpose of writing letters. That room was empty. Then he descended a stairway to the lavatories and bathrooms. Here men were shaving and washing themselves. He walked about and discovered nobody. He came up again into the corridor and entered the dining-room.

The dining-room was very large and furnished with small deal tables and long forms of the same material. The wooden floor was covered with sawdust, like the floor of a slum public-house. Here and there the sawdust was mixed with refuse that had been swept from the tables. At the far end of the room a great number of men were gathered around an immense range, some with frying-pans in their hands awaiting their turn to cook, others rushing about attending to cooking utensils that were already on the range. They all had knives, spoons and forks in their hands. They were jostling, perspiring, cursing, laughing and scratching themselves. There was a great din of voices and a smell of food and of human bodies.

At the other end of the room there was a counter and behind the counter a large bright kitchen, shining bright with white crockery, polished brasses and the clean white uniforms of the women who served in it. Three young women were there cooking and serving food, for the lodgers who had not the means or the inclination to prepare their own food. These lodgers stood at the counter buying tea, bread and butter, cooked eggs and meat. They also purchased knives, forks, spoons and salt, because these necessities were not provided by the management in the lodging-house, owing to the moral character of the lodgers, except on payment of a fixed sum, which was returned at the conclusion of the meal, when the articles were handed back at the counter.

McPhillip walked down across the room to the far side. He had seen the man he sought at the first glance. He walked straight to a table by the wall at the far side. At that table a young man of thirty or so was eating his supper.

He ate off an enamelled plate that was loaded high with potatoes, coarse cabbage and a large piece of boiled bacon. A great steam rose from the plate and twisted up towards the ceiling in front of the man's face. The man was dressed in a suit of blue dungarees, with a white muffler wound round and round his neck. He had a close-cropped bullet-shaped head, fair hair and dark eyebrows. The eyebrows were just single tufts, one over the centre of each eye. They grew long and narrowed to a single hair, like the ends of waxed moustaches. They were just like ominous snouts, and they had more expression than the dim little blue eyes that were hidden away behind their scowling shadows. The face was bronzed red and it was covered by swellings that looked like humps at a distance. These humps came out on the forehead, on the cheekbones, on the chin and on either side of the neck below the ears. On close observation, however, they almost disappeared in the general glossy colour of the brownish red skin, that looked as if there were several tiers of taut skin covering the face. The nose was short and bulbous. The mouth was large. The lips were thick and they fitted together in such a manner that the mouth gave the face an expression of being perpetually asleep. His body was immense, with massive limbs and bulging muscles pushing out here and there, like excrescences of the earth breaking the expected regularity of a country-side. He sat upright in his seat, with his large square head bolted on to his squat neck, like an iron stanchion riveted to a deck.

He stared straight in front of him as he ate. He held his fork by the handle, upright, in his left hand. He rapped the table with the end of the fork, as if he were keeping time with the rapid crunching of his jaws. But as soon as he saw McPhillip, his jaws stopped moving and the hand holding the fork dropped noiselessly to the table. His face closed up and his body became absolutely motionless.

McPhillip sat down at the opposite side of the table. He did not speak and he did not express recognition by any sign or movement of his body. But he knew the man quite well. They were bosom friends. The man was Gypo

Nolan, McPhillip's companion during the strike of farm labourers, when McPhillip had killed the secretary of the Farmers' Union. Gypo Nolan had once been a policeman in Dublin, but he had been dismissed owing to a suspicion at Headquarters that he was in league with the Revolutionary Organisation and had given information to them relative to certain matters that had leaked out. Since then he had been an active member of the Revolutionary Organisation and always acted with Francis Joseph McPhillip, so that they were known in revolutionary circles as the 'Devil's Twins'.

'Well, Gypo,' said McPhillip at last, 'how is things?'

McPhillip's voice was cracked and weak, but it had a fierce sincerity that gave it immense force, like the force in the chirping of a tiny bird whose nest is being robbed.

'Did ye leave them messages I gave ye?' he continued after a moment, during which he gasped for breath. 'I didn't hear anythin' from home since I saw ye that evenin' I had to take to the hills. What's doin', Gypo?'

Gypo stared in silence for several moments, breathing slowly, with open mouth and distended eyes. He never spoke. Then he made a strange sound, like a suppressed exclamation, in his throat. He slowly cut a large potato in four pieces with his knife. He transferred one piece to his mouth on the tip of his knife. He began to chew slowly. Then he stopped chewing suddenly and spoke. It was a deep thunderous voice.

'Where the divil did ye come from, Frankie?' he said.

'It don't matter where I come from,' cried McPhillip in an irritated tone. 'I got no time to waste passin' the compliments o' the season. I came in here to get wise to all the news. Tell us all ye know. First, tell me … wait a minute. How about them messages? Did ye deliver them? Don't mind that grub. Man alive, are ye a savage or what? Here I am with the cops after me for me life an' ye go on eatin' yer spuds. Lave down that damn knife or I'll plug ye. Come on, I'm riskin' me life to come in here and ask ye a question. Get busy an' tell me all about it.'

Gypo sighed easily and wiped his mouth with the back of his right sleeve. Then he put his knife on the table and swallowed his mouthful.

'Ye were always a cranky fellah,' he growled, 'an' ye don't seem to be improvin' with the spring weather. I'll tell ye if ye hold on a minute. I delivered yer messages, to yer father an' mother and to the Executive Committee. Yer ol' man gev me dog's abuse and drov' me outa the house, an' he cursed ye be bell book an' candle-light. Yer mother followed me out cryin' an' put half a quid into me hand to give to ye. I had no way o' finding' ye an' I was hungry mesel', so I spent it. Well — '

McPhillip interrupted with a muttered curse. Then he was seized with a fit of coughing. When the fit was over, Gypo went on.

'Well,' continued Gypo. 'Ye know yersel' what happened with the Executive Committee. They sent a man out to tell ye. I wouldn't mind them sendin' a letter to the papers sayin' they had nothin' to do with the strike. It ud only be all swank anyway, an' who cares? But I declare to Christ they near had me plugged when I went in to report. Commandant Gallagher was goin' to send down men to plug ye too, but lots o' the other fellahs got around him and he didn't. Anyway, I was fired out o' the

Organisation as well as yersel', although ye know yersel', Frankie, that I had nothin' to do with firin' that shot. An'—'

'What the —' began McPhillip angrily, rapping the table; but again he began to cough. Gypo went on without taking notice of the coughing.

'The police arrested me, but they could find no evidence, so they gev me an awful beatin' and threw me out. I ben wanderin' around since without a dog to lick me trousers, half starvin'!'

'What do I want to know about the Executive Committee?' grumbled McPhillip angrily, recovering his breath. 'I don't want to hear anything about executive committees or revolutionary organisations, me curse on the lot o' them. I want to hear about me father an' mother. What about 'em, Gypo?'

Gypo expanded his thick underlip and stared at McPhillip with distended eyes. His eyes seemed to hold an expression of sadness in their dim recesses, but it was hard to say. The face was so crude and strong that the expression that might be termed sadness in another face was mere wonder in his. For the first time he had noticed the pallor of McPhillip's face, the hectic flush, the fits of coughing, the jerky movements and the evident terror in the eyes that used to be so fearless.

'Frankie,' cried Gypo in his deep, slow, passionless voice, 'yer sick. Man alive, ye look as if ye were dyin'.'

McPhillip started and looked about him hurriedly as if he expected to see death there behind his back waiting to pounce upon him.

'Have a bite,' continued Gypo, ''twill warm ye up.'

At the same time he himself began to eat again fiercely, like a great strong animal, tackling the solitary meal of its day. The large red hands with just stumps of fingers held the knife and fork so ponderously that those frail instruments seemed to run the danger of being crushed, like some costly thing picked up on the tip of an elephant's trunk. But McPhillip did not follow the invitation. He looked angrily at the food for several seconds with wrinkled forehead, as if he were trying to remember what it was and what it was for, and then he spoke again.

'I know I'm dyin'', Gypo, an' that's why I came in. I got the consumption.' Gypo started. He was struck at that moment by an insane and monstrous idea. 'I came in to get some money from me mother. An' I wanted to see her before I die. Good God, it was awful, Gypo, out there on them hills all the winter, with me gun in me hand night an' day, sleeping in holes on the mountains, with the winds blowin' about me all night, screechin' like a pack o' devils, an' every blast o' them winds spoke with a man's voice, an' I lyin' there listenin' to them. Good God —'

Again he began to cough and he had to stop. Gypo was not listening to him. He had not heard a word. A monstrous idea had prowled into his head, like an uncouth beast straying from a wilderness into a civilised place where little children are alone. He did not hear McPhillip's words or his coughing, although the monstrous idea was in relation to McPhillip.

'So I said to mesel', that I might as well chance me arm be comin' into town as lyin' out there, starvin' to death with the cold an' hunger an' this cough. So I came along here to see ye, Gyp, first, so as to get a bead on what's doin'. Have they got a guard on the house?'

'Divil a guard,' replied Gypo suddenly, and then he started and stretched out his right hand towards McPhillip with a little exclamation. His eyes were wild and his mouth was wide open like the mouth of a man looking at a spectre. Gypo's mind was looking at that uncouth ogre that was prowling about in his brain.

McPhillip leaned across the table. Gradually his eyes narrowed into an intense stare of ferocity. His lips curled up and his forehead wrinkled. He began to tremble.

'What is it, Gypo?' he hissed. 'Tell me, Gyp, or I'll …' He made a rapid movement with the wrist of the hand that clutched his automatic. 'The cops are after me, Gyp, an' I'm dyin', so I don't mind how I use the twenty-four rounds I got left. I've notched their noses so they can make a square hole. There's one for mesel' too.' He shuddered as if at the thought of a tender pleasure. Then he scowled fiercely and half drew the butt of his pistol from his pocket. His voice was almost inaudible. 'Tell me the truth about how things stand without any jig actin' or I'll plug ye.'

He glared at Gypo, his hand on his pistol, his right arm rigid to the shoulder, ready to draw the gun and fire in one movement. Gypo stared him in the eyes without any emotion, either of fear or of surprise. With the nail of his right forefinger he abstracted a string of meat from between two teeth. He spluttered with his lips and then he shrugged his shoulders. The spectre had suddenly gone out of his mind without his being able to make head or tail of it.

21

'No use talkin' like that to me, Frankie,' he murmured lazily. 'The only reason why I didn't want to say anythin' was because I didn't like to ...' Again the ghoulish thing came into his mind and he stopped with a start. But almost immediately he continued in a forced voice. He was beginning to be ashamed of that spectre as if he had already given way to the horrid suggestions it made, although he did not at all comprehend those suggestions. 'I didn't like to maybe send ye into harm's way. Ye see, I don't know if there's a guard on yer father's house or if there's not. I generally knock around Titt Street, but I haven't been near No. 44 since that night I went there with yer message an' yer ol' man told me never to darken his door again. There may be a guard on it or there may be no guard on it. But if I told ye there wasn't and ye went there and got nabbed, ye know —'

'What are ye driving' at, Gypo?' growled McPhillip suspiciously.

'Nothin' at all,' said Gypo with a great deep laugh. 'But it's how ye've come in on me so sudden, an' I don't know right what I'm talkin' about. Ye see, I'm all mixed up for the last six months, wanderin' around here, without a mate that ud give me a tanner for a flop if I were to die o' the cold lyin' in O'Connell's Street with a foot o' frost on the ground. They —'

'Oh, shut up about yersel' an' the frost an' tell us somethin'.'

'Now don't get yer rag out, Frankie. I was comin' to that. I was comin' to it, man. They held me up in the street the other day and had a long talk about ye. They're after ye yet all right. Sergeant McCartney an' another fellah from Sligo was there. That Detective-Sergeant McCartney is a bad lot. Huh, he's a rascal, an' no goin' behind a wall to say it. He swore to me that he'd get ye dead or alive. "I wouldn't care much for yer job then," says I to him, just like that, an' he gave me an eye that ud knock ye stiff.'

'He says he's goin' to get me, did he?' murmured McPhillip dreamily. Suddenly his mind seemed to wander away and he lost interest in his present surroundings. His eyes rested vacantly on the table, about a foot away to the right.

Gypo looked hurriedly at the spot upon which McPhillip's eyes were fixed. He saw nothing. He looked back again at McPhillip's face and wrinkled up his forehead. Then he made a noise in his throat and began to eat once more with great rapidity. He breathed on his food, to cool it, as he put it into his jaws. He made noises.

McPhillip stared at the table for a long time. His right hand toyed nervously with the butt of his pistol. His left hand rapped the table. Then a strange sparkle came into his eyes. He laughed suddenly. It was a strange laugh. It made Gypo start.

'What's the matter, Frankie?' he asked in a terrified voice.

'Nothing' atall,' said McPhillip, shaking himself. 'Gimme somethin' t' eat.'

He began to eat ravenously, using his penknife as a knife and fork. He had not eaten for a long time. He did not taste the food but gulped it down at a great speed.

Gypo ate also, but he kept staring at McPhillip while he ate. Every time his wandering little eyes reached

McPhillip's eyes they narrowed and became very sharp. Then he would roll his tongue around in his cheek and make a sucking sound.

At last McPhillip stopped eating. He wiped his penknife on his trousers and put it into his pocket.

'Gypo,' he said slowly, 'are there any cops watchin' our house, the old man's place in Titt Street?'

Gypo shook his head three times in reply. His mouth was full. Then he swallowed his mouthful, he put his fork to his forehead and set to thinking.

'Lemme see,' he said at last. 'Yeh. They had two cops watchin' the place until after Christmas. Then they took 'em off. They didn't put any on since as far as I know, but I believe that a fellah goes around there now an' again to make inquiries. O' course they might have secret-service men on it as well. God only knows who's givin' information to the Government now, an' who isn't. Ye never know who yer talkin' to. I never in me life saw anythin' like it. Tell ye what, Frankie, the workin' class is not worth fightin' for. They think yer gone to the United States, but all the same it might be dangerous goin' down there now. I'm sorry I have no money to give ye, so as ye could —'

'Where the divil did ye get all the gab?' cried McPhillip suddenly, looking suspiciously at Gypo. 'I never knew ye to let out all that much talk in a day, or maybe a whole week. Are ye goin' to the university now in yer spare time or what ails ye?'

McPhillip began to rap the table again. There was silence. Gypo nonchalantly transferred the scraps from his plate to his mouth on the flat of his knife. When the

24

plate was completely cleaned up he rattled the knife and fork on to it. Then he stuck out his massive chest and rubbed his palms along it.

Suddenly McPhillip swore and jumped to his feet. He stood, as if in a dream, looking at the table for several moments. Gypo watched his face, with his little tufted eyebrows quivering. At the same time he cleaned his teeth with his left thumb-nail. At last McPhillip drew in a deep breath through his teeth, making a noise as if he were sucking ice.

'Right,' he said, with his eyes still on the table. 'My ould fellah is at home now, is he?'

'Yes,' said Gypo. 'I saw him yesterday. He was over in the 'Pool on a job, but he's back this fortnight. I think he's workin' on a new house out in Rathmines.'

'Right,' said McPhillip again. Then he raised his eyes, looked at Gypo fiercely and smiled in a curious fashion. 'See ye again, Gypo, unless the cops get me.'

As he spoke he seemed to think of something. His face quivered and darkened. Then he shrugged his shoulders and laughed outright. He nodded twice and turned on his heel. He strode hurriedly out of the room.

Gypo looked after him for a long time without moving. He had finished cleaning his teeth. He just stared at the door through which McPhillip had disappeared. Then gradually his mind began to fill with suggestions. His forehead wrinkled up. His body began to fidget. At last he jumped to his feet. He collected the plate, the knife and fork and the salt. He walked into the passage and put them in a locker, which was provided by the management for the lodgers. The locker did not belong to Gypo. He had no locker because he was merely a casual lodger since he had no regular income to pay for a bed by the week. The locker belonged to a carter of Gypo's acquaintance. Gypo had seen the man put his next-day's dinner in the locker and go away without turning the key. Gypo knew also that the man would not be back until ten o'clock that night. So he took the dinner.

He placed the things in the locker and walked away casually. He sat on the corner of a seat in one of the alcoves. He rummaged in the pockets of his dungarees and collected several minute scraps of cigarettes. He carefully unrolled the scraps, collecting all the tobacco in the palm of his right hand. Then he begged a cigarette paper from an old man, who sat beside him. The old man had none and said so with an angry curse. Gypo wrinkled his forehead and sniffed as if he were smelling the old man. Then he turned to a young man who passed and requested a cigarette paper. The young man halted and supplied one grudgingly. Gypo took the paper in silence, without a word or a nod of thanks. He rolled his cigarette and lit it at the gas-jet. Then he sat down again, crossed his legs, let his body go limp and began to smoke.

His ears seemed to stick out very far, as he lay back limply in the seat, in the half-darkness of the corridor.

For a minute the odour and the taste of the tobacco held him in a state of enjoyment. He did not think either of the fact that he had no bed for the night or of his meeting with McPhillip. Then gradually his forehead began to wrinkle and furrow. His little tufted eyebrows began to twitch. When he pulled at his cigarette his face was enshrouded in a bright glow and the humps on his face stood out, glistening and smooth. He began to shift about in his seat. First he uncrossed his legs. Then he crossed them again. He began to tap his knee with his right hand. He sighed. His cigarette wore out until it was burning his lips without his becoming aware of the fact. Then he spluttered it out of his mouth on to his chest and he jumped to his feet.

He stood looking at the ground with his hands deep in his trousers pockets. He seemed to be deep in thought, but he was not thinking. At least there was no concrete idea fixed in his mind. Two facts rumbled about in his brain, making that loud primeval noise, which is the beginning of thought and which tired people experience when the jaded brain has spun out the last threads of its energy. There were two facts in his brain. First, the fact of his meeting with McPhillip. Second, the fact of his having no money to buy a bed for the night.

These two facts stood together in an amorphous mass. But he could not summon up courage to tackle them and place them in proper juxtaposition and reason out their relationship. He just stood looking at the ground.

Then a drunken bookmaker's clerk named Shanahan brushed against him. He stepped aside with a muttered oath. He pulled one hand from his pocket to strike, with the fingers extended in the shape of a bird's claws. Shanahan, doubled up in the middle by the helplessness of intoxication, stared at Gypo with blue eyes that had gone almost completely red. Gypo turned away with a shrug of his shoulders. At any other time he would gladly have availed himself of this opportunity of begging a shilling from Shanahan. Shanahan was always good for the loan of a shilling when he was drunk. A shilling would procure Gypo a bed for the night and leave a little for a light breakfast in the morning. Ten minutes ago, a *rencontre* of this sort would have been a godsend to Gypo. But now, those two cursed facts stood in his brain, making him unconscious of everything else.

He walked out of the House and up the lane towards B— Road.

He walked with his hands deep in his pockets, slowly, with his thighs brushing on the insides as he walked. He seemed to haul his big boots after him, bringing them as near the ground as possible. His hips moved up and down as his feet went forward. His eyes were on the ground. His lips were distended outwards. His little torn, brown, slouch hat was perched incongruously on the top of his head, much too small for his large square skull, with the brim turned up closely all around. When a squall of wind, laden with little sharp hailstones, struck him across the face and body, his clothes puffed out and he curled up his short stubby nose in an angry grin.

He was looking into the window of a saddler's shop in Dame Street, when the relationship between the two facts became known to him. He was looking at a pair of bright spurs and his face contorted suddenly. His eyes bulged as if he were taken with a fit of terror. He looked about him suspiciously, as if he were about to steal something for the first time. Then he rushed away hurriedly. He moved through lanes and alleyways to the river. He crossed the street to the river wall. He leaned his elbows on the wall and spat into the dark water. With his chin resting on his arms, he stood perfectly still, thinking.

Chapter One

He was contemplating the sudden discovery that his mind had made, about the relationship between his having no money for a bed and his having met Francis Joseph McPhillip, who was wanted for murder in connection with the farm-labourers' strike at M— in the previous October. A terrific silence reigned within his head.

Now and again he looked around him with a kind of panting noise. He snorted and smelled the air and screwed up his eyes. Then he leaned over the wall again and rested his chin on his crossed hands. He was that way for half an hour. Then at last he drew himself up straight. He stretched his arms above his head. He yawned. He stuck his hands in his trousers pockets. He stared at the ground. Then with his eyes on the ground he walked away at the same slouching pace as before.

He crossed the river and traversed a maze of side streets, with his eyes always on the ground, until he reached the corner of a dark side street, that had a bright lamp hanging over a doorway, half-way down on the right-hand side. That was a police-station. He stared at the lamp with his eyes wide open for several moments. Almost a minute. Then he said 'Huh' out loud. Then he looked around him cautiously on all sides.

The street was empty. Rain drizzled slowly. He examined the street, the warehouses on his side of the street, the blank wall on the other side. Then his eyes came back to the bright lamp that hung above the door of the police-station. He sighed deeply and began to walk slowly, ever so slowly and ponderously, towards the lamp.

He walked up the steps, steadily, one at a time, making a loud noise. He kicked the swing door open with his foot without taking his hands out of his pockets. In the hallway, a constable in a black, cone-shaped, night helmet stood facing him, pulling on his gloves. Gypo halted and stared at the constable.

'I have come to claim the twenty pounds reward offered by the Farmers' Union for information concerning Francis Joseph McPhillip,' he said in a deep low voice.

CHAPTER TWO

At thirty-five minutes past seven Francis Joseph McPhillip shot himself dead while trying to escape from No. 44 Titt Street, his father's house. The house had been surrounded by Detective-Sergeant McCartney and ten men. Hanging by his left hand from the sill of the back-bedroom window on the second floor, McPhillip put two bullets into McCartney's left shoulder. While he was trying to fire again, his left hand slipped and lost its hold. The pistol muzzle struck the edge of the sill. The bullet shot upwards and entered McPhillip's brain through the right temple.

When they picked him out of the orange box in the back garden where he fell, he was quite dead.

CHAPTER THREE

At twenty-five minutes past eight Gypo left the police-station by a door in the rear of the building. In his pocket he carried twenty pounds in Treasury notes, the reward for information concerning Francis Joseph McPhillip.

He walked quickly along a narrow passage into a dark lane. The lane was empty. So it appeared at first. But as Gypo stood hidden in the doorway of an old empty house, piercing the darkness with wild eyes, he heard a footstep. The footstep made him start. It was the first human footstep he had heard, the first sound of his fellow human beings, since he had become an informer and … and an outcast.

Immediately he felt that the footstep was menacing, as if he were certain that it belonged to somebody that was tracking him. How strange! Within the course of ninety minutes the customary sound of a human footstep had, by some evil miracle, become menacing. Ninety minutes ago, his ears would not have challenged the sound of a human footstep, no more than they would have challenged the sound of the breath coming normally from his lungs. But now they pricked into attention at the trudging shuffle that approached from the left. His heart began to pant.

Of course it was nobody of consequence. It was only a ragged old woman of ill fame, with a debauched face and melancholy eyes. She paused drunkenly in front of him, muttering something unintelligible. Then she bared her ragged teeth. She spat and passed on without speaking. Was it an omen? Gypo did not notice that it was. He merely listened to the sound of her footsteps, splashing carelessly through the pools.

Then he looked ahead of him furtively and moved off with the careful listening, stooping movement of a man wandering alone at night in a forest gorge where lions are about. He turned a corner and came face to face with a blaze of light and a street with shops and crowds of people going about. At first he shuddered with fear. Then he swore and drew in a deep breath. What had he to fear? He knew the street well. Who was going to interfere with him? His giant fists clawed up, like talons enraged, and the muscles of his throat and shoulders stiffened. He imagined himself throttling these enemies who might be inclined to assault him. He felt comforted, reminded by this pressure of his muscles, of his enormous strength. He settled his little round hat jauntily on the back of his head. He stuck his hands in his trousers pockets. He swung his legs and rolled like a sailor out of the lane, arrogantly, into the glare of the street.

At the same slow, swinging, rolling gait, he crossed the street through the traffic without pausing, without stepping aside, without looking to the right or to the left. Motorcars, carts, bicycles and wagons swerved to avoid him. He went through them without looking at them, like a great monster walking through a cloud of ants, that are carrying on their futile and infinitesimal labours about his feet. They turned towards him to curse, but those that saw his face gaped and passed into the night with the curse unuttered. His face, with the humps on it shining in the glare of the lamps, was like a subtle mask. It was so … so dead.

He walked straight across the pavement into a public-house. He kicked the swing door open with his foot, without taking his hands out of his pockets, just as he had entered the police-station. He put a pound note on the counter with a slap of his palm and uttered the one word: 'Pint.' He stared at the counter until the drink was served. He put the measure to his head, opened his throat and swallowed the contents at one draught. He uttered a deep sigh and handed the empty glass to the barman. He nodded. When he received another pint and his change, he walked over to the corner and sat down.

Now he definitely set out to form a plan of action. It had been a habit with McPhillip and himself. Whenever they had done any 'stunt', they immediately went into a public-house, got drinks and set about forming plans for an alibi.

'Never bother about yer "getaway" until yer job is done,' used to be a motto of McPhillip's.

Suddenly Gypo realised what a clever fellow McPhillip must really have been. He used to make plans so easily. They jumped to his mind one after the other, like lightning. Gypo had never given any thought to the matter of plans.

Chapter Three

He often used to say to McPhillip with a queer glassy look in his eyes: 'Mac, you bite the easy side o' the cheese. I got to do all the rough work an' you do all the thinkin'. Strikes me you get away with it easy, mate.'

Now, for the first time, he realised the difficulty of making a plan without McPhillip. When he had to think it out for himself it appeared to be devilish work. His brain got all in a tangle and he could make a beginning nowhere. He gathered himself together several times, with set lips and stiffened back, like a horse stiffening for a great tug at an immense weight, but it was no use. He could not overcome the weight that seemed to fall on his brain every time his sensibilities approached it, probing tentatively for information. Sitting on a deal bench at the rear of the bar, with his legs crossed and his pint of porter in his right hand, held in front of him, with his elbow resting on his knee and the froth of the porter dripping from the glass slowly on to the tip of his raised boot, he stared at the ground, in an agony of complicated thought. His little tattered brown hat, perched on the top of his skull, looked like a magic charm, endowed with reason and knowledge, mounting guard over his stupid strength.

He had not even cleared his brain for a beginning with this devilish work of making a plan when he was interrupted by the arrival of Katie Fox. She had sat down beside him before he knew she was there. He was so immersed in his struggles that she nudged him and spoke before he was aware of her presence.

'How's things, Gypo?' she cried in her hard thin voice, as she nudged him in the ribs. 'Are ye flush enough to give us a wet?'

Gypo jumped to his feet, spilling half his pint. He gazed at her with fright in his eyes and his chest heaved. Then he recognised her and sat down immediately, flurried and confused by his display of excitement.

'Hello, Katie,' he muttered, pretending to be vexed, 'ye shouldn't come in that way on a fellah. I look around me an' there ye are proddin' me in the ribs. Why the divil didn't ye shout same as ye always do?'

She put the backs of her thin, red-veined hands on her hips and stared at him in amazement, partly real, partly born of that love of emphatic gesture and movement and speech which is a peculiar characteristic of the women of the Dublin slums. Katie was a woman of the slums. Her father had been an employee of the Corporation and her mother was a charwoman. As a girl Katie worked in a biscuit factory. Her own beauty of body and the grinding toil in the factory made her discontented. She joined the Revolutionary Organisation. That was six years ago. After that, her first plunge from the straight path of the tremendous respectability and conservatism of the slum woman, she was led by excess of feeling into one pitfall after another. Finally she passed out of the ranks of respectability altogether by being expelled from the Revolutionary Organisation on a charge of public prostitution. Now she had become an abandoned woman, known as such even among the prostitutes of the brothel quarter, a drug fiend, a slattern, an irresponsible creature. Traces of her young beauty still remained in the deep blue eyes, that were melancholy and tired and twitched at the edges, in her long lean figure now grown emaciated, in her black hair that strayed carelessly about her face from beneath the rim of her ragged red hat. But the mouth, that tell-tale register of vice, had completely lost the sumptuous but delicate curves of innocent girlhood and blossoming maturity. The lips hung down at the sides. They were swollen in the middle. Their colour had died out and had been renewed with loud vulgarity by cheap paint. The poor tormented soul peered out of the young face, old before the years had time to wrinkle it, sad, hard and stupefied.

She thrust out her little chin and turned her head sideways, turning down the corners of her lips farther at one side of her mouth.

'I thought as much,' she said slowly, contorting her lips and face as she spoke. 'That's why I came in unknownst and sat down beside ye. I saw ye be chance, me fine buck, as I was talkin' to Biddy Mac over at the corner opposite Kane's. So I just prowled in to see ye on the quiet. But it's clear as daylight that ye don't want to see me. Not while ye got money to fill yersel' with porter. It was a different story, wasn't it, this mornin' when ye begged the price of a cup o' tay off me, an' me that didn't see the colour of a half-crown for three days runnin'. Oh then —'

'Now shut yer gob, will ye,' interrupted Gypo excitedly. 'It's just like ye takin' a man up wrong that way. Sure I didn't mane anythin' like that at all. Only ye just came in on me all of a sudden. What are ye havin'?'

Katie looked at him in high dudgeon, still with her chin thrust out, her head turned sideways, her lips turned downwards and her hands on her hips. She murmured, 'Double Gin,' without moving her eyes from Gypo's face.

Gypo arose and slouched up to the counter for the drink. Her eyes followed him shrewdly and she kept nodding her head slowly at his immense back.

Her relationship with Gypo was of that irregular kind which is hard to describe by means of one word. She was undoubtedly not his wife and in the same manner she could not be called his mistress. But their relationship partook both of the nature of lawful marriage and of the concubinage that is sanctified by natural love. Katie loved Gypo because he was strong, big, silent, perhaps also because he was stupid and her ready slum 'smartness' could always outwit his lumbering brain. Whenever Gypo had any money he spent it with her. Sometimes when he was without any money, she brought him home with her and provided him with his breakfast next morning. On the whole they were good friends. During the past six months after Gypo had been expelled from the Revolutionary Organisation and left without friends or money or employment, Katie had stood between him and death from exposure or starvation. She loved him in her own amazing way. The last remains of her womanhood loved him as she might have loved a mate. But those shreds of love lived charily among the rank weeds of vice that flourished around them. It was only at times that they peeped out and covered the desert waste of her soul with the soft warmth and brilliance of their light. Each kindly act of pity for the lumbering giant was counteracted by a score of other acts that were vicious and cruel. While Gypo, with the nonchalance of the healthy strong man, took her for granted as if she were a natural contrivance of life, like fresh air or food. He would only notice her absence when she was needed.

He brought the gin and handed it to her. She took it in silence. She sipped it slowly, holding it within an inch of her lips, staring at the ground as she drank, shivering now and again, as if the drink were ice-cold. Gypo watched her suspiciously out of the corner of his eyes.

'What brought ye around here anyway?' he said at last.

He was extremely irritated that she should have come in on him, just at that moment, when he was trying to make a plan, when he had the money of his betrayal hot on his person, without being yet embalmed by a plausible excuse of its presence. He was irritated, but in a confused and ignorant way. He had not reasoned out a plausible excuse, even for his irritation.

Katie held her empty glass upside down in her hand and looked at him, with her blue eyes almost shut. 'Why, what's the matter with ye, kiddo?' she asked arrogantly, encouraged by the gin. 'Why shouldn't I knock around here if I want to. I'm not employed by a charitable institution at so much an hour to keep out o' yer honour's way, ha, ha, when it's yer lordship's pleasure to come into this pub. There's no law agin me comin' around this part o' the city at this hour, is there?' She worked herself into a fit of anger gradually as she spoke. She had an idea that Gypo was concealing something important from her and that her arrival at that moment gave her some power over him. That peculiar intuition of the slum woman could pierce the surface of Gypo's embarrassment, but without being able to probe into the real nature of it. She pushed back her coat with her left hand and put the back of the hand against her reddish frayed blouse below the heart. How slight her breasts were!

'Now, Katie —' began Gypo.

But she interrupted him immediately. She had been only waiting for him to begin to speak in order to interrupt him. She was quite happy when given the opportunity of a 'barge' of this description.

'Go on with ye,' she cried, 'pug nose! I know ye. Ya. You're bum all right. Yer all right as long as ye got nothin'. But as soon as ye can smell yersel' after a good meal an' there's a gingle in yer rags, ye stick yer nose into the air an' ye know nobody. D'ye know what I'm goin' to tell ye, Gypo? D'ye know what I'm goin' to tell ye? Yer a mane, lyin', deceitful twister an' I got yer measure from now on. Don't look for nothin' from me from now on, my fine bucko. No then; 'twill be little use for ye.'

Gypo became nervous and shifted his huge body. He wanted to let his left hand fly out and hit her in the jaw. One slight blow would make her senseless. But he had never struck a woman, owing to some obscure prejudice or other. Still, he was terribly tired of her. Now that he had this money on his person, without as yet having decided what to do with it, he wanted to be free from her.

'You shut up,' he cried angrily, 'or I'll fix ye. Haven't I given ye a drink?' Then he added half-heartedly: 'D'ye want another drink?'

Katie was still staring at him. Suddenly a change came over her. Something suggested itself to her peculiar reason and she changed her attitude.

'Don't mind what I said now, Gypo,' she continued in a low mournful voice, looking at the ground with hanging lower lip, like a person overwhelmed and utterly defeated by some persistent calamity. 'God Almighty, the world is so hard that a person loses her mind altogether. Misery, misery, misery an' nothin' but misery. Yer as bad off as mesel', Gypo, so ye know what I mane. No man has pity on us. Every hand is agin us because we have got nothin'. Why is that, will ye tell me, Gypo? Is God Himself agin us too? Ha, ha, o' course we were both of us Communists and members o' the Revolutionary Organisation, so we know there's no God. But supposin' there was a God, what the hell is He doin'—'

'Katie,' cried Gypo angrily, 'none o' that talk. Lave God alone.'

'God forgive me, yer right,' cried Katie, beginning to sob. But she pulled herself together suddenly with surprising speed and turned to Gypo almost sharply. Her eyes narrowed slightly and a quaint weird smile lit up her face. There was a trace of beauty in her face under the influence of the smile, a trace of beauty and merriment. 'Tell us where ye got all the money, Gypo. Ye had none this mornin'.'

Gypo started in spite of himself and glanced at her in terror. He struggled violently, trying to formulate an excuse for his sudden wealth. He fumed within himself for not having made a plan. Unconsciously he cursed McPhillip, whom he had sent to his death, for not having made a plan. He looked at Katie with glaring eyes and open lips. Then he bent towards her, tried to speak and said nothing. But she misunderstood him.

'Ya,' she said, 'I knew ye were yellow. Have ye robbed a church or what, an' are ye afraid of bein' turned into a goat be the priests?'

'Shut up,' he hissed suddenly, gripping at the word 'robbery' and hooking a plan on to it. It was a customary word, a friendly thing that he recognised, with which he felt at home. He bent down, with quivering face, eager to hurl out the words of his plan before he could forget them again. 'It wasn't a church. It was a sailor off an American ship. I went through him at the back o' Cassidy's pub in Jerome Street. But if ye say a word ye know what yer goin' to get.'

'Who? Me?' Katie laughed out loud and looked at him with emphatic scorn over her shoulder. 'What d'ye take me for? An informer or what?'

'Who's an informer?' cried Gypo, gripping her right knee with his left hand. The huge hand closed about the thin frail knee and immediately the whole leg went rigid. Katie's whole body shrivelled at the mere touch of the vast strength.

There was silence for a second. Gypo stared at Katie with a look of ignorant fear on his face. The word had terrified and infuriated him. It was the first time he had heard it uttered in the new sense that it now held for him. Katie, hypnotised by the face, panted and looked back at him.

'What are ye talkin' about informin' for?' panted Gypo again, tightening his grip on her knee. He had not meant to hurt. He merely wanted to give emphasis to his words.

'Lemme go,' screamed Katie, unable to endure the pain any longer and terrified by the look in Gypo's face and by his strange behaviour.

Gypo let go immediately. The barman came striding over, wiping his hands in his apron. He pointed towards the door. Gypo got to his feet and stared at the barman, glad to have a man in front of him, against whom he could vent his ignorant rage. He lowered his head and he was about to rush forward when Katie hung on to him and cried out.

'Come on, Gypo,' she cried rapidly, 'let's get out of here. Let him alone, Barney. He's got a few pints on him. He didn't mane any harm. Come on, kid.'

Gypo allowed himself to be dragged out backwards by the right hand into the street. They stood together on the kerbstone, with Katie's arm entwined in his.

'Come on up to Biddy Burke's place,' she whispered in a friendly tone. 'Come on up.'

In front stretched a main road, brilliantly lighted and thronged with people. The light, the people, the suggestion of gaiety and of freedom attracted Gypo. To the rear stretched a dark, evil-smelling lane. It repelled him. There was where Katie wanted to bring him, down towards the slum district and the brothel quarter. Down there were his own haunts, people who knew him. He feared the darkness, the lurking shadows, the suggestion of men hiding in alleyways to attack him. Out there in front he could wander off, among strange people who did not care a straw about informers.

'Come on, Gyp, down to Biddy's and buy us a sniff,' murmured Katie entreatingly, in a soft voice. 'Yer flush, aren't ye? I know well them American sailors carry a quare wad around with 'em. Let's walk along. I'm perished with the cold.'

'No,' muttered Gypo in a surly voice. 'I'm goin' down to the house to book a bed for the night.'

He now remembered with pleasure that the reason for his going to the police-station was the fact that he wanted money for a bed. So why not go and buy a bed? It was a good excuse to get rid of her.

'What are ye talkin' about a bed for?' cried Katie angrily, clutching at his arm. Then her voice softened again. There was an eager glitter in her eyes. 'Sure it's not thinkin' about a bed ye are when ye got money in yer pocket. Haven't I got a bed anyway, an' if it's not good enough for ye, sure we can get a bed at Biddy's, seein' ye have money in yer pocket.'

'I don't want yer bed,' snarled Gypo, 'an' I'm not goin' near Biddy Burke's. I been robbed by the thievin' old robber often enough.'

'Ye don't want me bed, don't ye?' cried Katie, losing her temper again completely. 'Ye were glad enough to have it last week when I brought ye in outa the rain like a drowned rat. Wha'?'

'Now I'll give ye nothin' for yer imperence,' grumbled Gypo. 'Yer too ignorant. That's what ye are.'

She moved up under his chin and held her two clenched fists to his jaws. They looked white and tiny against the size of his face.

'All right,' she hissed, 'you watch out for yersel', Gypo Nolan.'

She turned on her heel and went off at a fierce walk to the left, muttering curses as she disappeared rapidly into the darkness. Gypo stared after her, listening. He strained his neck in an effort to catch a final mumble of sharp words that floated up to him through the dark lane, as her obscure figure drifted around a corner. Then he shrugged

44

his shoulders with a gasp as if he had just watched a valuable possession suddenly drop over a cliff. With his hands in his trousers pockets he stared at the ground.

'Look here, Katie,' he called out suddenly, reaching out his right hand impotently towards the corner of the lane, around which she had swept. Then he put his hand back into his pocket and gripped the tight wad of Treasury notes. He wanted now to give her some money. She had been good to him. He began to walk up the lane slowly. There was no need to hurry. He knew where to find her. He must not let her go like that.

But he had not gone ten yards before he halted again. He turned about and walked back quickly into the main road. He had suddenly remembered a terrifying thing.

Supposing somebody were to come into Biddy Burke's and say that Frank McPhillip had been killed owing to information being given to the police? They were sure to say that. They would see him there with money in his pocket. They would suspect …

He turned to the right, past the corner of the main road. He went twenty yards down the street and then brought his two feet together like a soldier coming to a halt on parade. He wheeled inwards, still in the same mechanical manner, towards a shop window. He stood at ease, clasping his hands behind his back in military manner. Somehow, it gave peace to his distracted thoughts, as if he had suddenly given over the responsibility of his thoughts and actions to an imaginary superior officer.

Into his resting mind pleasant memories came, distant pleasant memories like day-dreams on a summer day, dreamt on the banks of a rock-strewn river, among the flowering heather. They were memories of his youth. They came to him in a strange bewildered manner, as if afraid of the dark, ferocious mind into which they came. Gypo stared at them fiercely, with bulging lips, as if they were enemies taunting him. Then gradually he softened towards them. Then a mad longing seized him for the protection of the environment of his youth, the country-side of a Tipperary village, the little farm, the big red-faced healthy peasant who was his father, his long-faced kind-hearted mother, who hoped that he would become a priest.

He wrinkled up his face and looked at his youth intently. He stiffened himself, as if he were about to hurl himself by sheer force back through the intervening years, of sin and sorrow and misery, to the peace and gentleness and monotony of life, in that little village at the foot of the Galtees.

Various, intimate, foolish, little recollections crowded into his mind. He remembered goats, asses' foals, rocks in a mountain torrent, a saying of the village smith, a glance from a girl, his first drink of wine stolen in the sacristy of the parish church while he was serving Mass. Thousands of memories came and went rapidly. They passed like soldiers before a saluting-point, some gay, some sad, some dim, some distinct and almost articulate as if they had happened a moment ago.

Suddenly he felt a wet daub coming down each cheek. He started. He was shedding tears. The horror of the act made him stare wild-eyed. He swore aloud. He bared his teeth of their covering of thick lips and ground them. His youth went out like a candle that is quenched by a squall in a long passage. The grinning spectre of the present became real once more. He shut his mouth. He sighed very deeply. Putting his hands in his pockets again, he walked off at his habitual slouch, with his head hanging slightly forward, hung on the pivot of his neck like a punchball.

'I must make a plan,' he said to himself once more.

Somehow he was convinced that the Revolutionary Organisation already suspected him of having given information concerning McPhillip. He felt that he was being sought for already. So he must make a plan. He must have a plausible excuse.

'If ye got a good aliby,' McPhillip used to say, 'the divil himself couldn't fasten anythin' on ye.'

But how was he going to get an alibi for himself? He walked the whole length of the road three times irresolutely, with his eyes fixed on the ground. He was unable to think of anything. His mind kept branching off into the contemplation of silly things that had nothing at all to do with the question, the favourite for the Grand National and whether Johnny Grimes, the comedian, had drowned himself in the Canal or whether he had been murdered and then thrown in; the two main questions that were agitating the Dublin slums just then.

At one moment he decided to go to the Dunboy Lodging House, pay for a bed and go to sleep. But immediately he was terrified at this suggestion. They might know already that he had given information. Then maybe, while he was asleep, somebody would be sent into his little cell with a loaded stick to murder him in his sleep. Or they might give him 'the bum's rush', breaking his neck silently like a rabbit's neck. He pictured the little narrow wooden cells in the lodging-house, the silence of the night, broken only by the dismal sound of snoring on all sides, an indiscriminate number of unknown people snoring loudly, dreaming, grumbling, snoring and sleeping in all directions, while *'they'* approached silently to murder him.

He shuddered. Perspiration stood out on his forehead. Eagerly, with relief, he decided to keep in the open, where he could use his hands and his strength. If he were going to be murdered, he would be murdered with his hands gripping a dead throat.

Then at last he stood stock-still and thumped himself in the chest.

'Well, I'm damned!' he cried. 'Amn't I an awful fool? Why didn't I think of it before? They'll be wonderin' why I'm not there already. Everybody in the town must 'a heard of it be now, an' me that was his pal an' I not there to say a word to his mother. They'll surely suspect something if I don't go at once.'

Narrowing his eyes, he set out at a smart pace in the direction of McPhillip's home in Titt Street. He took his hands out of his pockets and swung them by his sides after the manner of a policeman. He threw his head back and towered like a giant over those whom he passed.

He passed them, almost over them, like a being utterly remote, a unique creation.

CHAPTER FOUR

Titt Street was in turmoil like an ant-hill that has been rooted up by the ponderous hoof of a cow.

Under the scattered street lamps, between the parallel rows of two-storied, red-bricked houses, groups of wild-eyed men were talking. The pale light of the lamps showed the drizzling rain falling like steam on their rough, dirty clothes, on their thick-veined necks, on their excited faces, on their gnarled hands that were raised in gesticulation. Their voices filled the hollow darkness of the street with a hushed murmur, that rose and fell turbulently, like the chattering of a torrent coming through rocks. Their voices were nervous, as if they awaited a storm at sea.

Old women with shawls over their heads flitted about like shadows. They darted from doorway to doorway, talking, making threatening gestures at something remote, crossing themselves with their haggard faces turned upwards to the sky. Young women walked arm-in-arm, slowly, up and down the street. They looked at No. 44 as they passed it, in silence, with awe in their open, red lips.

No. 44 was the centre of interest. The horror that had

come to it had aroused the whole street. It had aroused the whole quarter. Three streets away, bar attendants stood gaping behind their counters, while some man, with an excited red face and a big mouth, recounted the manner of Frank McPhillip's death, with oaths and frenzied gesticulations. Everywhere, in the streets, in the public-houses, in the tenement kitchens, where old red-nosed men craned forward their shrivelled necks to hear the dreadful news, one word was whispered with fear and hatred.

It was the word 'Informer'.

Gypo heard that word as he reached the junction of Titt Street and Bryan Road — a long wide road, lined with little shops, the sidewalks strewn with papers, little heaps of dirt in the gutters, two tramcar lines rusted by the drizzling rain, groups of loafers at every lamp-post, at the public-house doors and on the Canal Bridge, where the road disappeared abruptly over the horizon, as if it had fallen over a precipice into space. He was passing Ryan's public-house that stood at the corner, half in Titt Street, half in Bryan Road. The word came to him through the open door of the public bar. He had slowed down his pace on reaching the neighbourhood, and when he heard the word uttered, he brought his left leg up to the right and instead of thrusting it forward for another pace, he dropped it heavily but noiselessly to the wet pavement of red and white glazed brick diamonds, with which the front of the public-house was decorated.

A squall of wind came around the corner just then and buffeted him about the body. He opened his mouth and nostrils. He distended his eyes. He thrust forward his head and listened.

Chapter Four

'There must 'a been information gev, 'cos how else could they —' a tall lean man was saying, as he stood in the middle of the sawdust-covered floor, holding a pint of black frothing porter in his right hand.

Then a burly carter, with a grey sack around his shoulders like a cape, jostled the man who was speaking, in an awkward attempt to cross the floor through the crowd. But the man had said enough. Gypo knew that they were talking about the death of Francis Joseph McPhillip, and that they suspected that information had been given.

Again the idea came into his head that he must form a plan without a moment's delay. But the inside of his head was perfectly empty, with his forehead pressing against it, hot and congested, as if he had been struck a violent blow with a flat stick. The idea floundered about in his head, repeating itself aimlessly, like a child calling for help in an empty house. 'No,' he muttered to himself, as he gripped his clasp-knife fiercely in his trousers pocket, 'I can't make out anythin' standin' here in the rain in front of a pub. Better go ahead.'

He hurled himself around the corner against the squall into Titt Street with almost drunken violence. Then he realised with terror the fate that menaced him if ... He saw the groups under the lamp-posts. He saw the flitting women. He saw the youths, hushed, strained, expectant. He heard the rumble of human sound. The dark, sombre, mean street that had been familiar to him until now, suddenly appeared strange, as if he had never seen it before, as if it had suddenly become inhabited by dread monsters that were intent on devouring him. It appeared to him rather, that he had wandered, through a foolish error of judgement, into a strange and hostile foreign country where he did not know the language.

He glared about him aggressively, as he walked up the street. He planted his feet on the ground firmly, walking with his legs wide apart, with his shoulders squared, with his head thrust forward into the wind like the jib-boom of a ship.

As he was passing an open doorway somebody cried 'Hist.' He halted like a challenged sentry. He wheeled savagely towards the doorway and called out:

'Who are cryin' hist after?'

'It's only me,' chirped an old lady in a clean white apron, a woman he knew well. 'I thought ye were Jim Delaney, the coalheaver. I got to whisper on account o' me throat. I got a cold a fortnight ago, scrubbin' floors out at Clontarf, an' it's getting worse instead of better. The doctor —'

But Gypo glanced angrily at her bandaged throat and her dim blue eyes and passed on with a grunt without listening to her further. He arrived at No. 44 and entered through the open door without knocking.

No. 44 was the most respectable house in the street. Its red-brick front was cleaner than the other fronts. Its parlour window was unbroken and was decorated with clean curtains of Nottingham lace. Its door was freshly painted black. Its owner, Jack McPhillip, the bricklayer, had already begun the ascent from the working class to the middle class. He was a Socialist and chairman of his branch of the trade union, but a thoroughly respectable, conservative Socialist, utterly fanatical in his hatred of the status of a working man. The whole house was in keeping with his views on life. The door opened on a little narrow hall, with the stairway rising midway in it. The stairway was spotlessly clean, with brightly polished brass rods holding down the well-washed linoleum carpet that struggled upwards rigidly to the top of it. From the door, in daytime, the backyard could be seen. In the backyard there were outhouses and stables, for Jack McPhillip kept a yellow she-goat, three pigs, a flock of white hens, and a little pony and trap, in which he was in the habit of driving out into the country on Sundays, in summer, with his wife, to visit his wife's relatives at Talmuc. To the right of the hall there were two doors. The first door opened into the parlour. In the parlour there was a piano, eight chairs of all sizes and sorts, innumerable photographs, 'ornaments', and absolutely no room for anybody to move about without touching something or other. The second door opened into the kitchen, a large clean room with a cement floor, an open grate and a narrow bed in the corner farthest from the door. The bed belonged to old Ned Lawless, the epileptic relative of Mrs McPhillip. He lived in the house and received his meals and half a crown per week, in exchange for his labours in looking after the backyard. He was never clean, the only dirty thing in the house. On the second floor there were three rooms. One was used by the old couple. The second by the only daughter Mary, a girl of twenty-one who worked in the city as a clerk, in the offices of Gogarty and Hogan, solicitors and commissioners for oaths. The third room, opening on the backyard, had been closed for six months. It had been Francis's bedroom. That evening he had just entered it to go to bed when the police arrived.

When Gypo entered, the house was crowded with neighbours who had come in to sympathise. Some were even standing in the hallway. Gypo walked through the hallway and pushed his way into the kitchen. Nobody noticed him. He sat down on the floor to the left of the door, with his back to the wall and his right hand grasping his left wrist in front of his drawn-up knees. He sat in silence for almost a minute waiting for an opportunity to speak to Mrs McPhillip. He could see her through the people in the room, sitting on a chair to the right of the fire. She had black wooden rosary beads wound round and round her fingers. There were tears in her pale blue eyes and streaming down her great white fat cheeks. Her corpulent body flowed over the chair on all sides like a load of hay on a cart. Her long check apron hid her feet. She was looking dimly at the fire, murmuring prayers silently with her lips. She nodded her head now and again in answer to something that was said to her.

She held Gypo's attention like a powerful magnet. Even when somebody came between his eyes and her body, he stared through the intervening body as if it were transparent. His eyes were centred on her forehead and on her grey-white hair, that had a yellowish sheen at the top of the skull where the parting was. He was thinking how good she had been to him. She had often fed him. More precious still, she always had a word of sympathy for him, a kind look, a tender, soft, smooth touch of the hand on his shoulder! These were the things his strange soul remembered and treasured. There were no others who were soft and gentle to him like she was. Often when he and Francis came into the house at dawn, after having done some revolutionary 'stunt', she used to get up, in her bare fat feet, with a skirt drawn over her nightdress. She used to move about silently, with quivering lips, cooking breakfast. It was a huge meal from her hands, an indiscriminate lavish Irish meal, sausages, eggs, bacon, all together on one plate.

And she would often press half a crown into Gypo's hand when nobody was looking, whispering: 'May the Virgin protect ye an' won't ye look after Frankie an' see that he comes to no harm.'

'She is a good woman,' thought Gypo, impersonally, looking at her.

Then the kitchen emptied suddenly in the rear of a fat short man with a pompous appearance, who wore a dark raincoat and a black bowler hat. Every one made way for him going out the door and there were whispers. Some scowled at him angrily, but it was obvious that everybody had a great respect for him and envied him, even those that scowled at him. He was an important Labour politician, the parliamentary representative of the constituency that comprised Titt Street and the surrounding slums. This important politician had been a bricklayer with Jack McPhillip in his youth, and Jack McPhillip was still his main supporter.

When the politician had disappeared there were only five people left in the room, other than Jack McPhillip and his wife. Three men in the corner by the window, to the left of Gypo, had their heads close together, whispering with that sudden intimacy that is born of the presence of a calamity, or of something that has a common interest.

Gypo knew two of them. Two of them were members of the Revolutionary Organisation.

'That skunk Bartly Mulholland is here,' muttered Gypo to himself, 'an' that's Tommy Connor with him. Mulholland is lookin' for Frankie McPhillip's job on the Intelligence Department, I believe; an' I suppose that big stiff Connor is trainin' to be his butty. Huh.'

Jack McPhillip sat on the narrow bed in the other corner, almost opposite Gypo. He was talking to two women, who had chairs close to the bed. They had pushed in to talk to McPhillip as soon as the politician had left. They were nodding their heads and fidgeting, with that amazing prodigality of emotion, which women of the very lowest rung of the middle-class ladder display, when in the presence of members of the working class who are still *in puris naturalibus*. One was the wife of the Titt Street 'small grocer'. The other was the wife of John Kennedy the lorry driver, who had just set up in business 'for himself'.

Jack McPhillip sat on the bed, with his right shoulder leaning against the pillow. One foot was almost on the floor. The other foot was on the bed. He held his right hand, palm outwards, in front of his face, as if he were trying to drive away some imaginary idea, as he talked.

'There ye are now,' he was saying; 'see what that man has done for himsel' in life. That's what every man should aim at doin', instead of jib actin' and endin' up by bringin' disgrace on his class an' on his family. Johnny Daly is a member o' Parliament this day because he spent any money and time he had to spare on his own education. He looked after his business and he did his

Chapter Four

best to educate and better the condition of his fellow-men. That's what every man should do. But my son … I put him into a good job as an insurance agent an' if he had minded himself he'd be well on his way now towards a respectable position in life for himself, but instead o' that —'

Suddenly there was an amazing interruption that caused everybody to start. Gypo had spoken in a deep thunderous voice that filled the whole house. 'I'm sorry for yer trouble, Mrs McPhillip,' he cried.

The sentence re-echoed in the silence that followed it. It had been uttered in a shout. Gypo's voice had suddenly broken loose from his lungs into a spontaneous expression of the emotion that shook him into a passion of feeling, looking at Mrs McPhillip. He felt suddenly that he must express that feeling forcibly. Not by a whisper, or a plain restrained statement, but by a savage shout that would brook no contradiction. The shout wandered about in the room long after its sound had vanished. Nobody spoke. Its force was too tremendous. Everybody, for some amazing reason or other, sniffed at the smell of fried sausages that now permeated the atmosphere of the kitchen. The smell came from the pan still left on the fireplace, containing the sausages that had been cooking for Francis Joseph McPhillip's supper when the police came. He had been so tired that he told his mother to bring his supper to him in bed. So they still remained there, on the side of the fireplace, forgotten.

Then the initial amazement wore off and everybody looked at Gypo. They saw him sitting on the floor, doubled up, bulky in his blue dungarees that clung about his thighs like a swimming suit, with his little round hat

57

perched on his massive head, still staring at Mrs McPhillip's face as if drawn by a magnet, unconscious of the amazement he had caused by his shout.

And alone of all the people in the room, Mrs McPhillip was not amazed. She had not started. She had not moved her eyes. Her lips still moved in prayer. Her mind was drawn by another magnet to the contemplation of something utterly remote from the people in that room, utterly remote from life, to the contemplation of something that had its roots in the mystic boundaries of eternity.

Then Jack McPhillip jumped to a sitting posture on the bed. He grabbed at the old tweed cap that had fallen off his grizzled grey head.

'Oh, it's you that's in it, is it?' he cried. 'Ye son o' damnation!'

He glared at Gypo so ferociously that his face began to twitch. His face was so burned by the sun that it was almost black at a distance. At close quarters it looked a reddish brown. He had a glass eye. The other eye looked straight across the glass one, as if guarding it. He had to look away from a man in order to see him. This distortion in his vision had always filled his wife with terror, so that now she trembled whenever he looked at her. It was so uncanny, his looking at space like that. His body was short and slight. He was fifty years old.

He jumped off the bed and stood on the floor in his grey socks, his blue waistcoat unbuttoned, the little white patch of linen on the abdomen of his grey flannel shirt puffing in and out with his heavy breathing, his throat contorting, his hands gripping and ungripping restlessly.

Mrs McPhillip had awakened from her reverie as soon as her husband spoke. She had started up and gripped her breast over her heart with a dumb exclamation. Then she rubbed her two eyes hurriedly and looked at him. As soon as she saw him, her eyes grew dim again and her body subsided into the chair from which it had risen slightly.

'Jack,' she cried in an agonised voice, 'Jack! Jack, leave him alone. He was Frankie's friend. He was a friend of me dead boy's. Let him alone. What's done is done.'

'Be damned to that for a story,' cried Jack. His voice was weak and jerky, just like the voice of his dead son. 'A friend d'ye call him? What kind of friend d'ye call that waster that never did a day's work in his life? That ex-policeman! He was even driven outa the police. That's fine company for yer son, Maggie. It's the likes o' him that's brought Frankie to his death an' destruction. Them an' their revolutions. It's in Russia they should be where they could act the cannibal as much as they like, instead of leadin' good honest Irishmen astray. Why don't they get out of here and go back to England where they came from, with their rotten gold, gev to them be the Orangemen to turn Ireland into an uproar, so that the Freemasons could step in again and capture it. Ah-h-h-h, I'd like to get me fingers on yer throat, ye —'

He was rushing across the floor at Gypo, but the three men had jumped up and caught him. They held him back. Gypo stared at him, as if in perplexity, without moving. But the muscles of his shoulders stiffened, almost unconsciously. His eyes wandered slowly from the fuming husband to the sobbing wife who had again turned to the fire.

Then the people from the parlour rushed into the kitchen, attracted by the shouting. They were headed by Mary McPhillip, the daughter of the house. She was a handsome young woman, with a full figure, plump, with red cheeks, a firm jaw, auburn hair cropped in the current fashion, blue eyes that had a 'sensible' look in them and a rather large mouth that was opened wide by her excitement. Every bit of her except her mouth belonged to an average Irishwoman of the middle class. The mouth was a product of the slums. Its size and its propensity for disclosing the state of the mind by exaggerated movement, which is the hallmark of the slum girl, belied the neat elegance of the rest of the body and of all the clothes. She was still dressed just as she had arrived from the office, in a smart navy-blue costume which she had made herself. The skirt was rather short, in the current fashion, and she stood with her feet fairly wide apart, in the arrogant posture of a woman of good family. Her well-shaped calves were covered with thin black silk stockings. But she had her hands on her hips, unconsciously, as she stood in front of the indiscriminate crowd that had followed her in from the parlour, to find out what had caused the disturbance in the kitchen.

'What's the row about, father?' she said.

The accent was good, but a little too good. It was too refined. The pronunciation of the words was too correct. It had not that careless certainty of the born lady. She spoke in an angry tenor voice, in the rich soft tones of the Midlands, her mother's birthplace. Her voice had the softness of butter, that voice which patriotic Irishmen always associate with kindness and unassailable innocence and virtue, but which is really the natural mask of a stern, resolute character. 'Aren't we bad enough,' she continued, 'without your acting like a drunken tramp? Shut up and don't disgrace yourself.' She stamped her right foot and cried again: 'Shut up.'

The father relaxed immediately. He began to tremble slightly. He was very much afraid of his daughter. In spite of the power of vituperation which he undoubtedly possessed, he had been afraid of both his children. When Francis had become discontented and had joined the Revolutionary Organisation, the father had poured out threats and abuse for hours, almost every night, for the edification of his wife, but when the son came in he said nothing. He was a weak, nervous character, slightly hysterical, capable of committing any act on the spur of the moment, but incapable of pursuing a logical course of action resolutely. But his children were resolute. The son was resolute in his hatred of existing conditions of society. He was a resolute, determined revolutionary, with his father's energy. The daughter was resolute in her determination to get out of the slums.

The father slipped out of the hands of the men that were holding him and moved backwards until he reached the bed. He sat down on it without looking at it. He wiped his forehead with his sleeve although it was perfectly dry. But it had a prickly feeling in it, as if scores of needles had thrust themselves out from his brain through it. He always felt like that when he got an attack of nerves, especially since his son became a revolutionary, and it became known that his activities were being watched at police headquarters.

He looked at his daughter, at first in a cowed fashion. He was afraid of her, because she had become what he had urged her from her infancy to become, 'a lady'. He was afraid of her because she was so well educated, because she had such 'swell' friends, because she dressed so well, because she washed herself several times a day, because she spoke properly. But then he became irritated with all this and remembered that he himself was a Socialist, the chairman of his branch of the trade union, a political leader in the district, that all men were free and equal and ... all the pet phrases with which respectable Socialists delude themselves into the belief that they are philosophers and men of principle. He spoke with a ring of indignation and of warning in his voice. 'Am I to be called a tramp by me own daughter in me own house,' he cried, 'when I tell this ruffian his true character? Yes, an' every other ruffian that's the curse o' the workin'-class movement with their talk of violence an' murder an' revolution. All me life I have stood straight for the cause of me fellow-workers. I was one o' the first men to stand up for Connolly an' the cause o' Socialism, but I always said that the greatest enemies o' the workin' class were those o' their own kind that advocated violence. I ...'

'I told you to shut up,' said Mary in a calm, low voice, as she walked over to the bed, with her hands still on her hips. 'It's just like you,' she almost hissed, putting her doubled fists into the little pockets of her jacket. 'It's just like you to go back on your own son.'

She did not know why she was saying this, but she felt some force driving her on in opposition to her father, in defence of her dead brother. Perhaps it was the audience she had behind her. Because, strangely enough, she herself hated Frankie for belonging to the Revolutionary Organisation, since she got a position two years before as clerk in the offices of Gogarty and Hogan. Before that she had been a revolutionary herself, but not a member of any organisation. She used to attend meetings and cheer and get into arguments with irritated old gentlemen, etc. But during the past two years her outlook on life had undergone a subtle change, gradual but definite. At first she began to get 'disillusioned', as she used to tell Francis, with the blasé air of a young girl of nineteen. Then she used to lecture him on the desirability of keeping better company. This was at the time when she made the acquaintance of Joseph Augustine Short, a young gentleman who was serving his apprenticeship with Gogarty and Hogan and wore plus fours and left Harcourt Street Station every Sunday morning, to play golf down the country somewhere. Finally, she became opposed violently 'to the whole theory of revolution', as being degenerating and 'subversive of all moral ideas'. She became religious and got the idea into her head that she could convert Commandant Dan Gallagher, the leader of the revolutionary movement. All this later development had been quite recent, however, and had not matured fully in her character. It was yet merely plastic. It had not become a fixed habit of thought, surrounded by deep and bitter prejudices, that form themselves into 'firm convictions'.

For that reason she had responded suddenly to that strange exaltation, born of hatred for the law, which is traditional and hereditary in the slums. The one glorious romance of the slums is the feeling of intense hatred against the oppressive hand of the law, which sometimes stretches out to strike some one, during a street row, during an industrial dispute, during a Nationalist uprising. It is a clarion call to all the spiritual emotion that finds no other means of expression in that sordid environment, neither in art, nor in industry, nor in commercial undertakings, nor in the more reasonable searchings for a religious understanding of the universal creation.

'I stand by what Frankie has done,' she cried, turning to the people. 'I don't agree with him in politics, but every man has a right to his opinions and every man should fight for his rights according to ...' She got confused and stammered a little. Then she raised her hand suddenly with an enthusiastic gesture and cried in a loud voice: 'He was my brother anyway, and I'm going to stand up for him.'

Then she suddenly put her handkerchief to her nose and blew it fiercely. There was a loud murmur of applause. The father made a half-hearted attempt to say something, but he subsided. Mrs McPhillip was heard to mumble something, but nobody paid any attention to her. Nobody noticed her except Gypo, who still sat on the floor staring at her, fondling the memory of her past goodness to him, like a sumptuous luxury that he must soon relinquish. Although he had been the cause of all the excitement, he was now forgotten in the still greater excitement, caused by the argument between the father and daughter of the dead revolutionary.

Then Mary turned to Gypo and addressed him.

'If you were a friend of my brother,' she said, 'you are quite welcome here. Come into the parlour a minute. I want to talk to you.'

Chapter Four

Gypo started and looked at Mary with his tufted eyebrows twitching ominously like snouts. But he said nothing. She was embarrassed by the uncouth stare and flushed slightly. She coughed in her throat and put her fingers to her lips. She began to talk rapidly, as if apologising to the uncouth giant for having had the temerity to address him a request.

'It's because Frankie told us that he met you in the Dunboy Lodging House before he came here. You are the only one he met in town before he came in here, so I thought maybe that … you might be able …'

She stopped in confusion, amazed at the startling change that had come over Gypo. He had become seized by some violent emotion as she spoke until his face contorted as if he were gazing at some awe-inspiring horror. Then she stopped. His face stood still gaping at her. Then for some reason or other he jumped to his feet, shouting as he did so at the top of his voice: 'All right.'

As he bent his head and the upper part of his body to jump to his feet, his right trousers pocket was turned mouth to the ground. Four silver coins fell to the cement floor with a rattling noise. These coins were the change he had received in the public-house.

He was petrified. Every muscle in his body stiffened. His head stood still. His jaws set like the teeth of a bear-trap that has been sprung fruitlessly. Behind his eyes he felt the delicious cold and congealed sensation of being about to fight a desperate and bloody battle. For he was certain that the four white silver coins lying nakedly, ever so nakedly, on the floor, were as indicative of his betrayal of his comrade as a confession uttered aloud in a crowded market-place.

Somebody stooped to pick up the coins.

'Let them alone,' shouted Gypo.

He swooped down to the floor and his right palm, spread flat, covered the coins with the dull sound of a heavy dead fish falling on an iron deck.

'I only wanted to hand them to ye, Gypo,' panted the weazened flour-mill worker who had stooped to pick them up. He had been knocked to his knees by Gypo's swoop.

Gypo took no notice of the explanation. As he collected the coins in his left fist and rose again, leaning on his right hand, he was listening, waiting for the attack.

But there was no attack. Everybody was amazed, mesmerised by the curious movements of the irritated giant. They stared with open mouths, all expect Bartly Mulholland and Tommy Connor, who stood in the background, looking curiously at one another with narrowed eyes. Darting his eyes around the room, Gypo caught sight of the two of them. Spurred by some sudden impulse, he held up his right hand over his head, he stamped his right foot, he threw back his head and shouted, looking straight upwards: 'I swear before Almighty God that I warned him to keep away from the house.'

There was a dead silence for three seconds. Then a perceptible shudder ran through the room. Everybody remembered with horror that there was a suspicion abroad, a suspicion that an informer had betrayed Francis Joseph McPhillip. Informer! A horror to be understood fully only by an Irish mind. For an awful moment each one present suspected himself or herself. Then each looked at his or her neighbour. Gradually rage took the place of fear. But it had no direction. Even the most daring gasped when their minds suggested that possibly the great fierce giant might have had ... Impossible!

'There's no man suspects ye, Gypo. Ye needn't be afraid of that,' cried Tommy Connor, the huge red-faced docker with immense jaws like a bullock, who had been whispering to Bartly Mulholland.

He had spoken spontaneously with a queer note of anger in his voice.

'Nobody suspects ye. Good God, man! ...'

There was a chorus of agreement. Everybody was eager to assent to the statement that Connor had made. Somebody put his hand on Gypo's shoulder and began to say: 'Sure it's well known that ...'

But Gypo elbowed the man away fiercely and set out hurriedly across the floor towards Mrs McPhillip. He elbowed the people out of his way without looking at them. He stood in front of Mrs McPhillip. He stared at her impassively for a few moments. Then he put his hand slowly to his head and took off his hat. He felt moved by an uncontrollable impulse. All his actions had completed themselves before his mind was aware of them. His mind was struggling along aimlessly in pursuit of his actions, impotently deprecating them and whispering warnings. But it was powerless.

This impulse that had possession of him now was of the same origin as the one that controlled him when he was looking into the shop window thinking of his youth.

He was beyond himself. His lips quivered. His throat got stuffed. He swallowed his breath with an articulate sound, resembling a cry of pain. He held out his left hand towards Mrs McPhillip. He opened the hand slowly. The four white silver coins lay there.

'Take it,' he muttered. 'Ye were good to me an' I'm sorry for yer trouble.'

He felt a mad desire to pull out the roll of notes and give them to her also, but the very thought of such a mad action made him shiver. Instead he dropped the four coins into Mrs McPhillip's lap.

Mrs McPhillip glanced at the money and then burst into loud sobs. The sound maddened Gypo. He turned about and rushed towards the door. He stubbed his foot against the door-jamb and hurtled into the hall. He rushed along the passage, cursing and striking furiously at everybody that came in his way. He stood outside the street door and breathed deeply.

Two men rushed out after him. They were Bartly Mulholland and Tommy Connor, the docker.

CHAPTER FIVE

'Gypo!'

Gypo had taken three steps down the street when his name came to him through the darkness, uttered in that long-drawn-out whisper which is the customary intonation among revolutionaries. He contracted his back suddenly like an ass that has been struck with violence. Then he halted. He did not turn about or reply. He waited. He listened with a beating heart to the slow footsteps that came up to him from behind. One, two, three, four ... they stopped. Gypo looked to his left. Bartly Mulholland was standing there.

The two of them stood in front of a window through which lamp-light was streaming, across Gypo's chest on to Mulholland's face. Mulholland's yellow face looked almost black in the lamp-light. It was furrowed vertically from the temples to the jaws, with deep black furrows. The mouth was large and open, fixed in a perpetual grin that had absolutely no merriment in it, that fixed grin of sardonic contempt that is nearly always seen on the faces of men who make a business of concealing their thoughts. The nose was long and narrow. The ears were large. The forehead was furrowed horizontally. The skin on the forehead was very white in contrast to the dark skin on the cheeks. The furrows on the forehead were very shallow and narrow, like thin lines drawn with a sharp pencil. In fact, the whole appearance of the face was that of an artificial face, such as that produced in the dressing-room of an actor by means of paints, etc. This suggestion was strengthened by the appearance of the hair that straggled in loose wisps from beneath the shovel-shaped peak of the grey tweed cap. The hair appeared to be a dirty brown wig, much the worse for wear. But neither the hair nor any portion of the face was artificial. Everything had come from the hand of Nature, which seemed, by some peculiar whimsy, to have cast this individual for the rôle of a conspirator. The face was the face of a clown to hide the conspirator's eyes, except from a very close scrutiny. The eyes were the colour of sea-water that is dirty with grey sand. These eyes are sometimes described as watery blue, but it is a totally wrong description. There was an indescribable coldness and depth in them which it is beyond the power of any colour to describe. They stared without a movement of the pupils or of the lashes at Gypo's face, expressing no emotion whatever. They were not doors of the soul like ordinary eyes, but spy-holes. They stared glassily like a cat's eyes.

This curious creature was dressed like a workman, in heavy hobnailed boots, brown corduroy trousers with strings tied around the legs below the knees, a black handkerchief tied in sailor fashion around his neck, and an old grey tweed coat that almost reached half-way down his thighs. His hands were stuck deep down in the pockets of his coat.

'Where's yer hurry takin' ye, Gypo?' he drawled in a low, lazy voice, as if he were half drunk or lying on his back in a sunny place on a hot summer's day.

'Who's in a hurry?' growled Gypo. 'How d'ye make out I'm in a hurry?'

'Oh, nothin' atall. Don't get yer rag out, Gypo. Ye might talk to the people. We never see ye atall now since ye left the Organisation. Are ye workin'?'

'No,' snapped Gypo angrily. The short ejaculation coming from his thick lips sounded like a solitary gunshot coming a long way over still air. 'I ain't workin', an' all o' you fellahs, that were supposed to be comrades o' mine, take damn good care to keep out o' the way, for fear I might ask ye for the price of a feed or a flop. Yer a quare lot o' Communists.'

Mulholland drew himself in at the middle, emitted his breath, shrugged his shoulders, thrust out his right foot and leaned his weight backwards heavily on his left foot. Then he turned his head up sideways to let the drizzling rain beat on the back of his neck instead of on his face. The grin left his mouth and for a moment he appeared to have become angry. 'Ye don't seem to be in any need o' money tonight, Gypo,' he breathed ever so gently.

Then just as suddenly he broke into an almost fawning and ingratiating smile. He continued in his ordinary lazy voice:

'Don't be tryin' to make out yer broke, after me seein'

the money that fell outa yer pocket in the kitchen beyond just now. Aren't ye goin' to stand us a wet?'

Gypo had begun to shiver. He shivered with minute movements, just as a massive tree shivers, when the forest earth is shaken beneath it by a heavy concussion. Then suddenly he recovered himself. Without pausing to think, he shot out both hands simultaneously like piston-rods. Mulholland gasped as the two huge hands closed about his throat. He struck out helplessly with his own hands at Gypo's body. His blows were as ineffective as the flapping of a linnet's wings against its cage. Gypo's face was lit with a demoniac pleasure as he raised Mulholland's body from the ground, clutching it by the throat with his two hands. He raised it up like a book which he wanted to read, until Mulholland's eyes were level with his own. Then they both looked at one another.

Mulholland's eyes were still cold and glassy, impenetrable and absolutely without emotion. Gypo's eyes were ferocious and eager, full of a mad savage joy. His mouth had shut tight and the skin had run taut over the glossy humps on his face, so that his face looked like tanned pigskin. Mulholland's tongue was hanging out.

Then Gypo groaned and prepared to crush out Mulholland's life between his thick fingers, when he was disturbed by a shout from behind. He dropped Mulholland to the street like a bag and whirled about. Tommy Connor had rushed up from the doorway of No. 44 where he had been waiting. He was standing now with his mouth wide open in astonishment and terror.

'What's wrong, boys?' he cried. 'In the Name o' God what are ye up to?'

'He suspects me,' cried Gypo, 'and ...' Then he sank into silence, unable to say any more. His unsatisfied fury choked him.

'Suspects ye of what?' cried Connor. 'What d'ye say he suspects ye of?'

'I didn't suspect him of anythin' atall,' cried Mulholland, rising to his feet slowly. His face was contorting with pain. 'I only asked him to —'

'Yer a liar, ye did,' bellowed Gypo. 'Ye suspect me, an' well I know ye, Bartly Mulholland. D'ye think I don't know ye an' all about ye? Ye got a grudge agin me an' Frankie McPhillip this long time. Don't I know yer Intelligence Officer for No. 3 Area an' that yer nosin' around now —'

'Shut up or I'll plug ye where ye stand,' hissed Connor, ramming the muzzle of his revolver into Gypo's side. 'Don't ye know there are people listenin'? D'ye want to let the dogs o' the street know the secrets o' the Organisation that ye swore on yer oath to kape?' He panted and continued in a lower voice still: 'Are ye mad, or are ye lookin' to get plugged?'

Gypo's mouth remained open in the act of beginning a word, but he did not utter the word. He half turned his body in order to look into Connor's face. He saw it, big, angry, menacing, with the nostrils distended, so that the insides, blackened with coal, were visible. The face was within four inches of Gypo's face. Connor's revolver muzzle was pressing into Gypo's right armpit. Gypo feared neither the face nor the revolver. He stared with wrinkled forehead at Connor, knowing that he could crush him and Mulholland, both together, crush them to death, to a shapeless pulp, by clasping them in his arms.

But they were not merely two men, two human beings. They were something more than that. They represented the Revolutionary Organisation. They were merely cogs in the wheel of that Organisation. That was what he feared, what rendered him powerless. He feared that mysterious, intangible thing, that was all brain and no body. An intelligence without a body. A thing that was full of plans, implacable, reaching out everywhere invisibly, with invisible tentacles like a supernatural monster. A thing that was like a religion, mysterious, occult, devilish.

Frankie McPhillip had once told him that they tracked a man to the Argentine Republic, somewhere on the other side of the world. Shot him dead in a lodging-house at night too, without saying a word. What d'ye think of that?

'All right,' he said at last, 'put away yer gat, Tommy. I'll stay quiet.'

A few people had gathered on the far side of the street and were looking on curiously. An immense crowd would have already gathered on ordinary occasions, but there was tension and anxiety in the district that night. Shooting might begin at any minute. It was always so. One death brings another in its train. Each man thought this in his own mind, although nobody breathed a word. It was a kind of silent terror.

'Come on, boys,' said Connor, 'let's get away from here. We're gatherin' a crowd.'

'Come on down to Ryan's,' whispered Mulholland to Gypo, in his usual lazy, insinuating voice, as if nothing had happened. 'Commandant Gallagher is down there. He wants to see ye.'

74

Chapter Five

'What does he want with me?' growled Gypo. 'I'm not a member o' the Organisation any more. He's got nothin' to do with me. I'm not goin'.'

'Come on, man,' whispered Connor, 'don't stand here chawin'. He's not goin' t' ate ye. Come on. Is it afraid o' the Commandant ye are? Why so?'

'I'm not afraid of any man that was ever pupped,' growled Gypo. 'Come on.'

The three men walked off abreast, in step like soldiers, their feet falling loudly on to the wet pavement, heels first. At the corner the footfalls became confused. Gypo spat into the street. Mulholland sneezed. They entered the public-house by a little narrow side door that had a bright brass knob on it. They went along a narrow passage, through a stained-glass swing door, into a brightly lit oblong room.

A man was sitting by a little gas-fire on a high three-legged stool facing the door. When Gypo saw the man he stopped dead.

The man was Commandant Dan Gallagher.

CHAPTER SIX

During the previous autumn a terrific sensation had been caused all over Ireland by the farm-labourers' strike in the M— district. The sensation was brought to a crisis by the murder of the Farmers' Union secretary. For the first time it was discovered that the Revolutionary Organisation had spread its influence among the farm labourers and over the whole country. Something had been discovered. A Government secret organisation had overlapped the Communist organisation and there was a little effervescence, which was immediately suppressed by the Government. Very little leaked out publicly. The newspapers were forbidden to talk about it. The Conservative organs in Dublin had timid editorials demanding that the Government should take the people into its confidence. What really was the extent of this 'conspiracy against the national safety'?

Then immediately Commandant Dan Gallagher became a public figure and a general topic of conversation. He came out of obscurity in a night as it were. People suddenly discovered that he was a power in the country. He was photographed and interviewed and his photographs appeared in all the newspapers both in this country and in England and in America. He promptly denounced the murder as a 'foul crime against the honour of the working class and the whole revolutionary movement'. He began to be feared intensely in official quarters as 'a slippery customer'. This phrase was used at a Government Cabinet meeting.

Just about that time, the leading organ of the English aristocracy had a two-column leading article on the subject of Commandant Dan Gallagher. In the course of the article a short survey of Gallagher's life was given sarcastically. The following is an extract from the article:

... This flower of Irish manhood grew on an obscure dunghill, in the daily practice of all these virtues, which are indigenous to the Irish soil, if one is to believe the flowery utterances of the politicians on St Patrick's Day. His father was a small peasant farmer in Kilkenny. Having assisted very probably in the gentle assassination of a few of his landlord's agents in the past, he reverently decided to devote the activities of his promising son to the service of his God. But Daniel would have none of it. He was meant for other fields of conquest. He succeeded in making himself famous in the ecclesiastical seminary in which he was being prepared for the priesthood, by smashing the skull of one of the Roman priests during a dispute on the playground. The instrument used in this display of boyish gaiety was the favourite Irish weapon, a hurling-stick.

The young Fionn McCumhaill was expelled and fled the country. He drifted around for eight years without a trace of his whereabouts. Very possibly he spent the time in the United

States. We can well imagine that he was favourably received among those organisations in the United States which are governed by Irishmen intent on the destruction of the British Empire by conspiracy, murder, slander, and all the other delectable schemes that come to life so readily in the Gaelic brain. We can imagine him perfecting himself in the arts of gunmanship, deceit and those obscure forms of libidinous vice which are said to be practised by this morose type of revolutionary in order to dull his sensibilities into an apathy which the consciousness of even the most horrible enormities cannot penetrate ...

At any rate he has returned to his beloved motherland endowed liberally with those qualities which make him dear to the hearts of all Irishmen of murderous inclinations. These latter unfortunately form as yet a considerable portion of the population of Ireland. Mr Gallagher has a powerful and enthusiastic following.

His brand of Communism is of the type that appeals most to the Irish nature. It is a mixture of Roman Catholicism, Nationalist Republicanism and Bolshevism. Its chief rallying cries are: "Loot and Murder." ...

The following is an extract from an article which appeared a little while later in the columns of the official organ of the American Revolutionary Organisation:

When the glorious history of the struggle for proletarian liberation in Ireland comes to be written, the name of Comrade Dan Gallagher will stampede from cover to cover in one uninterrupted blaze of glory ... No other living man has given nobler service to the world revolution than this sturdy fighter, who rules the workers of Dublin with greater power than is wielded by the Irish bourgeoisie, who are still nominally in the saddle. The collapse of the farm-workers' strike need not dishearten those comrades who expected great things from the hoisting of the red flag at M— last October. Comrade Gallagher has not seen fit as yet to call the Irish bourgeois bluff. When the time arrives ...

In November a representative of the International Executive of the Revolutionary Organisation was sent over from the Continent to make a special report on the situation in Ireland. The following is an extract from a secret report drawn up by him, after spending three months in Ireland secretly touring the country:

... For the moment it would be a tactical blunder to expel Comrade Gallagher from the International. At the same time there can be no doubt that the Irish Section has deviated entirely from the principles of revolutionary Communism as laid down in the laws of the International. Comrade Gallagher rules the national Organisation purely and simply as a dictator. There is a semblance of an Executive Committee but only in name. The tactics are guided by whatever whim is uppermost in Comrade Gallagher's mind at the moment. Contrary to the orders issued from Headquarters, the Organisation is still purely military and has made hardly any attempt to come into the open as a legal political party. This is perhaps not entirely due to Comrade Gallagher's fault. There are local causes, arising out of the recent struggle for national independence, which has left the working class in the grip of a romantic love of conspiracy, a strong religious and bourgeois-nationalist outlook on life and a hatred of constitutional methods. This makes it difficult for the moment to check Comrade Gallagher's hold ....

CHAPTER SEVEN

Gallagher's eyes had opened wide when the three men came into the room. Then they narrowed until they became thin slits under their long black lashes. He nodded to Mulholland and Connor. Then he stared at Gypo.

Gypo returned the stare. The two men, unlike in their features and bodies, were exactly alike in the impassivity of their stare. Gypo's face was like a solid and bulging granite rock, impregnable but lacking that intelligence that is required by strength in order to be able to conquer men. Gallagher's face was less powerful physically, but it was brimful of intelligence. The forehead was high and it seemed to surround the face. The eyes were large and wide apart. The nose was long and straight. The mouth was thin-lipped. The jaws were firm but slender and refined like a woman's jaws. The whole face had absolutely no colour, but there was a constant movement in the cheeks, as if tiny streams were coursing irregularly beneath the smooth glossy skin. The hair was coal-black and cut close. The ears were large. The neck opened out gradually from the base of the shoulders on either side, like a hill disappearing into a plain.

Then he jumped off his high stool and stood with his legs wide apart in front of Gypo. He was five feet eleven inches and a half in height, but Gypo towered over him with his extra two inches. Gallagher wore a loose brown raincoat, from his throat almost to his ankles, that made his well-built frame look larger and stouter. Yet Gypo, standing bare in his dungarees that were now almost sodden with rain, looked immense compared to him. Gallagher held his hands in his raincoat pockets thrust in front of his body, as if he were pointing pistols at Gypo. Gypo held his hands loosely by his sides, two vast red hands hanging limply from whitish round wrists. Gallagher wore a broad-brimmed black velour hat of a fashionable make. Gypo's tattered little round hat was still perched on his skull, like a tiny school-cap on an overgrown youngster.

They looked at one another, the one, handsome, well dressed, confident and indifferent; the other crude, ragged, amazed, anxious.

'Well, Gypo,' drawled Gallagher, in the irritating, contemptuous tone that he affected. 'Ye don't seem glad to see me.'

'Can't say that I am,' replied Gypo curtly, almost without moving his lips. 'I don't see no reason to be glad to see ye, Commandant Gallagher. Ye were never a friend o' mine, an' I ain't in the habit o' crawlin' on me belly to anybody that don't like me. I'm not one o' yer pet lambs any more, so ye needn't do any bleatin' as far as I'm concerned. One man is as good as another in this rotten ould world. I'm usin' yer own words, amn't I?'

Gallagher laughed out loud, a merry laugh that showed his white teeth. He shrugged his shoulders and took a turn around the room. He took a packet of cigarettes from his pocket as he walked and selected one. He kept laughing until he paused to light the cigarette over near the stained-glass window.

'Yer a queer fish, Gypo,' he said, again laughing, as he paused to throw the used match into a spittoon.

Then he cast a glance all round the room and came back again to Gypo. Mulholland and Connor watched him all the time with that loving interest with which a crowd watches the movements of a champion boxer who is walking around the ring in his dressing-gown, preparatory to a big fight. They smiled when Gallagher laughed. They stopped smiling when he stopped laughing.

Gypo, on the other hand, watched Gallagher's movements angrily. He felt a desire to pounce on him and crush him to death before he could do any harm.

Then Gallagher came up to him and caught him by the right shoulder in a friendly and confidential manner.

'Listen, Gypo,' he said. 'You've got a grudge against me no doubt for getting you expelled from the Organisation, but you have nobody to blame but yourself. I sent ye down, on the orders of the Executive Committee, you and Frank McPhillip, to look after the defence work of the strikers. What orders did I give the two of you? Can you remember? Well, I'll remind you. TO KEEP OFF THE BOOZE AND NOT TO USE THE LEAD UNLESS YOU WERE ATTACKED. But what did you do? The very first thing, the two of you got hold of two women. That, of course, must have been

Chapter Seven

Frankie's work, because I don't suppose you were ever a great magnet among the women. Women were Frankie's weak spot, damn it. But anyhow, it doesn't matter very much which of you started the hunt. You tasted the honey as well as he did it, as far as was reported to me. The two of you got drunk at M— in company with these two women. You got so mad drunk that McPhillip went to shoot up the town. You might have assisted him in that pastime, but your time was occupied trying to pull a lamp-post up by the roots in Oliver Plunket Street, for a bet of a gallon of stout. In the very middle of your entertainment, McPhillip met the secretary of the Farmers' Union and shot him dead. That made you get over your drunkenness damn quick, didn't it? The two of you bolted without making any attempt to cover your tracks. You ran like two hares. You came into Dublin with a red herring of a story about an attack and what not. It WAS a tall yarn. Well? D'ye know what I'm going to tell you, Gypo?'

He paused dramatically and looked Gypo closely in the eyes. Gypo never moved a muscle in his face. He grunted interrogatively from somewhere deep down in his chest. Gallagher continued very slowly:

'I'm going to tell you this much, Gypo. Only for me, you wouldn't have got away with it as easily as you did that time. There were others who wanted to give you this, for disobeying orders.'

He moved his right hand suddenly beneath his raincoat, thrusting it forward against Gypo's lower ribs. Gypo felt the contact of a blunt hard metal. He knew it was the muzzle of Gallagher's Colt automatic pistol, but

Gypo took no notice of the pistol. He was not afraid of the pistol. But he was afraid of Gallagher's eyes into which he was looking steadily. He didn't like them. They were so cold and blue and mysterious. Goodness knows what might be hidden behind them. His face began an irregular chaotic movement. His jaws, cheek-bones, nose, mouth and forehead convulsed in opposite directions, as if a draught of wind had stolen in under the skin of his face and caused it to undulate. Then the face set again. The neck swelled and the little eyes bulged.

'No use tryin' yer tricks on me, Danny Gallagher,' he growled, knocking the pistol muzzle away with a slight movement of his right hand. Although the blow was slight, it caused Gallagher to reel backwards two paces before he regained his balance. His face darkened for a moment and then again he broke into a smile. Gypo continued in a thunderous melancholy voice: 'Gallagher, I got no use for you. Them's all lies ye were tellin' just now about tryin' to save me life when I was before the Court of Inquiry last October. I know very well they was. Yerrah, are ye goin' to tell me that yer not the chief boss an' God knows what in the Organisation? Who else has got any authority in it except yersel'? Yah. I got no use for ye. Yer a liar. Yer no good. An' I'd be in my job yet in the police only for ye an' yer soft talk. It was you that got me outa me job with yer promises o' the Lord knows what. I declare to Almighty God that I done more for yer bloody Organisation than any other man in Ireland. I done things that no man unhung could do. An' ye went an' threw me out on account of an ould farmer gettin' plugged. Me an' McPhillip. What did we get for it? Wha' … ye rotten …'

Chapter Seven

Gypo rambled off incoherently into a long string of blasphemous curses, raising his voice as he did so. His arms were raised outwards in a curve and his head was lowered, as if he were in the act of performing a swimming exercise. He frothed at the mouth and glared from one to the other of the three men, as if undecided which to attack first.

Then suddenly a little wooden panel in the wall to the right was raised up and a pretty red head was pushed through. It was Kitty the barmaid.

'Lord save us,' she cried, putting her fingers to her lips as she looked at Gypo. 'Who is that fellah? What's he doin' here, Dan?'

'That's all right, Kitty,' said Gallagher with a light laugh; 'he's a friend of mine. We are having a cursing competition.'

And he laughed heartily as he walked to the spittoon with the stub of his cigarette.

Gypo turned around and looked at the terrified face of the barmaid. As he looked at her beautiful face and her pretty soft hair that shimmered in the artificial light, his head swam and his eyes went watery. His anger left his body immediately so that it seemed to empty and collapse. It had been rigid and like a tree. Now it became loose and jointless. He stood with stooping head and wondering eyes, looking at the barmaid.

The barmaid, seeing the change she had effected by her presence in the unruly giant, grew conceited. She smiled in a superior way and dabbed at her hair. She looked around at the others with an air of: 'D'ye all see that now?'

Then Gallagher came up to the aperture jauntily, took her two hands in his and looked enticingly into her eyes. Her eyes winced for a moment as if she had become suddenly afraid. Then she smiled softly, wearily, like a woman passionately in love. Gallagher bent down his head and whispered something in her ear. She burst into a loud laugh. Gallagher smiled, listening to her. Then he suddenly sighed and rapped the counter curtly.

'Four glasses of Jameson's quickly,' he said in a low, sharp, cold voice.

The barmaid stopped laughing as suddenly as if she had been stricken by a pain. She pulled down the shutter, lisping as she did so: 'Yes, Dan.'

Gallagher came back to Gypo and put his hand again on Gypo's shoulder. Gypo had his two hands now in his trousers pockets. After his unsuccessful outburst he felt tired. He wanted to go away somewhere and lie down and sleep for days and days. His mind was in a maze. He was very tired. As he looked at Gallagher he even felt a longing to confide his secret to him. Gallagher's eyes were so devilishly attractive. They seemed to draw things out of Gypo towards themselves. They would be able to form a plan and ...

Gypo had uttered one syllable of Gallagher's name before he realised the real identity of the man and the consequences of a confession to him. The name died on his lips. Gallagher smiled.

'Gypo, old boy,' he said in a friendly tone, 'ye had better forget all that's past. We've got something on hand that's as much your business as ours. So we can act together on it. That's why I sent Bartly Mulholland into

McPhillip's house to look for ye. A pal of yours has been done in by the police. D'ye hear? It looks like an informer's job. We have to get that informer. It's really no business of the Organisation, because Frank had ceased to be a member. He was only an ordinary civilian criminal as far as we are concerned. But an informer is an informer. He's got to be wiped out like the first sign of a plague as soon as he's spotted. He's a common enemy. He's got to be got, Gypo. And it's up to you to give us a hand in tracking the traitor that sent your pal to his death. Because ...'

At that moment the slide was drawn up again sharply and the barmaid appeared at the aperture with four glasses of whiskey on a tray. Gallagher went to the aperture, paid for the whiskey, handed glasses to Connor and Mulholland, received his change, pinched the bar-maid's cheek and made her scream, laughed, pulled down the shutter himself and then advanced smiling to Gypo with a glass of whiskey in each hand. He held out one glass to Gypo. Gypo stared at it without making any movement to take it or reject it.

He had followed all Gallagher's movements with the stupid and suspicious wonder of a terrified wild animal that thinks some trick is being played on it. Now he stared at the glass as if he suspected some trick in that too.

'Take it,' said Gallagher coldly. 'Take it, man, if you've any sense. It's better have me as a friend than as an enemy. If you are not going to help us in this job ... er ... people might think ... er ... that ...'

'Uh,' began Gypo, with a shrug of his whole body. Then he stopped panting. He went on, speaking at a very

high pitch. 'It's not that but ... Look here ... It's how ...'
His voice suddenly deepened into a hoarse shout, 'It's
how I don't know what I'm doin'.'

He stopped. Gallagher glanced at Mulholland.
Mulholland's cat's eyes both winked imperceptibly.

'I've been starvin' here for the past six months,' continued Gypo, suddenly breaking out into a torrent of
words. He talked like a negro, hollow, thunderous, and
melancholy. 'I've been kicking about this town an' every
one o' you fellahs I met passed me by without a word
as if I never knew ye. I had been over in the House there,
livin' from hand to mouth on whatever I could bum
from sailors and pimps and dockers. I got no clothes. I
got no money. I got nothin'. An' then you come up all
of a sudden with yer soft talk. Well ... uh ... how is it
that ...'

He came to a stop once more with his chest heaving.
He seemed to be about to go into a rage once more, but
suddenly Gallagher moved closer to him and whispered
gently and soothingly:

'Look here, Gypo. I'm going to make a fair deal with
you. I'll admit you have done a lot for the movement. You
have paid the penalty during the last six months for the
dangerous position you placed the whole Organisation in
last October. We'll call that quits on one condition. If you
can give us a clue to the man that informed on Francis
Joseph McPhillip, I'll get ye taken back again into the
Organisation at yer old job on Headquarters Staff. Here.
Take this drink.'

Gypo's hand shot out immediately. He grasped the
glass and Gallagher's hand both together in his immense

paw. The two men almost struggled trying to disengage their hands. As soon as the glass was free Gypo put it to his lips and drained it. Then he stalked slowly over to the mantelpiece and placed the empty glass on it. With his back to his companions he paused to wipe his mouth with his sleeve.

He wanted time to compose himself. Gallagher's proposal had taken him so completely by surprise that he was beside himself. Since that infernal moment when he kicked open the door of the police-station, his whole life had been submerged in a pitch-black cloud that was impenetrable and offered no escape. He had been alone, outcast, encompassed by a universal horde of enemies. Now, suddenly, he was offered a means of escape by the great Gallagher himself. Gallagher, the great Gallagher, had made him an offer. He would get back again into the Organisation. Again people would be afraid of him. Again clever men would be always at hand to make plans for him, to provide him with money for doing daring things, to protect him, to praise his recklessness, his strength and his ... Mother of Mercy! What luck!

As he wiped his mouth on his sleeve at the counter an insane idea struck him, such was his eagerness to qualify immediately for re-admission to the Organisation. For a moment he contemplated the man who had gone into the police-station as a being apart from himself. Sound began to gurgle up his throat. It was an attempt on the part of his present personality to speak and deliver information against that dazed Gypo Nolan who had stumbled into the police-station. But the sound froze in his throat, in a ball, hurting him as if his tonsils had swollen suddenly.

He realised that he himself was one with that ponderous fellow, wearing a little tattered round hat, who had gone into the police-station. It was only another artifice on the part of something within him, his conscience maybe, to persuade him to make a confession of his betrayal.

That same impulse had confused him all the time that he was looking at Mrs McPhillip.

And then, just as in the public-house, when he had been terrified by Katie Fox, his mind had given birth to an insane plan about a sailor in a tavern, so now also his mind conceived an amazing fabrication. It entered his brain suddenly, like a thunder-storm, with noise and fury. His face and eyes lit up. He opened his mouth. He walked over to Gallagher quickly and spoke in a hissing whisper.

'I'll tell ye who informed,' he gasped. 'It's the Rat Mulligan. It's him as sure as Christ was crucified.'

The three men gathered up close to him. They all looked behind them suspiciously and then stared at him with narrowed eyes. There was a moment of tense silence. Then each drew a deep breath. Connor slipped his finger over the trigger of his revolver. 'The Rat Mulligan!' exclaimed Gallagher at length. 'How d'ye make that out, Gypo?'

'I'll tell ye,' cried Gypo triumphantly. Then he paused again and looked about him with furrowed brows dramatically. 'I didn't like to say anythin' mesel' for reasons that everybody knows. A man can never be sure of a thing like that. An' God knows it's a quare charge to bring agin a man. But as ye put it the way ye put it, Commandant, about him bein' me pal an' me duty to the

Cause, well … Still! Poor Mulligan!

'Oh, come on,' cried Gallagher, twitching with excitement. 'Get finished with what you have to say. Make your statement, man.'

But Gypo was not to be hurried. An amazing arrogance had taken possession of him. He reached out towards the glass of whiskey that Gallagher still held untasted in his hand.

'Gimme that, Commandant,' he said, 'seein' as yer not tastin' it.' Gallagher nervously handed him the drink. 'Thanks. Here's luck. Ah! Good stuff that. Well. This is how it was. Just after Frankie left me in the dining-room, I suddenly thought to mesel' that I had better run after him and try an' head him off from goin' home. I had been tryin' to make him clear out of town again an' not go near Titt Street, but the same cranky fellah that he always was wouldn't listen to a word of what I said. So that I said to mysel', Lord have mercy on him, "Well, me fine fellah, I'm not goin' to get mesel' into a fever, tryin' to keep ye outa harm's way, an' get cursed upside down for doin' so." Well, anyway, as soon as he had gone, I decided to follow him and give him a last shout. I ran out into the hall, an' who do I see but the Rat sneakin' around the corner. I ran down the hall. There was the Rat at the door with his hands in his overcoat pockets peerin' up the lane. Then he dived out into the street. I chased after him. I was just in time to see Frankie turnin' the corner into the road with the Rat crawlin' after him. It's as clear as daylight. So it is. Lord have mercy on the dead, if I had only thought of it at the time, Frankie might have been alive at this minute instead o' been a frozen corpse. Give us another drink, Commandant. Me throat is parched.'

Without a word or a glance Gallagher walked up to the counter and rapped at the aperture. Gypo did not even condescend to follow his movements. His conceit was now boundless. He realised that he himself was amazingly cunning. He even felt a contempt for Gallagher in his mind. As for Mulholland and Connor ... He glanced at them appraisingly, as a man might glance at a useful pair of dogs. It was the same kind of glance that Gallagher was in the habit of directing towards everybody.

Gallagher brought a fresh glass of whiskey and handed it to him. He took it without a word of thanks. He walked to the spittoon and emptied his mouth into it. Then he swallowed the drink again at one draught. He put the empty glass on the mantelpiece and coughed deeply. He clasped his hands behind his back with a loud sound. He began to balance himself backwards and forwards on his heels like a policeman.

'How didn't I think of it before?' he cried, looking thoughtfully at the ceiling.

He was completely immersed now in the contemplation of his own cleverness. He did not notice the utter silence with which his story had been received by Gallagher and the other two men. He was contemplating with pleasure the old days, when he had a criminal in his charge, in the cells, at the police-station. He used to stand for a whole hour in the stillness of the night, baiting the prisoner, terrorising him with his eyes, with a sudden display of strength, with a mad laugh, with silent staring. He was feeling that same sensation now. Exhilarated by the whiskey he had drunk, and carried away by the concentrated nerve-strain of the past few hours, he imagined that he had Gallagher and the other two men at his mercy, that he was a policeman and that they were civilians who were asking a favour of him, an illegal favour that put them in his power. It was just that way in the old days, when he used to sell Gallagher little titbits of information over a drink; little harmless, he thought, bits of information, about headquarters routine and the disposition of the detective-force personnel.

'Think of what before?' Gallagher remarked coldly.

He spoke slowly and casually, looking at Gypo in a brooding way.

'Why, I mean the grudge that the Rat had in for Frankie,' Gypo replied confidentially and with an air of great importance.

'What grudge are you referring to?'

'Oh, it's a long story,' said Gypo with a sigh, as he walked over to the spittoon and spat into it. Then he hitched up his trousers. He cleared his throat with a tremendous noise. It was very tantalising. 'Stand us another drink, Commandant, before they close,' he cried suddenly, with amazing nonchalance.

'By the lumpin' Moses!' ejaculated Gallagher. 'You're a cool customer, Gypo. Ha, ha, ha! Well now! You're worth another drink, anyway.'

He winked secretly at Mulholland and Connor as he walked over to the aperture. Gypo called after him almost contemptuously.

'Hurry up,' he said, as he looked at the clock with a scowling face, 'we only have another minute. It's a minute to eleven.'

Again four glasses of whiskey were passed around. Gypo took his and swallowed it at a draught. This time he took the glass from Gallagher's hand without asking for it. He swallowed that also at a draught, as if he were going through a public exhibition of his drinking powers. Mulholland and Connor swallowed their drinks hurriedly, as if they were afraid that he was going to take theirs too. He walked over to the mantelpiece and put the two empty glasses on it. He looked at the five glasses he had emptied and smiled broadly. He whacked his chest with a loud sound.

'Come on now, comrade,' said Gallagher sharply, 'out with your news. No fooling.'

'All right,' said Gypo, thrusting forward his huge head so that it looked like a battering-ram, suddenly attached to his collar-bone. 'D'ye remember the Rat's sister Susie? She used to be a member o' the Organisation. She —'

'All right,' snapped Gallagher angrily. 'I remember her. What about her? What has she got to do with it?'

'Well, why wouldn't she have a lot to do with it? She had a baby, didn't she? Didn't she leave —'

'What d'you know about her baby?' hissed Gallagher. He was deadly pale.

'Don't get yer rag out, Commandant,' leered Gypo with a broad laugh. He was slightly drunk and insolent. 'Hit a sore spot, wha'? Well, I don't know anythin' about that. Ye can set yer mind at rest. Frank McPhillip was the father o' that kid an' he refused to marry her. I remember me an' him were at the back o' Cassidy's havin' a pint one night, when somebody came in an' asked Frankie to step around the corner a minute. He was gone a long time, so I followed him, suspectin' that there might be a bit o' foul play. But I found him an' Susie jawin' away to beat the band. She was cryin' an' askin' him to take her away with him somewhere. O' course he didn't budge. Next day she went to the 'Pool. Gone on Lime Street, as far as I can hear. Well! You bet yer life that's why the Rat did it. That's why he informed.'

Gallagher looked at Mulholland. Mulholland wrinkled his forehead and shook his head slightly. Then he looked at Gypo curiously. Connor's mouth was wide open and there was a look of wonder in his eyes as he gaped at Gypo. Gypo was tightening his trousers belt.

'Well, Commandant,' he said, when he had finished. 'Yer word holds good about takin' me back into the Organisation?'

'Steady on,' murmured Gallagher dreamily, staring at the ground. 'We have to verify your statement first. If your statement is true you'll get back all right.' Suddenly he looked up, smiling, with sparkling eyes. He seized Gypo by the right hand and smiled into his face in a friendly intimate way. 'Listen. There's a Court of Inquiry tonight at half-past one. Be there. Mulholland will take you up there. You can arrange to meet him somewhere. You can rely on me, comrade, to fix you up again. You did good work before, comrade, and you'll do good work again for the liberation of your class.'

Gypo gripped Gallagher's hand and squeezed it eagerly. Then he clicked his heels and saluted in a grandiose fashion. Then he turned to Mulholland. 'I'll be at Biddy Burke's place,' he whispered; 'about one o'clock. I'll see ye there.'

'Right ye are,' answered Mulholland.

'Good night, boys,' cried Gypo in a loud hearty voice.

Then he stalked out of the room, striking the floor with his heels fiercely and clearing his throat.

They all looked after him in silence for two seconds. Then somebody called, 'Time, gentlemen, time.' Gallagher started.

'Well, I'll be damned,' he cried, striking his left hand into his right.

'It's him,' hissed Connor, rushing up to Gallagher with open mouth.

'Shut up, you fool,' snapped Gallagher.

'Listen, Commandant,' cried Mulholland excitedly; 'it's him. I'll swear it is, because —'

'Damn you,' snarled Gallagher, 'who is asking your opinion? Give me your report. Quick, quick. Don't make a song of it.'

In short jerky statements, with rapid gestures, Mulholland described all that had happened at No. 44 Titt Street, Gypo's excitement, the falling of the money to the floor, Gypo's giving it to Mrs McPhillip, his rush from the house. Then suddenly he began in a whining voice to recount all he had done since he had been mobilised at eight o'clock on receipt of the news of Francis McPhillip's death. But Gallagher cut him short.

'Cut that out,' he cried. 'Did the police find any papers at No. 44? No. Good. Was anything found on the body? You don't know. Well, you better find out tomorrow at the inquest. Now beat it. Keep at Gypo's heels like a pot of glue. Find out every damn thing you can. Bring him along sharp to the Bogey Hole at one-thirty. Off.'

Mulholland disappeared without a word. Gallagher turned to Connor.

'You, Connor. Mobilise six men of your section. Round up Mulligan. Get him to the Bogey Hole. Get busy.'

Connor mumbled something and disappeared.

Gallagher remained staring at the ground, alone, lost in thought. Drunken voices were singing in the next compartment. Feet were shuffling. A droning voice cried constantly: 'Time, please, gentlemen, time.'

Gallagher's eyes distended dreamily. He sighed.

'The least little rift,' he murmured to himself, 'and everything is burst open. Then it's all up with me. I've got to stamp out this damned informer whoever he is. It may be Gypo. It might be the Rat, though that's very doubtful. That's of no consequence. What is of consequence is the fact that there is an informer ... Good God! An informer is the great danger. Every man's hand is against me. It's only fear that protects me. I must make an example of this fellow.'

His voice had gradually died out. Now silence reigned in the room again. The room was hot and stifling, full of the smell of stale drink and tobacco. He stared at the floor.

A cockroach peered out of its hole, contemplated a blotch of drink four inches away from its snout and then disappeared again. It would come out later on and suck the blotch.

The distance was full of sound as if many things were happening there.

Then Gallagher raised his head with a start. He sighed and walked rapidly over to the aperture. He tapped the panel with his knuckles. It was raised up almost immediately. The pretty red head appeared. Gallagher nodded. The red head disappeared again and the slide was pulled down. Gallagher waited. After three seconds a little door to the left was opened quietly and the barmaid stepped into the room, shutting the door carefully behind her. She rushed immediately to Gallagher and threw her arms around his neck. He kissed her lips several times rapidly. Then he unwound her arms.

'Got anything for me?' he asked.

She nodded and took a piece of paper from within the breast of her black dress. He stuck it within his raincoat.

'Right,' he muttered dreamily.

Then he kissed her again on the lips and patted her cheek. He took a pace away, but she grabbed at him. She held him, looking beseechingly into his face.

'Have ye got nothin' to say to me, Dan?' she whispered, almost sobbing.

'For goodness' sake, Kitty, have sense,' he muttered savagely. 'This is no time for jig-acting.' He put a finger to his throat. 'I'm up to here in it. The whole Organisation is in danger.'

'O Lord! What is it, Dan? Tell me.'

'An informer. See ye tomorrow. Let me go. Good night.'

He kissed her on the forehead. Her arms loosened. He was gone. She looked after him dejectedly. Then she shivered and gripped her breasts.

Gallagher walked up Titt Street. Here and there a workman recognised him and saluted respectfully. He did not acknowledge the salutes. He wheeled sharply in at the door of No. 44 and knocked. The door was opened almost immediately by Mary McPhillip. She also started and put her hand to her breast when she saw him.

'Good evening, Mary,' he said gently, holding out his hand. 'May I come in? I want to speak to your mother.'

'Yes,' said Mary excitedly; 'mother is in the kitchen, but you had better come into the parlour. Father is in the kitchen too, and there would surely be a row if he saw you.'

'Oh, that's all right,' said Gallagher. 'Is there anybody else there?'

'No, everybody else is gone.'

'Who is that yer talkin' to, Mary?' came Jack McPhillip's voice from the kitchen.

'Nobody atall, father,' cried Mary.

'Don't I hear a man's voice,' cried the father. 'Who is he?'

'Hist! It's all right,' whispered Gallagher, pushing past her as she tried to speak again. 'He won't bite me. It's just me, McPhillip. How are you? I'm very sorry to hear of your trouble.'

The two of them met at the kitchen door. They stared at one another for a moment. Then Gallagher made a movement to come forward and McPhillip, with a little start, moved backwards. He did not speak until he was near the bed again.

'Oh, it's you, is it?' he said angrily. 'An' what brings you here at this hour of the night?'

Gallagher took no notice of him. He turned to Mrs McPhillip, who was still in the same position by the fire, telling her rosary beads.

'I am sorry to trouble you, Mrs McPhillip,' he said gently and respectfully, 'in the middle of your … eh … but there's a question or two I have to ask you for the sake of him that's dead. Would you be kind enough to —'

'And what right have you to ask a question or two?' cried McPhillip, raging because Gallagher had refused even to talk to him.

He was sitting on the bed now. He sat on the bed timidly, as if he were in somebody else's house.

Gallagher turned to him slowly and looked at him fiercely in the eyes.

'I have the right,' he said, 'of a revolutionary to track a traitor to the cause.'

'Ha!' sneered McPhillip. 'An' what kind of a revolutionary d'ye call yersel'?'

'A revolutionary Communist,' answered Gallagher.

Then he turned about insolently and bent down his head to talk to Mrs McPhillip.

'Communist be damned,' cried McPhillip, jumping off the bed. 'D'ye know what I'm goin' to tell ye? Ye —'

'Father,' cried Mary, wringing her hands, 'don't —'

'Shut up, you young rip,' stamped the father; 'am I master in me own house or am I not? You, ye Communist, as ye call yersel'! Yer the greatest scoundrel in Ireland. Yer the greatest enemy o' yer class. Now let me alone, Mary, or I'll tan yer skin for ye. Let me tell him … Let me … Let go,' he screamed shrilly, as she seized him tightly about the body and began to push him forcibly from the room.

He placed his hands and feet against the jambs of the door, and turning his head around, he continued in a half-hysterical voice:

'It's the likes o' me that's the revolutionaries, but we get no credit for it. It's the likes o' me that does the hard work, eddicatin' me fellow-men, an' at the same time strikin' an honest blow for better conditions. But men like you are criminals. Criminals, criminals, that's what yez are. Don't lay hands on yer father, Mary. Don't —'

'I'm not touching you,' cried Mary. 'Come on now. Get to bed.'

She got him into the hall. He sighed and broke into half-stifled sobs. Going up the stairs he kept saying in a low melancholy voice:

'If I had only put him on the scaffoldin' with me, instead of eddicatin' him, maybe he'd be alive an' an honest man today. If I had only ...'

Then his voice died away into a mumble as a door closed behind him upstairs.

When Mary returned to the kitchen after putting him to bed, she found Gallagher sitting beside her mother, writing rapidly in a notebook. He had taken off his hat. His close-cropped black head looked very handsome to her. Still she shivered looking at it. The side face looked very cruel, with the brooding expression on it, as he looked downwards at the notebook.

She stood watching him until he finished writing. Then he sighed. He got up. He said a few words to Mrs McPhillip. Then he shook hands with her and turned to Mary.

'I want to speak to you,' he said.

She led him into the parlour excitedly. It was dark there and she had to fumble around for matches to light the gas. She couldn't find them. Gallagher offered his box. He lit a match. She went to take it from him. Their fingers touched. She started and stumbled over something. The match fell from his fingers and went out. He reached out his hands to catch her as she stumbled. He caught her by the wrists and held her tightly. They had not spoken a word. It was very queer in the darkness. Their faces were very close together, but they could not see one another. They stood still, each of them mastered by some strange impulse, that bound their tongues. They stood still, in the utter darkness and silence of the little stuffed room, for almost a minute. Then Gallagher spoke. He spoke in a soft whisper. The sound of his voice was soft and caressing. His lips were so close to hers that his breath came moist to her lips. There was a catch in his voice, as if the volume of sound were not strong enough to steady itself on the air.

'Mary,' he said, 'I want you to come to a Court of Inquiry with me tonight.'

She made no attempt to reply. Neither did he seem to expect a reply. It seemed that the words and their implication were foreign to the purpose of their meeting here. It seemed that the coursing of their blood and the confused beating of their hearts was in response to some prearranged assignation of declared love.

But there had never been a question of amorous relations between them. They had never met in privacy like this before. Their previous meetings were more in the nature of quarrels. Mary had always disputed with Gallagher, particularly of late, when she had become violently opposed to him. But now in the darkness, in the solitude, both she and he were mastered by some amazing emotion that was inexplicable.

'Dan,' she whispered suddenly, 'you make me afraid.

Why are we standing here in the darkness? What do you want with me?'

'I want you to revenge your brother,' said Gallagher suddenly, as if he had obeyed an unforeseen impulse and broached an unexpected subject, with which his mind had hitherto only toyed nervously. 'I want you to join me, Mary. I want you to take your brother's place in the Organisation. But a greater place than he held. No. It's not your brother's place I want you to take, but ...'

'Dan, what are you talking about?' she panted in a terrified voice.

There was a pause during which Gallagher imperceptibly moved his face closer to hers. Their lips met. They kissed gently. Then she drew back suddenly, shivering violently. She wanted to rush away and to shout, but the fascination of his voice was upon her. His voice and the glamour of his face. His face and the romance of his life. She was bound suddenly by it. Suddenly, too, it became apparent to her why she had been eager to convert him. It had been in order to meet him, with a plausible excuse.

And she was almost engaged to Joseph Augustine Short, who was a 'gentleman', who would place her in a respectable sphere of life, who would free her for ever from the hated associations of her slum life with its squalor, its revolutionary crises, its damnable insecurity, its soul-devouring monotony.

Mother of Mercy! Was she in love with Gallagher? Was she going to be drawn into the web of his conspiracies by the deadly fascination of his face and of his voice, by the romance of his life?

'Mary,' he murmured at last, 'you are the remainder of me. The two of us together would make a complete whole. There would be nothing else wanting to the two of us, no unfulfilled ... er ... well ... it's not that either. I have not fully worked out that part of the theory. I have approached it from another point of view.'

'What is it, Dan?' She drew away her face farther and loosened one hand. He was wrapped in dreams now and he did not attempt to stop her. In fact, he let her go altogether suddenly and sat on the table, simply holding her right hand in his. 'What do you want with me?' she said again.

'I want you to join me,' he muttered almost inaudibly, wrapped in his thoughts.

'Dan, I don't understand,' she gasped, afraid of his voice.

'How? How?' he muttered. 'Why don't you understand? I want you to join me.'

'Do you mean ... to ... to ... to marry you?'

'Oh, rot,' he cried irritably, waking from his half-reverie and turning towards her. 'These ridiculous conventions don't enter my consciousness. Not only have I no respect for them, but they don't enter my consciousness. You understand the significance of that. My personality is entirely in keeping with my mission in life. For me all these words attain their true values. Marriage, for instance, is truly a capitalist word meaning an arrangement for the protection of property so that legitimate sons could inherit it. So I don't have to argue with it in my own mind in order to rid myself of a belief in it. Most men have to do that. I am a hundred years before my time. I want to destroy the idea of property. It is my mission. I don't want to leave property to my children. I don't want children. They are nothing to me. The perpetuation of my life is in my work, in men's thoughts, in the fulfilment of my mission. That's why I want you to join me, because I feel something, an affinity maybe, that's a wrong word though, between you and myself. I am sure there is a natural relationship, chemical maybe, between the two of us. We are two parts of one whole. I am sure of that. No, damn it all. What a ridiculous idea! I don't want you to join me for the purpose of cohabitation. I have no time to make sentiment a main impulse of my desire to live. Neither have you. I am certain of it. You are governed by other impulses. Maybe you don't know it. Probably you are afraid to analyse yourself. But I know it. I don't know it. I feel it. "Know" is not a proper word. It's out of use. "Feel" is better. It is an outcome of the new consciousness that I am discovering. But I haven't worked that out fully yet. It's only embryonic.'

He paused. She started when he stopped. She had not been listening to what he had been saying. She had been arguing with herself. She had not succeeded in settling with her conscience what she had been discussing when he stopped. She bit her lip and started. She was blushing.

'Tell me, Dan,' she whispered, 'do you believe in anything? Do you even believe in Communism? Do you feel pity for the working class?'

Gallagher uttered an exclamation of contempt and shrugged his shoulders. He panted as he spoke, such was the rapidity of his words, in an effort to keep pace with the rapidity of his tempestuous thoughts.

'No,' he said, 'I believe in nothing fundamentally. And I don't feel pity. Nothing fundamental that has consciousness capable of being understood by a human being exists, so I don't believe in anything, since an intelligent person can only believe in something that is fundamental. If I could believe in something fundamental, then the whole superstructure of life would be capable of being comprehended by me. Life would resolve itself into a period of intense contemplation. Action would be impossible. There would be no inducement for action. There would be some definite measurement for explaining everything. Men seek only that which offers no explanation of itself. But wait a minute. I haven't worked out that fully yet. It's only in the theoretical stage yet. I have no time.

'But you spoke of pity. Pity? Pity is a ridiculous sensation for a man of my nature. We are incapable of it. A revolutionary is incapable of feeling pity. Listen. The philosophy of a revolutionary is this. Civilisation is a process in the development of the human species. I am an atom of the human species, groping in advance, impelled by a force over which neither I nor the human species have any control. I am impelled by the Universal Law to thrust forward the human species from one phase of its development to another. I am at war with the remainder of the species. I am a Christ beating them with rods. I have no mercy. I have no pity. I have no beliefs. I am not master of myself. I am an automaton. I am a revolutionary. And there is no reward for me but the satisfaction of one lust, the lust for the achievement of my mission, for power maybe, but I haven't worked out that yet. I am not certain that the lust for power is a true impulse, a true … but listen. That can come later. Can you give me an answer now? Will you join me?'

'No … no, Dan. Stop. Listen.' She gasped, holding him back. 'Not now. Later on I'll tell you. On a night like this, with death in the house, how can you talk of …?'

'Why?' he uttered fiercely. 'What night would be better suited for you to join me? Don't you want to avenge your brother's death? Don't you want …'

'Dan, Dan,' she gasped, struggling away as he attempted to seize her in his arms, 'don't touch me or I'll scream. I'm so excited.'

There was a pause. Their breathing was loud in the silence. A noise came from the kitchen.

'That's mother going to bed, Dan,' said Mary hurriedly. 'You must go, Dan.'

'Will you come to the Court of Inquiry tonight?'

'Dan, I'd rather —'

'You must come, Mary. You must. You —'

'All right, Dan, I'll come.'

'Good. I'll come for you. Be ready at one o'clock.'

'All right, I'll be ready.'

'Be waiting in the parlour here. I'll knock on the window.'

'All right, Dan. Go now immediately. I'm coming, mother. Good night.'

He bent hurriedly and kissed her lips. Then he stumbled from the room. She waited until the hall door closed behind him. Then she shuddered as the barmaid had done.

Gallagher walked away northwards furiously, with glittering eyes, thinking.

CHAPTER EIGHT

Walking out from the public-house into the street, Gypo felt as if he had leapt suddenly into an arena, where he was to perform astounding feats, while an amazed audience, with two million eyes, gazed silent and spell-bound. He thrust his head into the air. He let his arms hang limply from his shoulders in front of his body. He took two staggering steps forward and uttered a long-drawn-out yell.

It was that peculiar yell that mountaineers will utter in the west of Ireland, when the fair is over in the district town and night is falling, as they issue from the public-houses, bareheaded and wild-eyed, dragging their snorting and shivering mares after them by the halter.

Gypo's yell was just such a one. It was like a challenge to mortal combat issued to all and sundry. He felt beside himself with strength. He was free again. Had not Gallagher given him his word that everything would be all right? Would he not be taken back again into the Organisation? Had he not thrown suspicion on to the Rat Mulligan? He was free again. Ye-a-a-aw!

Chapter Eight

He staggered to the kerbstone and yelled, letting his body go completely limp with ecstasy. Then, breathing heavily through his nostrils, he stood erect and looked about him to see what effect his yell had produced. There was a small crowd of people near by. They had just come out of Ryan's public-house and from Shaughnessy's, another public-house ten yards away at the corner of a lane. The corner was brilliant with light, from the public-houses, from a fried-fish and potato shop, and from a drapery shop where the lights were kept on all night by the owner, with the idea that the light might terrify gunmen and housebreakers.

Gypo stood out in the blaze of light, on the kerbstone, with the beads of rainwater on his white woollen muffler reflected like dewdrops in the artificial light. The people looked at him in amazement and with that intense satisfaction which the proletariat of the slums always derives from something unexpected and extraordinary happening, at no cost to themselves. A spectacle had presented itself. The crowd began to swell.

Gypo had not intended to carry the affair any further. In fact, he had not intended to yell at all. But when he saw the crowd he became amused. He pitched on a man who stood near, a tall, thin, respectably dressed man, who had a sour expression on his face.

'What are ye lookin' at me for?' cried Gypo, staring the fellow in the face insolently.

'I'm not lookin' at ye,' snapped the man irritably.

'Yer a liar,' bellowed Gypo. 'Don't I see ye lookin' at me?'

'Well, a cat can look at a king,' cried the stranger, thrusting out his chin and spitting venomously to his left.

'What are ye sayin' about kings?' said Gypo angrily. 'Better say nothin' about kings around here, me lad. I think yer lookin' for trouble. I've got a good mind to give ye a wallop in the jaw.'

'Ye would, would ye?' cried the stranger, making a move to take his hands out of his coat pockets.

But he was too late. Gypo's right hand swung around. The man went down like a bag of nails dropped to an iron deck. Somebody cried: 'Lord, save us.' Gypo stood over the fallen man with his chest heaving. A policeman appeared from somewhere in the rear. He advanced rapidly, shouldering the people and trying to snatch something from under his cape as he made for Gypo.

'Look out, look out,' cried an old woman, through her cupped hands.

Gypo looked on either side hurriedly and then he heard the excited breathing of the policeman approaching from behind. He tried to turn about, but the policeman was upon him. The policeman's hands closed about his biceps and jerked back both his arms to lock them behind his back. The arms were half-way back before Gypo could mobilise his vast strength to arrest their retreat. There was a loud snap of bones being strained taut when Gypo's strength collided with the policeman's strength at the point on Gypo's biceps where the policeman's hands rested.

Both men groaned loudly. The policeman's boots tore at the wet pavement, making a noise like dry cloth being rent, as he struggled to keep firm. Slowly Gypo leaned forward until the policeman's body was on his back.

Then he thrust back his head with a snarl. His poll

collided with the policeman's chin. There was a dull thud and a snap. Gypo uttered an oath and thrust his head downward towards his knees, holding his thighs rigid. Before the head had reached the knees, the policeman had hurtled through the air with a scream of terror, right over Gypo's head.

He fell with three separate soft sounds to the street, with his right side against the concrete wall of a house. He fell on his back. He rose again in the middle, resting on his right hand and on his heels. He brandished his left hand towards Gypo and at the same time he tried to grip a fleeing spectator with it. Then he moaned and subsided again. 'Run, Gypo,' said somebody.

Gypo ran towards a lane at a fast run. He was followed by a crowd. Others gathered around the fallen policeman.

Gypo halted at the far end of the lane, in a dark corner. The crowd gathered around him. Everybody was panting with excitement. They all stared down the lane towards the blaze of light where the policeman lay. They began to jabber.

'I can see trouble comin',' said one. 'The sojers 'll be here shortly. Then yer goin' to see some pluggin'.'

'Gwan,' said another contemptuously. 'There's no sojers goin' to come down here. Ye wouldn't get a sojer in the town to dare come within a mile of Titt Street on this blessed night, after what happened today.'

At the mention of 'what happened today', a man cursed, a woman crossed herself piously under her shawl, an angry silence fell.

Gypo stood with his hands in his pockets, paying no

heed to the talk. With his lips stuck out, he was looking gloomily down the lane towards the blaze of light. He was enjoying himself immensely.

'Hist, hist!' somebody cried. 'Look, look.'

Two policemen crossed the blaze of light, bearing their fallen comrade between them. A few women and small boys followed them. Then two more policemen came, hauling along the man whom Gypo had struck. They were dragging him unceremoniously, holding him by the armpits, with his feet trailing along the ground and his arms dangling. They were probably under the impression that it was he who had felled their comrade. The man made an effort to wrench himself free, but they tightened their hold on his arms. He writhed and went limp again, allowing himself to be dragged lifelessly. A woman, with straggling red hair and a child on her back in a black shawl, danced in front of the policemen, screaming and gesticulating, demanding the man's release. Then the procession passed out of sight with a mad rush of feet and a medley of indiscriminate noises.

'Let's go back,' muttered a young man who had a slight hump.

Gypo grunted and hitched up his trousers. He put his hand to his head to settle his hat jauntily before leading the way back. But instead he uttered an oath. His little round torn hat was not there. His massive round skull stood bare under the night. It stood naked, hummocked and gashed here and there, like a badly shorn sheep. He traversed the skull with his right palm, in little flurried rushes, as if he had had a vague suspicion that the hat was hiding somewhere along the expanse of skull. Then he set out at a wild rush down the lane, followed by the crowd, to retrieve the hat, as if his life depended on it. For the first time, since Gallagher had given his word, terror again invaded his mind. If they discovered the hat they might be able to discover the identity of that ponderous fellow who had gone into the police-station....

But no. He rushed into the road and brought up with a slither of his right foot on the wet pavement. The hat was lying in the gutter before his eyes. It lay crushed beside a flattened little cardboard chocolate box and an orange skin. It had been trodden on by a small bare foot. The impress of a wet heel was on its right side.

He grabbed it up hurriedly, punched it into shape and crammed it on to his skull with both hands. Then he laughed aloud and turned to the people. 'I thought I had lost it,' he cried affectionately. 'I had it this two years.'

The crowd gaped at the hat as if it had magical properties. Others who had run up without knowing what had already happened gaped at Gypo's humpy face, at his ruminative eyes and his eyebrows that were like snouts, at the red fat backs of his hands, as he held them to his throat tightening the white woollen muffler about his neck. There were agitated whispers on the outskirts of the ragged crowd.

'He's stronger than any bull.'

'How? Why? What did he do?' from a dozen throats.

'Wait till I tell ye. I saw him with me own eyes send Scrapper Moloney o' the B Division flyin' over his shoulder like a man divin' off the Bull Wall. I declare to me —'

'I know him well. He used to be a bobby himself once. His name is Nolan. Gypo Nolan. Didn't ye ever hear of him?'

'Sure; usen't he be pals with Frankie McPhillip that was shot today?'

'Sure I was,' broke in Gypo, overhearing the remark; 'an' when ye speak o' the dead, ye might add Lord have Mercy on him.'

'Hear, hear,' cried several voices. 'Hit him a puck in the jaw. Who is he?'

A noisy argument and a scuffle arose. The culprit was hustled away, kicked and struck about the face, until he made his escape by running at full speed up the lane. They all crowded around Gypo again.

He stood head and shoulders above them, revelling in the attention he was attracting. He stood so impassively with his arms folded, that he might be mistaken for a great scowling statue at a distance. Then he suddenly raised his right hand and made a circular movement with it.

'Come on,' he cried wildly. 'I'm goin' to give everybody here a feed. Come on. Come on every mother's son in this crowd that's hungry.'

He waved his arm towards the fried-fish and chip shop and headed off towards the door.

'Hurrah!'

'Long life to ye, me darlin' son of Erin.'

'More power to yer elbow.'

'Up the rebels.'

Gypo strode in front of the disreputable throng as proud as a king leading his courtiers. They came after him with pattering feet, panting, pushing, snivelling, emitting that variegated murmur of sound that comes from a pack of wild things in a panic, coming from afar, unseen, without a guiding reason. They were the riff-raff and the jetsam of the slums, the most degraded types of those who dwell in the crowded warrens on either bank of the Liffey. But to Gypo they were an audience to acclaim his words and his deeds.

'Before long ye'll see me cock o' the walk around here,' he thought, as he strode into the shop. 'Me an' Gallagher. Come on, every man jack an' woman too. Come on.'

They packed the little shop to the door. There was an overflow outside. It was warm within after the drizzling rain and the sharp wind outside. The air within the shop became almost immediately full of the vapour of human breath. The low murmur of breathing could be heard distinctly through the hum of whispered conversation.

'Hey there, towny,' cried Gypo to the shopkeeper, 'chuck us a feed for all hands. I'm payin' for the lot.'

The shopkeeper was an Italian, a dark middle-aged fellow with plaintive eyes. He looked at Gypo and then at the crowd. Curiosity, fear, suspicion and surprise raced across his face. Then he smiled and nodded his head. He said something in a foreign language to the girl who stood behind him and then he began immediately to put steaming portions of potatoes and fish into slips of old newspapers that lay ready to hand. The girl, a red-cheeked young woman with big black eyes, dressed in white, busied herself, pushing to and fro on a long arrangement like a sink, more fish and potatoes that were being fried. A crackling noise came from this frying. A hot, sweet and acrid smell permeated the whole room.

The starved wastrels revelled in that smell. They looked towards the frying food with eager mouths and glistening eyes. Their nostrils smelt its heat and its savour greedily. Their faces were all fierce and emaciated. Their bodies were unkempt, crooked, weazened. But just then, the joy of an unexpected banquet had filled even their haggard and stupefied souls with a pleasure that made them laugh and chatter irresponsibly like children. The sorrows and the miseries of life were forgotten in that moment of common rejoicing. And perhaps that joyous mumble of chattering voices, rising through the steam in that slum eating-house, was a beautiful hymn of praise to the spirit of life.

And Gypo stood among them like some primeval monster just risen from the slime in which all things had their origin.

While around him crowded the others, like insects upon which he had been destined to fatten.

As he looked about him, with the slow, languorous eye movement of a resting bull, he felt the exaltation and conceit of a conqueror at the hour of victory. An intelligent being, gifted with such strength and the power to analyse his sensations, would have said: 'This is the greatest moment of my life.' But Gypo did not think. There was nothing about him in relation to which he could think. A queen will not dream of flaunting her beauty and her raiment at a boors' banquet. But she will, on a public holiday, bow to their clamorous cheers. So with Gypo.

The cumbersome mechanism of his mind had been put in motion that evening by the necessity for forming a plan after leaving the police-station. The unaccustomed strain had unmoored it. It floundered about until Gallagher's promise perched it on a foolish eminence whence it regarded the rest of humanity with contempt. It sprawled its ponderous foundations on that crazy eminence as arrogantly as if it were about to rest there for eternity.

He rolled his eyes about at the heads that were standing thickly around him, some on a level with his biceps, some on a level with his waist, while here and there a tall man like himself, stood with a red, lean, knotted neck strained forward, with throbbing throat, towards the food counter.

'Biga lot o' people,' murmured the Italian suddenly, making a polite gesture with his hands to indicate the number of people present and the nature of his suspicions.

'That's all right,' muttered Gypo. 'Count 'em as ye hand out the grub. I'll pay. Don't you fret yersel'. Keep back there.'

He had been standing with his palms against the edge of the marble-topped counter. Now, in order to put his hand into his right trousers pocket, he had to pick up a small-sized man and crush him in between two women, who leaned away behind their shawls. Then he thrust his hand into his pocket and fingered the wad of Treasury notes. The very touch of them sent a wave of remembrance through his body. A slight tremor ran up, almost tangibly like a breath of cold wind in a hot place, up the extent of his body until it entered his brain. The remembrance of the origin of that wad of notes staggered him momentarily. He remembered the fat white hand, surmounted by a carefully brushed blue sleeve, that had handed him the wad over a desk, saying every so icily: 'You'll find twenty pounds there. Go.'

But after the first shock he curled his thick upper lip

slightly and licked it with the tip of his tongue. The movement of his mouth had the appearance of a grin. The girl who happened to glance at him just then, found his gaze centred on her. She dropped the fish slice into the pan with some sort of an exclamation in a foreign language. But Gypo, though he was looking at her, did not see her. He was busy with his clumsy thick fingers, separating a single note from the roll without taking the roll from his pocket. At last he succeeded in doing so. He grunted and pulled out a single Treasury note. He held it up.

'Here ye are,' he cried. 'This'll pay for the lot. Hand out the grub.'

The Italian smiled immediately and began to serve the packages into the eager hands that reached out for them. He counted out loud as he did so: 'One, two, three, four ...'

An uproar commenced immediately. People crowded in from the door struggling to get served. Those who had been served struggled to get out into the street, with their food in steaming, dripping, paper packages in their hands. Altercations arose. The shop was full of sound. There were cat-calls, whistling, cursing and laughing. Then a big docker brought the uproar to a climax by smashing his big boot through the wooden bottom of the counter, uttering a drunken yell as he did so. Then he sprawled over the counter, laughing foolishly and reaching out with his two hands towards the girl who shrank away terrified. The Italian uttered an exclamation of terror. Gypo turned towards the docker, lifted him up by the back and shouted: 'Keep quiet.'

The two words re-echoed through the shop, like two rocks rolled down from opposite precipices and meeting in a glen, with two separate sounds, a heavy thick sound as they collide, a loud rasping sound as their splintered fragments fly clashing into the air.

The words had scarcely passed out the door into the night before a silence fell. Everybody stood still. One man stopped in the act of sucking a fishbone between his lips.

'Now carry on,' continued Gypo, 'but don't kick up a row like a lot o' cannibals. Don't disgrace yer country. A man ud think ye didn't see a bite for a year.'

Then he himself turned towards the counter and asked the Italian how many meals had been served. Twenty-four meals had been served. He threw the pound note on the counter.

'Take out o' that for three rounds for mesel',' he said.

Then he pushed back his hat, drew a paper full of food towards him and began to eat. Without speaking, the Italian held the Treasury note between him and the electric light and peered at each side of it several times. Then he nodded his head and opened his till.

Mulholland had also strained his neck to peer at the Treasury note. He had been standing in the angle of the doorway all the time, silent and immovable. As soon as he saw the pound note, he drew out into the open and craned over the heads of the people to look at it. A neighbour noticed him, a ragged little fellow, who mistook the cause of Mulholland's curiosity.

'Didn't ye get any grub?' said the little man to Mulholland. 'It's yer own fault if ye didn't. Come on, man. Don't stand there hungry. Go on up to the counter.'

He caught Mulholland by the arm and tried to push him towards the counter.

'Leave me alone,' hissed Mulholland. 'I don't want any grub. Let go.'

'Go on up,' pursued the little fellow; 'go on, man. Didn't ye hear him say he was standin' a round for everybody. Go on up.'

'Let go, I tell ye. Let go. I don't want it, I say.'

But it was no use for Mulholland to refuse. The more he refused the more the little fellow was determined that he should be fed. Others joined in, eager for some amazing reason or other that Mulholland should be fed. It seemed that they suspected something indecent and improper in Mulholland's refusal to eat.

'Call out,' cried somebody, 'call out for another ration. Bring it down to him.'

'Yes, why shouldn't he have his share as well as the next?'

'Let me alone,' cried Mulholland in a rage; 'let me alone, or I'll smash yer skull for ye.'

That put a different aspect on the question. There were a dozen angry oaths.

'So that's what's the matter with ye. Yer lookin' for fight, eh?'

'Stand back an' let me at him,' cried somebody in the rear, pressing forward.

Mulholland tried to rush for the door, but they held on to him.

'What the hell is the matter now?' thundered Gypo, striding over.

Immediately the scuffling stopped. Gypo came face to face with Mulholland. He saw Mulholland's little eyes, gleaming and flashing like the eyes of a cat beset by dogs.

There was a tense moment during which Gypo struggled with obscure suspicions. But suddenly the expression on Mulholland's face changed into an expression of cunning intimacy. His face, instead of being fierce and resentful, suddenly seemed to say: 'We are members of the Revolutionary Organisation, you and I. Get this rabble out of my way.' Gypo immediately remembered Gallagher's promise. He looked at Mulholland with good-natured condescension. 'Ha,' he thought, 'this fellah 'll be useful.

'Let him alone,' he cried arrogantly; 'he's a friend o' mine. How are ye gettin' on, Bartly?'

Then he continued carelessly, to impress the crowd with his own importance and his intimacy with the affairs of the Revolutionary Organisation, which was the most impressive thing in the lives of those about him.

'Hear anythin' yet about what I was tellin' ye? I mean about the fellah that informed on Frankie McPhillip?'

Mulholland was amazed for a moment. What audacity! But it was not audacity. Gypo had completely forgotten the ponderous fellow in the little tattered round hat who had gone into the police-station. His sudden conceit had completely swallowed that ponderous fellow.

'He must be drunk,' thought Mulholland. He said aloud, whispering to Gypo, as he bent his head close and turned up his face sideways in his peculiar manner. 'I was just passin' an' saw ye. I just thought I'd drop in an' tell ye I'd be there at one o'clock. Ye know where I mean? No, we didn't hear anythin' yet about that.'

He winked his right eye. Gypo winked his right eye and nodded solemnly. Then Mulholland walked quickly out the door, evidently going off somewhere in a hurry.

But he halted at the corner of the lane, distended his eyes and gritted his teeth. He rubbed his chin meditatively, looking at the ground. He couldn't make it out, whatever it was, that was troubling his mind.

Gypo turned once more to the counter and continued his meal. He ate as if he were about to travel for days and he were deliberately devouring a store of food sufficient to last to the end of the journey. Behind him and on either side of him, they were talking about his strength and praising him, but he paid no heed to them. He was immersed in dreams about his future, now that Gallagher was going to take him back again into the Organisation.

'Aha!' cried an old woman, with watery blue eyes and a wrinkled white face, as she shook her fist upwards at him, 'I wish I had a son like ye. Me own Jimmy, Lord have Mercy on him, was killed in the big war. He was the boy that could bate the polis! Don't be talkin'. I seen him wan night an' it took six o' them to pull him off a coal-cart an' he holdin' on to the horse's reins all the time with wan hand while he was fightin' them with th' other.'

She stamped on the floor and yelled, her eyes gleaming ferociously, as if the contemplation of her dead son's fight gave her tangible pleasure. Then she walked towards the door, trailing her shawl and her arms with bravado. The poor woman was slightly insane as the result of paralysis.

A tall, sour-faced, lean man, with a red nose shaped like a reversed scimitar, who had just come in, looked after the old woman and shook his head. He mumbled something under his breath. The old lady halted and looked at him contemptuously.

'What are ye sniggerin' at,' she cried, 'you with a face like a plate o' burnt porridge?'

There was a loud laugh.

'Mary Hynes,' said the hook-nosed man, 'if ye were more careful of yer son's upbringin' an' of yer own immortal soul, ye wouldn't be in the state ye are in now. Is it boastin' of yer son's lawlessness ye are? Are ye boastin' of his livin' crimes an' he already gone to meet his God?'

The hook-nosed man raised his right hand dramatically to point at the ceiling and he glared at the old woman with fierce and menacing sorrow. But his words produced a contrary effect to that which he expected on the old woman. She looked at him contemptuously and then curled her mouth up in anger.

'Yerrah, d'ye call it a crime to bate a policeman?' she cried in amazed indignation.

'Certainly it is a crime,' cried the hook-nosed man.

'Damn an' blast it, what are ye talkin' about, Boxer Lydon?' cried a burly fellow coming up to Lydon and staring him excitedly and angrily in the face. 'Didn't ye hear of what the polis did today to Frankie McPhillip? D'ye call it a crime to bate that murderin' lot? Aye, or shoot them either!'

'I don't say they were justified in what they did to-day,' cried Lydon, raising his voice to a querulous shout in order to drown the uproar; 'but neither will I say that the dead man was justified in what he done. Do none o' ye think o' the man McPhillip killed? Wasn't he a fellow-man like yersel'? Wasn't he an Irishman of the same flesh an' blood?'

'Aw! That's nationalism,' cried somebody. 'What's an

123

Irishman no more than a Turk? Ye belong to the I.R.B., an' that's where ye get yer lingo. Up the workers!'

The hook-nosed man paused with his hand raised until the interrupter finished. Then he continued unmoved:

'Do none o' ye think that maybe that man left a mother an' a —'

But he had to stop. His voice was drowned in the uproar and the scuffling. The old woman began to sing 'Kelly the boy from Killane,' as she strolled out the door. Another man was pushing his way in through the crowd at the door towards the hook-nosed man. This new-comer had been standing at the door for some time. He was dressed from head to foot in a heavy black overcoat. He was better dressed than anybody present, but he looked as pale and haggard as the others. His face continually twitched and his eyes were bloodshot. He looked at the hook-nosed man fiercely and seized him nervously by the buttonhole. The hook-nosed man edged away.

'For God's sake, let up on that rubbish,' cried the new-comer, stammering at each word. His upper lip was contorting as if he were in a fit.

'Let me go,' cried the hook-nosed man. 'I'll have my say, an' I won't be intimidated by any Socialist agitator. Keep back from me.'

'I only wanted to tell ye,' shouted the other, 'I only wanted to tell ye ... I say ... I say ...'

Then nothing could be distinguished above the uproar. Everybody present took part in the argument. The ragged fellows who had come in with Gypo, curiously enough, took no interest in the argument. Those of them that had not already disappeared as soon as they got their food, now took their leave when the argument began. There was even a look of fear in their faces as they slunk away, as if this demonstration of interest in the affairs of the world terrified them, who had no interest in anything, since their souls were numbed by the hopelessness of despair. Only a few of the most wretched remained, crouching against the counter, in the comforting shadow of Gypo's immensity. They remained because the presence of his powerful personality comforted them and gave them the imaginary feeling of having something to protect them from the menace of civilised life.

Those that were now taking part in the argument were of a better class. They were workers of all sorts, members of trade unions and respectable people. They had appeared somehow, one by one but rapidly, in that mysterious way in which crowds of people of a certain type gather in the Titt Street district and carry on an argument with furious heat.

Gypo suddenly turned around and looked at the wrangling group, at the open mouths, the listening ears, the distorted faces, the glittering eyes. He listened. He blinked. Then he laughed softly within himself. He felt a crazy desire to yell and fall on them with his fists. The mixed murmur of their agitated voices had a maddening effect on him. But he looked back at the counter. He still had food to eat. He continued his meal. The argument went on.

The man with the long overcoat who had just arrived held the attention of the crowd. He was a well-known man in the district and all over the city. He owned a small tobacconist and newsvendor's shop. He was called The Crank Shanahan, and indeed he was a crank. He belonged to no organisation, he went about alone, he attended every political meeting in the city, and he was continually, in all weathers, agitating and preaching in a loud shrill voice his own peculiar philosophy of social life. That philosophy was a mixture of all sorts of political creeds, but its main basis was revolt against every existing institution, habit or belief. He was called an anarchist, but he was not an anarchist. He was just a fanatic who was dissatisfied with life. At night he was given to fearfully morbid thoughts that caused him to lock and bar himself in his room and sleep with the blankets right over his head. He was even supposed to put cotton-wool into his ears at night lest he might hear a sound. And once the policeman on duty found him wandering around the street in which he lived, at three o'clock in the morning, dressed in a torn nightshirt, trembling and gnashing his teeth with terror. He had jumped up horrified by a nightmare and rushed out in that state.

'Listen,' he cried. 'I don't agree with the Revolutionary Organisation, but the man that killed McPhillip ... no ... no, no ... I mean the man ... can't ye let me speak? ... I mean the farmer that McPhillip killed, he was an agent of the capitalist class. Then it follows logically that he was an enemy of the working class. McPhillip was an agent of the working class. He was justified in killing the man. That's the matter treated logically and brought to a logical conclusion. Everything must be approached logically. Listen. Taking the question from a wider standpoint we can get a broader judgement that will fit all cases of the kind that may arise' — he raised his voice to a scream to drown the noise of a scuffle at the door — 'in the near future. We are at the base of a world revolutionary wave. According as that wave advances and gathers strength the whole process of capitalist society will crumble up. Then there will be a gradual increase in the number of these skirmishes, as it were on the ...'

His voice was drowned suddenly by a big man who began to swing his arms about his head uttering a fearful torrent of oaths. He was drunk. Then Lydon shouted:

'Murder is murder, I say. Murder is always murder, and the gospel of Our Lord Jesus Christ says —'

'There must be no mercy,' yelled a little man with a black moustache, who rushed into a corner where he had room to prance about. 'There must be no mercy. To hell with everybody. That right, boys? Wha'?'

'What are ye all talkin' about?' cried Gypo, suddenly turning about.

Silence fell immediately. Everybody looked at him. His face was perspiring. He rubbed his hands on his chest. He curled up his lips. He gave his little hat a slight push towards the back of his head.

Then he was seized by another fit of strange humour. He yelled once more and staggered towards the crowd, with his arms hanging loose, pretending to be dead drunk. They fell away from him in amazement. He stood in the middle of the room and looked about him.

'What ye talkin' about?' he drawled ponderously, swaying backwards and forwards.

He glared from face to face, but each pair of eyes was turned away as he sought them. He was delighted with the terror he caused. Behind the counter the Italian, still smiling, had grasped a large knife and stood perfectly still. The girl was crouching on the floor. Then Gypo broke into a loud laugh, stuck his hands in his trousers pockets and strolled towards the door.

He hesitated for a moment outside the door. Then he headed straight across the road. They all ran to the door to look after him. His huge long frame, clad in blue dungarees that clung to his thighs, shone in the light of the lamps as he crossed the wide road, one foot advancing past the other slowly, the trousers brushing with the sound of hay being cut with a scythe. Then the figure left the area of light and grew dim as he gained the pavement at the far side, and turned to the left under the shadow of an abrupt tall house. Then he fell away into the night.

Presently a lean slouching figure crept across the street in pursuit. He also disappeared under the shadow of the abrupt house. Nobody noticed him. It was Mulholland tracking Gypo.

CHAPTER NINE

Around the corner Gypo halted. He put his hand against the wall behind him and stood motionless, with his head turned back, listening. He had heard a step following him. But the steps halted also. He listened for several seconds breathlessly and heard nothing further. Then he snorted and turned his head slowly to his front. He looked ahead into the darkness, dreamily. He stood perfectly still.

Then his face broke slowly into a sort of smile and his eyes grew dim. He trembled slightly. He glanced about him sharply and furtively several times. There was a strange, almost mysterious 'significance' in his movements, slight, sudden, furtive movements.

Then he stared steadily down along the dark, narrow street that stretched ahead of him, ending at the far end in a high wall, with a dim lamp at one corner suggesting that another street branched off it to the left. He winked his right eye at the lamp and a roguish expression creased his face as he did so.

'Why not,' he muttered aloud. 'Why shouldn't I go an' have a bit o' fun? Wha'? A few bob on the women an' a few drinks to keep me supper warm.'

A wave of passion surged through his body. He was on the point of opening his mouth to utter a yell, but instead he thrust his hand into his trousers pocket anxiously and groped for his wad of money. He found it. He sighed easily.

'They might have pinched it,' he muttered, with a look of gravity in his little eyes. 'That mob around there are a lot o' wasters. Ye couldn't trust yer shirt with 'em on a winter's night. They'd take the charley from under a pope's bed. Terrible lot o' criminals around lately.'

Then his face lit up with eagerness as his mind swerved back again to the contemplation of that lamp at the far end ... and where that street led. He swallowed his breath with a loud noise and set out towards the lamp.

Almost immediately a head peered around the corner behind him. The head watched until Gypo turned to the left at the far end past the lamp. Then a man darted around the corner and raced down the street in pursuit. It was Mulholland tracking Gypo.

When Gypo turned to the left past the lamp he came into a narrow street in which there were no houses. On the right-hand side there was a high wall, like a barrack wall. It enclosed a big goods yard belonging to a manufactory, where mineral waters or something of that kind were made. On the other side of the street there was no wall at all. The foundations of houses still remained. Here and there a doorway, a chimney stack, or the brick framework of a window, stood up in a ghastly fashion.

Beyond that there was an open space full of refuse, mounds of earth, bricks, pots, old clothes. The street itself was a network of puddles. In order to avoid wetting himself to the knees, Gypo had to walk along the sloping bank of clay where the houses had crumbled.

It was a dreary sight. It almost shouted its experiences, and if it had shouted, it would have talked in that endless, loud, babbling scream in which maniacs and demented creatures utter their words. It was alive in that peculiar way in which ruins are alive at night, when the earth is covered with darkness and the living sleep.

But Gypo was not sensitive. For him, the street, with its dirt and its squalor, was a savage sauce to whet his appetite for the riotous feat of ... He strode rapidly. He jumped from mound to mound, now slipping with a curse, now catching a loose brick in some piece of wall to steady himself. Now and again he heard a 'hist' from the opposite wall of the street, where some woman, old and decrepit, sought the darkness so that her ravaged figure might escape the drunken eyes of some passionate fellow seeking a fool's pleasure. These noises, croaks uttered by damned souls, sounds so tremendously horrid to the innocent mind, made no impression on Gypo. To him they were merely noises, expressions of everyday life.

Once he recognised one of the women who took a pace forward from her position and put a wrinkled hand to her brow to look at him.

'Ho! Blast yer sowl, Maggie Casey,' he muttered, 'aren't ye dead yet?'

He clucked with laughter as he heard her blasphemous rejoinder.

As he approached the far end of the street the silence lessened. He heard whisperings and murmurs, snatches of distant song, sounds of footfalls, strains of music. These sounds acted on him like battle-cries. He almost broke into a run as he came gradually nearer to the volume of sound. At last he dashed under an old archway and he was in the next street. The medley of sound was all about him. On his left-hand side stretched the long, low streets of brothels, entwined like webwork among the ruins of what was once a resort of the nobility of eighteenth-century Dublin.

He was in a narrow street of two-storied houses, low houses with green venetian blinds on the windows of some of them, their street doors opened wide, lights in all the front, ground-floor windows. But the street itself was in darkness on account of the drizzling rain. An odd woman flitted along. A few men walked about uncertainly. The street had a gloomy deserted look. But from the houses a medley of joyous sound issued.

Gypo looked on for a moment excitedly. Then he walked down the street slowly, examining each house as he passed. He knew Katie Fox was by now at Biddy Burke's. He wanted to avoid Biddy Burke's. Biddy Burke's house was over on the other side. He didn't want to go there tonight. It was only a poor place, used by the revolutionaries and criminals of the working-class type. The women there were an ugly, ill-dressed, whiskey-drinking lot. He was well known there. He knew all the women. There was only Guinness's stout on sale, and even that was so diluted and ghastly that it was like drinking castor oil. The more a man drank of it the thirstier he became. A shilling a drink for poison like that!

Yah! Away with Biddy Burke and Katie Fox and Sligo Cissie and the rest of them! Tonight he wanted to go somewhere where he was not known. He wanted to go among beautiful women. Strange, beautiful women clothed in silk! Mad women! Women with dark, flashing eyes and sharp, white teeth! Huh! He wanted to go mad. It was a mad night. There was fire in his blood. His hands wanted to rip mountains. He would swallow tankards of drink. He would drain this vast reservoir of strength from his body. He must or he would burst. Already he felt a desire to beat his head against walls.

For six months he had been walking about a beggar, cut off from pleasure, subject to Katie Fox's charity. Phew! She was no longer attractive to him, that bag of bones who thought of nothing but dope.

Suddenly, without thinking, breathing heavily, flushed, excited like a man inhaling chloroform, he staggered through a doorway. He stood in a long, dark hall. He could hear laughter and drunken singing coming from his right, a few yards down the hall, from behind a door through which a glint of light came. He strode to the door. He tried to lift the latch and walk in, but the door was bolted. Almost instantly the sounds ceased. He kicked at the bottom of the door with his boot several times.

'Who's that?' came a woman's voice angrily.

'Open the door an' find out,' answered Gypo in a shout.

'Wait a minute, Betty,' came a husky man's voice; 'lemme out.'

There was shuffling and whispering.

'Keep well behind it,' said somebody else.

Then the bolt was withdrawn. The latch was lifted carefully. The door opened slowly about three inches. Gypo watched these proceedings nervously and angrily.

'Come on, come on,' he cried at last, 'what's all this monkey trickin' about? Why don't ye open the door wide and take yer mug outa the way?'

The man suddenly slipped outside the door like a cat. With his back to the door and his right hand bulging in his coat pocket he faced Gypo. He was a stocky, bulgy fellow, with a criminal face. He had rushed out with the intention of giving Gypo a thrashing with the 'blackjack' that was concealed on his person, but when he saw the kind of customer with whom he had to deal his jaw dropped. Gypo gazed at the fellow angrily.

'So you're the pimp,' he gurgled ferociously.

He took a little hurried breath, shot out his right hand and seized the pimp by the throat. The pimp gasped. His right hand dropped the 'blackjack'. He reached up with his two hands to grip the giant hand that held his throat.

'Lemme go,' he screamed.

But Gypo contemptuously hurled him away from the door and sent him sprawling along the hall into the darkness. Then he sent the door flying open with a push of his shoulder and strode blinking into the room.

The room was crowded with people. It was very large. It had a stone floor and a wide, open hearth where an immense turf fire was blazing in a huge grate, with steaming kettles on either side, on the hobs. There was a dresser loaded with shining Delft-ware of all colours. The ceiling was high and whitewashed. The walls were covered with pictures of women, in amorous postures and in the varying degrees of nakedness that might be expected to arouse libidinous desires in the minds of all types of men. Everything in the room was spotlessly clean, but the air was warm and heavy, due to the rather intense heat of the fire and the combined odour of perfume and of alcohol.

This heavy, languorous odour exalted Gypo. He rolled his eyes round the room, drawing in a deep breath through his expanded nostrils. Everybody was looking at him. There were eight men present, three students from the University, an artist, a doctor and three young gentlemen farmers, up from the country 'on the tear'. They had hired the brothel for the night and ordered the proprietress to admit nobody; but they did not take umbrage at Gypo's appearance. They were just at that moment in the delicious stage of intoxication when the most strange incidents become normal and welcome, to the minds that are cloyed with alcohol fumes and the contemplation of bodily pleasures. The scuffle outside the door and the manner of Gypo's entrance made no impression on them. His appearance, huge, towering, in a suit of dungarees, with his little round hat perched on his massive skull, intrigued them with a feeling that this was some new kind of pleasure provided for their entertainment. They looked at him, half laughing, half serious, with that dim and distant look in their eyes that comes with the initial stages of drunkenness.

The women, on the other hand, looked at Gypo with disfavour. There were ten of them present. Some of them were almost nude and in various stages of intoxication, sitting on the men's knees, with glasses in their hands and cigarettes in their mouths. Others sat solemnly on their chairs dressed for the street, as if they had just dropped in on their way somewhere. Their hard faces set in a scowl when they saw Gypo. He was dressed like a workman. Therefore he had no money. Therefore they scowled at him. This was an 'upper-class' brothel. All the women here were 'ladies'. Their 'class' instincts were aroused by his wretched clothes and his uncouth features.

One woman alone took no notice of him whatsoever. She sat in a corner, reading a newspaper, with her legs crossed, a cigarette between her lips, a fashionable short fur coat wrapped around her. Gypo's eyes wandered around the room until they rested on her. There they remained.

'What d'ye want?' cried a harsh voice behind him.

Gypo turned. The proprietress of the brothel was standing beside the door. Her left hand was on her breast fingering a little silver crucifix that was suspended from her neck by a black velvet cord. Her right hand rested on the door, a short, white, fat hand, as if she were waiting until Gypo went out so as to shut the door again. She was a small, fat woman of middle age, with a huge head of devilishly black hair, arranged in towering fashion, with a glittering black comb stuck in the rear of the pile. Her hair was the last remains of her beauty. The remainder of her head had been coarsened by the odious nature of her pursuits. Her face was blotched, wrinkled and pale. Her eyes were yellow, hard, sunken and bloodshot. Her mouth was drawn together as if some clumsy fellow had tried to stitch the lips and made a bad job of it. She was dressed in a blue skirt and a white blouse. The blouse sleeves were rolled almost up to her shoulders, showing a tremendously fat pair of arms. They called her Aunt Betty, and she was known all over the district for her cunning, her meanness and the peculiar habit she had, perhaps in the middle of a conversation, of suddenly uttering a coarse expression, grasping her breasts and staring about her wild-eyed, as if she was afraid of some dread spectre being in pursuit of her.

Gypo did not know her, because her place was fashionable, frequented only by well-to-do people, business men, army officers and students who had money to spend. Gypo only knew the cheaper brothels, places that were used as 'friendly houses' by revolutionaries, criminals and working men. On any other night he would never think of entering the place, no more than a man in overalls would think of taking a seat in the stalls of London theatre. But tonight he had transcended himself. He looked at Aunt Betty arrogantly with his lower lip hanging.

'I want a drink,' he replied gruffly, in a low voice. Then he added after a pause with a sudden hoarse chuckle, 'an' anythin' else that's goin'.'

'Ye can't get a drink here,' said Aunt Betty. 'You better be going somewhere else. You're wasting your time here, my good man.'

Aunt Betty spoke in a state of great excitement. This was habitual with her, owing to the terrific strain it caused her to try to effect the correct pronunciation of her words and 'the educated accent of a woman of good family'. For she always tried to speak like a lady.

Gypo took no notice of her, or of the pimp who had again entered the room and now stood against the wall, with his terror-stricken eyes gleaming and his face livid with malice.

'Here,' he cried, 'give everybody a drink. I'm callin' a drink for the house.'

He thrust his hand into his pocket, pulled out the roll of notes and separated one, which he held out to Aunt Betty. It was like the performance of a miracle. Aunt Betty's eyes sparkled. She advanced almost unconsciously, laughing with her thin, hard lips, while her eyes gleamed with avarice. Her fingers almost trembled as she took the note slowly. Feverishly, she examined it under the light. Gypo laughed as she did so and gave her a loud, hearty smack on the back, with horrid familiarity. She merely nudged him playfully in response. The note was genuine and had passed her scrutiny. She sighed and cracked her fingers towards the pimp.

'Glasses all round,' she said.

There was a little thrill of applause from the throats of the women as soon as they saw that his money was genuine. Some of those who were sitting alone, dressed for the street, got up and approached him, uttering laughing endearments. Even the women who were already engaged, sitting on the knees of the men, slightly tipsy, sobered up and became contemplative and sulkily jealous of those women who were free to capture Gypo and his wad of Treasury notes.

The men, on the other hand, now regarded him with

hostility, jealous of the attraction he held for the women.

Only one person in the room took absolutely no notice of the whole proceedings. That was the woman in the fur coat, who sat in the corner to the right of the fire, reading the newspaper.

And Gypo, disregarding the soft, naked arms that attempted to embrace him, and the amorous, sensuous faces that were turned up to his on all sides, and the soft, seductive, sibilant whispers that were uttered at him, kept his eyes towards the indifferent woman in the corner fixedly.

'Keep out of me way,' he muttered.

He pushed the girls away from him, strode over to the corner and stood beside the mysterious one. He stood over her, breathing heavily, looking down at her. She glanced at his knees from under her eyelids. Then she puffed at her cigarette, flicked something off her sleeve with her thumb and forefinger and went on reading her newspaper. The other women looked on silently with narrowed eyes. The men began to smile. Everybody was interested in what the fur-coated woman would do.

Gypo sat down beside her. He sat on the floor with his back to the wall.

'Aren't ye hot wearin' that fur coat?' he said.

She did not reply. There was a titter from the women.

'What's all the news in the paper about?' continued Gypo.

The woman did not reply. One of the men burst into laughter, making a sound like an explosion, as if his mouth had been full of laughter a long time and it suddenly burst out.

'Horrid man! Go 'way,' said somebody else, mimicking the voice of a timid and refined woman.

Gypo's face darkened and his throat veins swelled ominously. But just then the drinks arrived. He jumped to his feet and rushed over to the pimp who was carrying them. He drained one glass of whiskey, then another, then another. An outcry arose.

'Hey, don't drink the lot.'

'Savage.'

'What d'ye mane by callin' a drink for us an' then swallowin' 'em yersel'?'

'Hey! Stop him, Johnny. Take the tray away from him.'

'You all go to the divil,' gasped Gypo. The whiskey rushing down his throat had taken his breath away. 'Wait there. There's lots more.'

He pulled out another pound note and tossed it to Aunt Betty carelessly.

'There ye are,' he cried, 'go an' get more drinks.'

Then amid the delighted yells of the girls he drained three more glasses one after the other, each one at a gulp, while the women danced around him.

Suddenly the whole company went into a state of mad excitement. Human beings always respond in that way to the mysterious influence of a fresh and dominant personality, who, with a word, a gesture, a shout, turns a solemn and bored gathering into an almost Bacchanalian party. It seemed that all the people in the room had only awaited the arrival of Gypo to abandon themselves completely to an orgy of mad behaviour. Shouts, shrieks, smacking kisses, laughter, mingled chaotically in the warm air of the room. Each of the men vied with his neighbours in an exaggerated attempt to make a fool of himself. A young man with an innocent, red face and beautiful grey eyes, a student, stood up precariously in front of the fire, laughing incontinently and began to strip himself naked. Another man, a big fellow, seized a girl in his arms, tumbled with her to the floor and lay there shouting and trying to kiss her, while she struggled to free her loosened hair from beneath his shoulder. Gypo picked up two women and perched them one on each shoulder. Then he seized two others round the waist, raised them from the ground under his arms and began to jump into the air, yelling like a bull with each jump, while his fluttering, half-naked cargo of women laughed hysterically as they dangled about him.

This amazing scene lasted fully a quarter of an hour and then it ended suddenly. Everybody seemed to be exhausted. It was only then that Aunt Betty's voice was heard above the uproar.

'Do ye want to get me run in be the police?' she cried.

'It's all right, mother,' said Gypo, going up to her and putting his arm around her waist. 'Yer a nice girl. I'll keep order here for ye. Now who is kickin' up a row? The next fellah that speaks above a whisper I'll open his skull for him.'

'Would you, though?' cried the young man who was stripping himself naked. He stood in front of the fire in his trousers and underwear with his shirt in his hand. 'I'll teach you manners, my good fellow,' he continued, pulling up his trousers and brandishing his shirt. 'Come on. I'll teach you how to behave yourself in the presence of gentlemen.'

But somebody pulled him on to a settee before he could do anything. Gypo looked at him for a moment and then he laughed. His eyes were gleaming. The quantity of whiskey he had drunk was coursing through his head and his limbs as if it were being pumped methodically by a machine. He released Aunt Betty and took a pace towards the centre of the floor. Then he shivered all over and gasped for breath. He broke into a laugh. He walked over to the fur-coated woman without looking in her direction. He stooped down, put his arms about her, lifted her up until her face was level with his, and he kissed her. His clumsy lips met her right cheek. They groped about for her mouth, but they could not reach it on account of her frantic efforts to free herself. He lost his balance and let her down to the floor. He regained his balance, laughing heavily and wiping his mouth on his sleeve.

There was an intense silence. The woman stood in front of him erect and trembling. She held her hands rigid by her sides, with the long, slender fingers bent backwards. She was dressed in excellent taste, black shoes, navy-blue skirt, short fur coat, small, black hat, from under whose rim brown curls protruded. She was a handsome woman, a beautiful woman, but for her face. The left side of her face was disfigured in a ghastly way from the temple to the jaw. So that one cheek was white and the other almost black. The left eye was darkened and almost sightless, while the right eye was blue, clear and gleaming with anger. The disfigurement touched the corner of her mouth. The remainder of the mouth was red-lipped, arched and beautiful.

Suddenly she bared her white teeth and spat at Gypo

with the ferocity of a wild animal.

He shivered. His hands clawed up. His face contorted and he swivelled his head on his neck from left to right and back again, like a ram that is going to charge an enemy. A woman near the fire gasped with horror. But Gypo did not attack. Instead of advancing on the woman he took a pace to his rear and let his breath out through his nostrils with a great noise. Then he stood motionless, with his eyes distended, staring at the infuriated woman in awe and wonder. She was staring at him with her eyes almost closed.

'You pig,' she gasped.

There was a painful silence. Each person in the room felt sure that a catastrophe was imminent. The fact that the room, a few minutes before, had been full of the sound of libidinous revelry, made the silence all the more terrible. Everybody watched Gypo. His huge body, monstrous with strange movement, stood under the glare of the lamp that hung from the ceiling. His face, staring steadily at the woman, changed again and again, in response to the dark and mysterious suggestions that chased one another through his mind. At one moment his chest would heave and his limbs would stiffen. Then his breath would come out with a snap. His jaws would set. His eyes would expand. A movement would begin in his throat. Then a sound like a curtailed snort would come from his nostrils.

At last, after waiting for twenty seconds, the spectators were startled by the unexpected outcome of these movements. Gypo broke into a roar of laughter. He raised his head and laughed at the ceiling. Everybody gaped at him in fright. All gaped at him, terrified, except the woman. As if in response to his laughter, laughter broke from her lips too, but it was the shrill, thin laughter of hysteria, that made her eyes glitter coldly.

Breaking off in the middle of his laugh, Gypo strode over to Aunt Betty. He took her by the arm, pointed his finger at the woman in the fur coat, and whispered hoarsely:

'I want her. Get me a room. I want to take her upstairs. Ye can have whatever money ye ask.'

'Never,' shrieked the woman in the fur coat.

She put her hands to her face. Then she took a tiny step forward with her right foot and stood leaning on the foot, trembling as if she had planted it on ice.

'None of this nonsense, Phyllis,' said Aunt Betty, coming forward to the centre of the room. She faced the fur-coated woman with her arms akimbo and her jaws squared. 'I'm fed up with your swagger. You're no better than yer board and lodging, an' as long as I keep you, you're no better than any other woman that takes bite and sup in my house. Put that in your pipe and smoke it. One man is as good as another. You're going with him.'

'That's true, Aunt Betty,' said several women, looking with hatred at the fur-coated woman.

'Rabble,' shrieked the fur-coated woman, stamping her feet and shaking her fists all round her at the women. 'What filthy souls you have to be reduced to this level. I'm not a prostitute like you, and that's why you hate me. You hate me because I'm an educated woman and —'

'It's nothin' o' the kind,' cried a big, large-boned, red-faced, strong, handsome woman, called Connemara

Maggie. 'We hate ye because yer a stuck-up, ignorant thing, that thinks she's better than what God turned her into; an' God forgive me for sayin' so —'

'More power to ye, Maggie,' interrupted several; 'tell her yer mind.'

'I don't mind what you say, Connemara Maggie,' gasped the fur-coated one. 'You're not the worst of them and —'

'Good God,' shouted Aunt Betty, suddenly putting her hands to her breasts.

She backed to the wall, staring furtively at the fur-coated woman. She was in the power of one of her 'visions'. Gypo stared at the woman in the furcoat with his arms hanging loosely by his sides.

'Listen,' continued the woman, 'I don't bear any of you any malice. You can't help it, any of you. I don't bear even you any malice, Aunt Betty. I know very well that were it not for you I would starve or … or be in a worse place. I have been in your house a month now and you've been kind to me. I know very well nobody can help anything. I'm English, an army officer's wife, so it's only natural that you girls would be prejudiced against me —'

'It's nothing o' the kind,' cried Connemara Maggie; 'it's yer stuck-up ways that —'

'Let her have her say, Maggie,' cried another.

'I had no right to come in here,' cried the woman, bursting into tears. 'I should have gone to the police and got them —'

'The police!' yelled Gypo suddenly, starting as if he had been awakened from his sleep. 'None o' that talk. Keep away from the police. What d'ye want the police for?'

'I want to get back home,' sobbed the woman.

'Where's yer home?'

'It's ... it's near London.'

'Well, what are ye doin' over here then?'

'I got this,' cried the woman, becoming hysterical again. She put a trembling hand to her disfigured cheek. 'I got this a year ago. It's driven me mad. My husband took another woman. I sold everything I had and came over to Dublin. I wanted to go to work. Honest to God, I did. But I could get nothing. Then a man brought me down here. Good God, the shame of telling you all this in a place like this ... the ...'

'D'ye want to go home now?' cried Gypo angrily.

She did not reply, but looked at him with large eyes, as if in amazement.

'What'll bring ye home?' he continued. 'How much will it cost?'

'A little over two pounds,' she replied in a low voice.

'Here,' he cried, taking out his money, 'here's yer fare. One, two, three,' he paused and was going to add a fourth, but he put it back. He handed her the three notes. She shrank backwards, looking at the money with large eyes.

'Don't be afraid,' he said in a strange, dreamy voice. 'Take the money an' get outa here. That's enough to take ye home. Go back home. Yer not wanted here. You an' yer husband and the police. Ye better keep away from the police I'm tellin' ye. Go on. Beat it. Get outa here.'

Staring him in the face, trembling, with her mouth open, she seized the notes suddenly. Then uttering an exclamation, she looked about her once and rushed to the door.

'Go off now,' cried Gypo after her. 'Go off now.'

Everybody stared at the door through which she disappeared, banging it after her. There was silence. Then Aunt Betty spoke:

'That's all very well,' she sniggered; 'but she owes me two pound ten. Who's goin' to pay me that? It's all very well doin' the —'

'Shut up yer gob,' cried Gypo, 'here's two pound for ye. That's enough. Not another word outa ye.' He threw two pound notes at her. Then he threw out his arms. 'Who's comin' to bed with me,' he cried, 'before the bank is broke?'

'I am, me bould son o' gosha,' cried Connemara Maggie, rushing to him, with her yellow curly hair streaming about her face and her blue eyes dancing.

She enveloped his neck with her brawny arms.

CHAPTER TEN

At fifteen minutes to one, Bartly Mulholland entered Biddy Burke's kitchen and sat by the fire. Nobody addressed him. He saluted nobody. Biddy Burke was sitting on the other side of the fire, on a stool, smoking a cigarette.

Biddy Burke was a middle-aged woman with a lowering expression in her black eyes, with puffed-out, sallow cheeks and a swollen throat. She was of the type of Irishwoman that is prone to sudden passions, due to the habit of eating enormous meals and then suffering from digestive disorders. They are tender-hearted people, utterly lacking in an æsthetic sense, violent, quarrelsome, savage, generous, inconsistent. Biddy was dressed in a white blouse and a blue skirt. She wore her greyish hair drawn back to her poll tightly and parted in the middle according to the peasant fashion.

There were other people in the room, two young women who sat on chairs and Jimmy 'the fancy man', who lay on his right side, on the settle opposite the fire.

Mulholland looked around the room slowly. Then he spoke.

'Was Gypo Nolan here this evenin', Mrs Burke?' he said.

Biddy Burke slowly shook her head, carefully examining Mulholland's face as she did so. Then, as if she suddenly remembered something important, she leaned forward and bunched her lips together.

'There hasn't a man stood within me door this blessed night,' she said in her rough, croaky voice. 'No, nor damn the bottle o' stout did I sell. That's the God's truth. Some people find Biddy Burke all right when they're in trouble an' they got nothin', but when their tune changes they give her a wide berth. I'll soon be in the workhouse at the rate things are goin'. I never saw anythin' like it. The country is goin' to the wall. That's all there's to it. I knew they'd make a mess of it with their revolutions an' their shootin' the peelers. Not that I didn't do me bit to help the boys, God bless 'em, but 'tisn't the boys that done the fightin' that get the jobs. So it isn't. It never is, if ye ask Biddy Burke. It's them publicans an' bishops that were always top dog in this country. 'Twas that way before an' 'tis that way now, an' 'twill be that way when Biddy Burke is goin' to meet her God on the day of judgement. They were talkin' about English tyrants, but sure nobody ever saw the likes o' these tyrants with their searches an' their raids, an' every divil's wart of a farmer's son that can pull on his breeches without his mother's help runnin' around an' callin' himself a gineral. Aw! Gypo Nolan! He's like the rest o' them, Bartly Mulholland. You take it from Biddy. Indeed, then, he hasn't set a foot within me door. It's not that I haven't heard of his goin's on, though. Huh!'

'What did ye hear about him?' asked Mulholland, peering at her.

'What did I hear about him?' cried Biddy Burke. 'What d'ye take me for, Bartly Mulholland? An information bureau, or what? Don't be botherin' me.'

Mulholland sighed. Then he took out his pipe and lit it. He put his back against the wall and began to smoke in apparent comfort. There was silence. Through the open street door sounds of footsteps and of voices came in through the rain now and again. They were subdued sounds. It seemed that everything was waiting for something monstrous to happen.

The two young women began in their gruff, cracked voices to discuss the death of Francis Joseph McPhillip. They talked casually, in whispers, indifferently.

Mulholland peered at them for a moment. Then he sank back into his thoughts. His thoughts just then were not at all comfortable. He had lost track of Gypo. He had been wandering about trying to find his quarry again, absolutely without success. Gypo had been swallowed up. A more nervous man than Mulholland would have not taken the matter so philosophically, so coolly. Because if Gypo could not be found again, Mulholland's own life would be in serious danger. But Mulholland was not considering that aspect of the affair. Mulholland was a sincere revolutionist. It was the danger to the 'cause' that worried him. The 'cause' was his whole existence. He did not understand any other purpose in life except the achievement of an Irish Workers' Republic.

Still … as he sat on the stool, stoically smoking his pipe, other worries came into his mind. If he could not find Gypo and anything serious happened to himself as a result, what would become of his wife and his six young children? He hardly ever thought of them seriously, in this way, with a view to the future. The future held a workers' republic, somewhere in the distance, when there would be no slums, no hunger, no sick wives, no children that got the mumps and the rickets and the German measles and the whooping-cough with devilish regularity. It never worried him to think that his wife and his six children were for the moment living in a miserable slum shanty, with his wife going rapidly into a decline through hard work. That had to be. The 'cause' was above all these things. Why! It was his wife who often urged him on to give all his time to the 'cause' whenever he became slightly despondent or disheartened, timorous or apathetic.

Ever struggling without reward!

So he thought suddenly. But almost as soon as the thought entered his brain another thought came in mad, bloodshot pursuit. He pulled savagely at his pipe and ejected the first thought in terror.

Even 'mentally' it was dangerous to think of leaving the Organisation without being expelled. After all … terror was the foundation of his zeal.

He forced himself into his habitual calm. His face assumed the impenetrable aspect which he had developed during five years of constant practice. He turned to Biddy Burke again.

'Where did ye say ye saw Gypo carrying on?' he said casually.

Biddy Burke looked at him ferociously, emitting two columns of cigarette smoke through her fat nostrils.

'I didn't say I saw him carrying' on anywhere, Bartly Mulholland,' she said angrily. 'Be the holy! These late years every one o' ye is as smart as a corporation lawyer. Now look here, Bartly. I don't want to have any truck atall with ye or yer crowd. Ye know that too. I know ye, me fine bucko, an' I don't think ... eh ... well o' course, Bartly ... ye know what I mane ... It's not ... uh ... that I mane any harm ... but a poor woman like mesel' ... o' course I'm ready as I said before to do me duty for me fellow-men ... but it's like this ... what does a woman like me gain be gettin' mixed up in politics ... that is o' course ... look here,' she continued in a lower voice, 'I heard he was up in Aunt Betty's, raisin' hell up there. He was one o' your crowd, wasn't he?'

Mulholland looked at her sombrely. She drew back immediately.

'Well, ye know me well, Bartly,' she muttered apologetically and nervously. 'I'm not sayin' anythin' out o' place. Am I, girls? Sure —'

Just then an interruption came from outside. Footsteps came rushing to the door. Then gasps were heard. Then a panting sound became audible. Then Katie Fox burst into the room, with her right hand on her hip, her eyes glittering, looking about her wildly. She rushed up to Biddy Burke. She bent down from the hips towards her and began to speak immediately, gasping after each word.

'What d'ye think of it, Biddy?' she cried. 'D'ye know where I found him? D'ye know where I found him? The big hulkin' waster! An' she that's not fit to walk the same street as me with her big, ugly arms around his neck! She laughed in me face. She laughed' — screaming — 'in me face! I wish to God I had hit her with the bottle I threw. That ud spoil her mug. Though it was spoiled enough the day she was born. Who was she, may I ask? Who was she, Biddy Burke? I'm askin' ye. Ye don't know an' ye'd never guess in a thousand years. Who would she be but me bould Connemara Maggie! That imperent trapster that came up here last year as a skivvy in a Gaelic Leaguer's house, one o' them crazy fellahs that goes around in kilts. She came up here an' before she was three months in the town she was put in the family way be a soldier. Then she comes down here, with her curly locks an' her big face like a heifer, savin' the comparison. I pushed up past Aunt Betty in the hall an' she shoutin' after me. I bust in the room an' there he was, sittin' on the floor, with his legs spread out, drinkin' outa the neck of a bottle, laughin' like a fool, with her sittin' beside him. "Hello, Katie," says he, "d'ye want a drink?" "'Twill do ye good," says she with a giggle. Me curse on her! I gave him a bit o' me mind an' … Biddy, for God's sake, gimme a drink o' water. Biddy, listen.'

She threw herself suddenly at Biddy's feet and began to moan. But almost immediately she jumped to her feet again and cried out:

'An' what's more, he gave three quid to that swank of an Englishwoman. He gave her three quid and he paid two quid more to Aunt Betty, money that was owin' to her for board, an' he never gave me a penny. Me that kept him for the last six months when I hadn't a bite mesel'. But I'll tell everybody. I'll tell.'

She looked around her wildly. She saw Mulholland.

She came up to him and bent down close to his face. Her hat trailed off. Her hair fell down over her eyes. She swayed. She pointed her right forefinger menacingly at Mulholland's forehead.

'Listen to me, Bartly,' she said. 'You remember me when I was a good girl an' when I was a member o' … ye know yersel' … Well, so was he, wasn't he? Well, can ye tell me how did Frankie McPhillip get plugged? Who got the twenty quid that the Farmers' Union gave out? Where did he get the money? I'm not shoutin' any names. No names, no pack drills. But ye can guess for yersel'. Where did he get his money from? Was it be robbin' a sailor at the back o' Cassidy's same as he told me in the pub? Was it?' She suddenly threw her hands over her head and clawed the air, shrieking. They jumped up and caught her.

Mulholland got to his feet quietly. He stole out into the street, avoiding the people who came rushing up to Biddy Burke's door, attracted by the screaming.

Mulholland chuckled as he crossed the street. He would have plenty of news for Gallagher. After this there would be little difficulty in his getting McPhillip's job on the Headquarters Staff. He stole quietly into the hallway of Aunt Betty's house. He went noiselessly up the stairs without attracting the attention of the revellers who were still 'on the tear'. He reached the landing. There were three doors, with light streaming through each of them. He listened at each door. The third was the right one. He stood straight. He lifted the latch suddenly and strode into the room. He called out as he did so dramatically:

'Come on, Gypo, it's time for ye to be comin' with me.'

For a moment he could see nobody, owing to his

excitement and the thick mist of smoke and unescaped vapours which filled the room. He stood within the door with his feet spread out wide on the bare moth-eaten boards of the floor, with his right hand in his pocket fingering his revolver. His heart was beating wildly. Then he became aware of Gypo's presence. He felt that peculiar movement in his head that the realisation of Gypo's presence always caused, a little snapping movement of unreasoning terror. Then he heard Gypo's voice, heavy and hoarse with drunkenness, but cordial and friendly and distinctly patronising.

'Hello, Bartly. Sit down an' have a drink. Plenty time yet.'

Then he turned his head towards the fireplace and saw Gypo.

Gypo was sitting on the floor to the right of the fire, in a corner, in half-darkness, bare to the waist, with his trousered legs stretched out at a wide angle, sitting bolt upright, a bottle gripped in his right hand between his knees, his feet bare.

Connemara Maggie was standing by the fire drying Gypo's shirt, his jacket and his socks. The big boots were resting on a fender before the fire, steaming. She took no notice of Mulholland's entrance. With her golden hair hanging in disorder over her face, with her blouse undone, with her strong, heavy-boned face covered with perspiration, with her great, soft eyes swollen and gentle like the eyes of a heifer, she busied herself tending her man, just as if she had never left the purity of her Connemara hills and she was tending her peasant spouse after a hard day's work in the fields; instead of tending a casual lover in the sordid environment of a brothel. There was no hint of vice or of libidinous pleasure in her face or in her movements. She seemed to be, like Gypo himself, a daughter of the earth, unconscious of the artificial sins that are the handiwork of the city. In her two brawny arms she held the steaming shirt to the blaze. She stood silent and immovable.

There was little else in the small, whitewashed, low-ceilinged room. A bed with the clothes tousled on it, a quilt that lay on the floor by the bed, a chair on three legs, and a weatherbeaten washstand, containing a basin and a broken jug, comprised the furniture.

Mulholland looked around at all this before he spoke. It was as well to get the correct details in case identification were necessary. Gypo might deny it. Then he spoke. He had recovered his nerve.

'No,' he said. 'I don't want a drink. It's time for ye to be comin'.'

'Be off with ye, ye little divil,' yelled Gypo, suddenly jumping to his feet, with a great scraping and slapping noise. 'Who are ye givin' orders to?'

He took a pace forward and reached out his right hand, but Mulholland had drawn his revolver and taken a pace to his rear. At the same time he called out in a hissing whisper:

'It's not me orders. It's the Commandant's orders an' ye better be careful about disobeyin' them.'

Immediately Gypo drew himself up and let his hands drop to his sides. His face, which had lit up with anger, dropped into that peculiar wondering expression which he wore when he was musing on the river bank before he went into the police-station. He looked at Mulholland in amazement. His forehead wrinkled. His nostrils expanded and contracted. His thick lips moved backwards and forwards, up and down. His face and his cropped skull shone in the light of the paraffin lamp that rested on the mantelpiece over the fire. The light also shone across his body, over a bulging bare shoulder that stood out white and massive and round below his brown neck. The shoulder muscles were immense. His body was white and hairless. His skin was perfectly smooth. But everywhere the muscles strained against the skin, in irregular, moving mounds. They swelled out on his breasts, at his biceps, above his hips, on his shoulders, just as if his head and neck were a massive tree growth and the body muscles were its roots, sunk into the body promiscuously and afar, during centuries of life.

He looked at Mulholland for some seconds. Then he turned to Maggie.

'Gimme me clothes, Maggie,' he said quietly.

She handed them to him in silence. He dressed. He put on his little tattered round hat. Then he put his hand in his trousers pocket. He took out all the money he had left. Two pounds four and sixpence. He put the four and sixpence back into his pocket.

He handed the two pound notes to Maggie.

'Keep one an' give the other to Katie Fox,' he said. 'Ye'll find her down at Biddy Burke's.'

She nodded and put the notes within her blouse.

'So long, Maggie. See you again,' he said, going to the door.

'So long,' she called after him quietly.

Gypo stalked out unsteadily, followed by Mulholland.

After a little while Connemara Maggie also left the room. She went down to Biddy Burke's.

Biddy Burke's was now thronged with people. They were mostly women of the district and their men. They had been talking at a terrific rate when Maggie came in, but a strange silence fell upon them when she appeared. She did not take any notice of them. Going up to Katie Fox, who sat by the hearth, on the seat occupied recently by Mulholland, she took out the pound note and offered it to her.

'Gypo Nolan gave me this for ye,' she said quietly.

Katie Fox looked at the note. Then she looked at Maggie. Her underlip was quivering. Her eyes opened and narrowed spasmodically. She was moved by some complex emotion that she could not master for the moment. She did not speak. Others began to whisper. Some spoke out loud and sharply:

'Don't take it, Katie. It's blood-money,' said one.

'Take it,' said Biddy Burke indignantly. 'A pound note doesn't smell when it's changed.'

'Money is the common whore of all humanity,' stuttered a tall, lean, drunken gentleman, who dozed by the window with his head dangling.

'I bet she got more than that to give ye,' said another woman.

'Yes, I bet she has,' cried Katie Fox, suddenly settling the matter that was agitating her mind, whatever it was. 'I know her. Out with it, Connemara Maggie,' she screamed, jumping to her feet and squaring herself. 'Out with it an' don't stand there tryin' to melt butter in me mouth with yer soft looks. How much did he give ye for me? Don't tell me he only gave me one quid. Yer a liar before ye open yer mouth to say so. Ye —'

'Well, of all the stories —' cried Connemara Maggie in amazement.

'Don't put on airs, Maggie,' said a woman beside her. 'Don't put on airs.'

'Out with the rest o' the money,' cried Katie Fox.

'Yer a pack o' dogs,' cried Connemara Maggie furiously. 'Yer a pack o' —'

She gasped and could say no more, astounded and hurt bitterly by the slanderous attack from Katie Fox, to whom she had never spoken in her life before, except to say good morning. She fumbled at her blouse and took out the other pound note that Gypo had given her for herself. Then she took a purse from a hiding-place on her left thigh. She abstracted another note from that. She put back the purse again. She threw the three notes at Katie Fox.

'There ye …' she hissed. 'That's all his money. Take it. Maybe it's dirty like yersel'. I am well rid of ye. If he's yer man, keep him.'

She spat and strode out of the room, swinging her arms and knocking out of her way all who came in front of her.

Some stared after her and swore. Others looked at Katie Fox. Katie had the three pound notes in her hands and her lips were moving. Then Biddy Burke whispered something to her. Immediately Katie sighed and clutched the three notes in her hand, desperately, staring at the floor. Then she held them out to Biddy Burke rapidly, without looking in their direction. They lay crumpled in a ball on her quivering thin palm.

'Take them, Biddy,' she whispered. Then she suddenly raised her voice to an hysterical shriek. 'Take them, but for God's sake hurry and give me something at once. Quick, quick. Give it to me, Biddy. Give it to me.'

CHAPTER ELEVEN

In the Bogey Hole rats scurried about, careless of the
sentry who tramped up and down, from end to end of the
long stone passage, with his rubber heeled boots sound-
ing loudly in the cavernous silence. Drops of water
gathered slowly on the stone ceilings and then fell with
soft, empty splashes to the stone floors. Except for the
scurrying of the rats, the falling of the water and the
footfalls of the sentry, there was silence.

The Bogey Hole, in which the Revolutionary Organisation were about to hold their inquiry into the cause of the
death of Francis Joseph McPhillip, had once been the wine-
cellars of a nobleman. Above it the ruins of the house still
remained. But everybody had long since forgotten the name
of the owner in the district. The hallway of the house was
choked with rubbish. The two top stories had fallen in.
Only a few rooms remained in a crumbling state.
Children played in them and parties of men played cards
for money there on Sundays. That's all. But the wine-
cellars underneath were often used by the Revolutionary
Organisation as a meeting-place and for other purposes.

A wide stone stairway led down into the cellars from the rear of the hallway. There was a wide passage running straight through the cellars and rooms opened off the passage on either side. In the first room to the left of the stairway six men stood about. They were the guard, seven men including the man who was on sentry. They stood about the room, or sat on the floor by the wall, with their revolvers strapped outside their raincoats. A lighted lantern was placed on the floor in the centre of the room. The faces that were touched by the lantern light were haggard and pale. Farther down on the same side of the passage, a larger room was prepared for the inquiry. A small table had been placed in it. A horse blanket covered the table. There were several small forms there and a little 'bedside table' to the right of the main table, with a deck-chair behind it. A big lamp, turned on full, hung from the ceiling. It lit up the room so that the dampness on the walls glittered. Two tall, lean men stood by the entrance to the room, one on either side of it.

Across the passage, still farther away from the stairway, the Rat Mulligan was sitting on a form in another room. His three guards sat opposite him on a form. They had their revolvers in their hands.

All along the passage the light of the big lamp penetrated. It reached up three of the steps of the stairway. Beyond that and about the roof of the passage, there was pitch darkness.

At the far end of the passage the outlines of a door could be seen. It was a heavy oaken door, very old. Formerly it was the door of an airtight room where special wines were kept. These wines were let down into the

Chapter Eleven

room from the garden. A trap-door opened off the garden into the room. The barrels were let down through this trap-door. Now, however, the room was used by the Revolutionary Organisation for prisoners. A square hole had been made in the upper part of the door to let in air, so that the prisoners would not suffocate.

It was three minutes past one. Three men, dressed in long raincoats and soft hats, with masks over their eyes, came down the stone stairway. They were immediately challenged by the sentry. One of them mumbled a word casually. The sentry saluted. They walked quickly down the passage and entered the inquiry room. The sentries at the door stood to attention as they entered. They sat down at the table. One of them, he who sat in the middle, threw an attaché case on the table and yawned. They all lit cigarettes and began to talk in whispers, with bored, sleepy voices, hardly opening their lips. They were the three members of the Central Executive Committee who had been appointed as judges for the inquiry.

At twenty minutes past one Commandant Dan Gallagher came down the stairs with Mary McPhillip. She wore a dark woollen overcoat buttoned to the throat and belted at the waist. Gallagher was dressed as before. She looked around her in a frightened manner. Gallagher had to urge her along with his right hand that held her arm. When the sentry uttered his challenge she stopped dead, gasped, and put her hands to her lips. Gallagher began to whisper to reassure her. Trembling and clutching at his arm, she was led by him into the inquiry room. He put her sitting on a form and went over to talk to the members of the Executive Committee, who had not got to

163

their feet or taken any notice whatsoever.

At twenty-five minutes past one, a hoarse voice was heard at the top of the stairs, yelling the words of a ribald song, while another voice, a hushed one, angrily expostulated. Then there was a savage grunt, an oath, the sound of a heavy body crashing into something that broke with a brittle crack, and then Gypo came down the stairs. He came down, slipping on his back, with his arms and legs stretched out, groping at the air. He landed at the bottom with a thud. He sat up stiffly. Then he broke out into an amazing peal of laughter.

Men rushed at him from all directions with their revolvers drawn, as quickly as if they had been waiting for a long time anxiously for his appearance in that strange manner. But when they saw him sitting there laughing, with his little tattered round hat fallen forward over his forehead, they halted and put their revolvers back into their holsters.

'Hello, boys,' cried Gypo. 'Here I am. What are ye lookin' at? I'll fight any six men that ever walked this earth. Who's first?'

He jerked himself to his feet with one sudden forward movement, by drawing up one heel under him. He stood up, towering suddenly over those about him. They drew back. Mulholland, who at that moment was limping down the stairs with his hand to his right eye, side-stepped quickly with fright as Gypo stood up. He fell headlong past Gypo's right shoulder into the arms of two men who reached out to receive him. Then Gallagher pushed his way to the front.

'What's the matter here?' he cried sharply. 'To your

posts, men, quickly. Well, Gypo? What's troubling you now?'

Gypo clicked his heels with a loud noise and saluted. He staggered slightly as he saluted. His face, wild with drunkenness, moved spasmodically, but he remained silent. He had not put on his muffler on leaving the brothel. His brown neck was bare, the muscles standing out like ridges on a mountain side. Then he jerked his hat back into its correct position and shuffled his feet. He broke into a low, thick laugh. He spoke.

'You an' me, Commandant,' he said with a foolish grin. 'What ho! We'll put 'em all on the run. What d'ye say?'

Gallagher had been looking steadily at Gypo all the time without a single movement in his face. He turned away in silence and addressed Mulholland.

'What's the matter with your eye, Bartly?' he said.

'Oh! He just came in me way,' interrupted Gypo, taking a pace forward and patting Gallagher familiarly on the shoulder. 'He came in me way — uh — an' I hit him with the back o' me hand. That's all, upon me soul. He'll be all right again with a bit o' beefsteak. Don't worry yersel' about him, Commandant.'

Gallagher drew away with an irritated gesture and walked back to the inquiry room. Mulholland looked at Gypo with savage hatred in his eyes. Gypo looked around him arrogantly with his chest swelled out.

'Nolan,' called out Gallagher from the doorway of the inquiry room, 'get into that room there across the passage. Third on your right. That's it. Wait there until you are wanted. See?'

'All right, Commandant. I see it. I — uh — damn that wall. Stand outa me way, will ye?'

Gypo stalked down the passage, slightly unsteady on his feet and breathing heavily. He brought up suddenly against the wall again and laughed in his throat with his mouth shut. Then he headed straight for the room where the Rat Mulligan was sitting with his guard. When he had entered that room Gallagher beckoned to Mulholland. Mulholland came up. They both disappeared into the inquiry room. The sentries came to the doorway. They stood at ease across the doorway, facing the passage, with their drawn revolvers in their hands. 'The preliminary investigation' had begun.

Gypo subsided on to a chair beside the Rat Mulligan. He sat for several moments with a hand on each knee, staring intently at the ground in front of him, breathing through his nose and twitching his eyebrows that were like snouts. Then he raised his head and looked about him. He examined each of the armed men and nodded to each as he recognised him. They all nodded in return, but in a sour manner. Then he looked towards the huddled form of the Rat Mulligan and he screwed up his face in perplexity. He scratched his skull. He took off his hat and beat it, in a confused way, against his trousers leg, as if he were dusting it. Then he put it on his head again. He reached out his right hand as if to touch Mulligan's shoulder, but when the hand was within an inch of Mulligan's shoulder, he jerked it back suddenly. Then he jumped to his feet with an oath and stood facing Mulligan with his chest heaving.

'Mulligan,' he whispered thickly, but with great force.

'Hey, Rat! What ye doin' here? Hey, Mulligan!'

Mulligan never moved for two seconds. He sat on his chair, with his flat feet wide apart and his knees together, with his upturned palms resting on his knees and his head resting on his palms. His little emaciated body was covered with a heavy, black overcoat, that hung about him unbuttoned, with its ends trailing on the floor. His hat lay on the ground beside him where it had fallen unheeded from his skull. His shaggy black hair was tousled and damp. Then he slowly raised his head to look at Gypo. His face was yellow and hollow-cheeked, with great sorrowful dark eyes and a large mouth filled with two perfect rows of yellow teeth. His mouth was wide open. His eyes were staring and bloodshot. His whole body, ravaged by consumption, was terrible to behold. Gypo gasped, looking at it. A look of terror came into his little eyes.

'Rat,' he whispered, 'what brings ye here? Man alive, why aren't ye in yer bed? This is no hour for a sick man to be out.'

The Rat stared at Gypo aimlessly as if he had not heard him and could not see him. Then, slowly, his head subsided once more on to his palms. He shivered and sat still.

Gypo came up to him softly. He stooped down and touched him on the shoulder, as if to console him or to sympathise with him. But as soon as his hand touched Mulligan he drew back with an oath. Through his drunken brain the whole memory of the evening's proceedings rushed back under the influence of that touch. He remembered distinctly himself in the public-house, denouncing the Rat Mulligan to Gallagher, as the man who had informed against McPhillip.

He looked about him suspiciously at the armed men. Their eyes were cast about the room indiscriminately, with the habitual bored look of men under discipline. They were taking absolutely no interest in Gypo or in the Rat Mulligan. Gypo sat down again. He took his head between his hands. He crushed his skull with all his might in a great effort to regain control of his faculties.

For three minutes he sat that way, with all his strength concentrated in the effort to conquer his drunkenness. He was barely conscious of the effort he was making. It was instinct that warned him of the dangers that lay ahead of him, instinct aroused by the contact with Mulligan's body. His drunkenness resisted fiercely. Continual waves of reckless delirium surged through his body, rising up from his chest to his head, with the spontaneous action of sea-waves swelling up the side of an abrupt precipice. His head hummed and swayed. His eyes blinked. His tongue wagged loose and wanted to talk and sing and laugh. An unaccountable joy permeated him, a joy that did not originate in his actual self but in some strange being that had come to lodge in him temporarily. He could contemplate that new strange being with savage hatred as he pressed his hands against his skull. That being was an enemy of his. He must conquer him.

At last he felt his drunkenness weakening, gradually, like the lessening of a pain at night. It did not disappear but its effects changed. Instead of feeling reckless and hilarious, he began to feel cunning, careful, gloomy, defiant, recklessly strong. His head cooled and steadied.

It seemed to have become suddenly walled with steel, so that he almost experienced a physical pain from the pressure of his skull against the skin on his forehead. But he took away his hands from his forehead and he found that the pain vanished. His teeth set. His face assumed a look of stony apathy, the lips hanging flabbily, the cheeks loose, the eyes vacant. All the muscles of his body went loose, with the looseness of the athlete who is standing at ease, but ready to plunge off somewhere like an arrow.

In response to this change, as it were in his personality, he got to his feet in a dignified, calculated, imperious manner. He cleared his throat. He held out his right hand. He spoke.

'Listen, men,' he said. 'I had a drop taken when I came in here. I didn't know what I was doin'. I just remembered now who I was talkin' to an' it nearly knocked me dead. Look at him.' He pointed a thick, short, hairy forefinger at Mulligan. 'He wouldn't speak to me. He's afraid to look at me. I know why. It's him that informed on Frankie McPhillip, an' he knows that I saw him.'

'It's a lie,' screamed Mulligan, suddenly starting up and spreading out his hands and feet, downwards and outwards, as if he were resting exhausted after a race. His face was distorted with fear, amazement and rage. 'It's a lie, boys. It's a lie I tell yez. Before the Blessed Mother of the Infant Jesus I swear on me knees that I never left the house today except to go to the chapel to say me prayers.'

'Ha! Me fine boyo!' cried Gypo excitedly. 'Will ye listen to his oaths? It's easy work for an informer swearin' oaths.'

'Never —' began Mulligan again. But he was cut short

by two of the armed men seizing him by the arms, forcing him back to his seat and putting a handkerchief over his mouth.

At the same time Gallagher rushed out of the inquiry room and across the passage with his pistol in his hand. His sallow, lean face was aflame with anger. His eyes sparkled like points of fire. He looked at Gypo for a fleeting moment. It was no longer the cold, contemptuous, patronising look with which he had regarded him in the public-house. It was a look of fierce, relentless hatred. 'The preliminary investigation' had convinced him of something.

Gypo, on the other hand, looked at Gallagher in a friendly, intimate, confident manner.

'Here he is,' he said, pointing at the convulsing body of Mulligan. 'He knows it's all up with him already. He went into fits when I taxed him with it. So he did.'

Then he opened his mouth and gave voice to a hoarse laugh.

Gallagher smiled faintly into Gypo's eyes. There was something diabolic in the smile. It was so inhuman.

'Come on, you two witnesses,' he said icily. 'You, Nolan, and you, Mulligan. You are wanted at the inquiry now. Lead them in two of you.'

Gypo walked across the passage jauntily, swinging his shoulders, with his chest thrown out, with his head in the air. Mulligan had to be carried across. He sobbed all the way fitfully. The two sentries with drawn revolvers again took up their position in the doorway. Now, however, they had their backs to the passage. They faced the two witnesses. The two witnesses were seated on a small form in front of the larger table. They sat side by side. The two armed men who had conducted them into the room stood close behind them. The three judges sat in front of Gypo and of Mulligan at the large table. Gallagher sat at the little table to the right, with Mulholland standing a little to his rear, peering over his shoulder at what he was reading. To the right of the judges Mary McPhillip sat on a form alone.

There was a deadly silence for several moments. Drops of water, one after another, in irregular succession, could be heard falling from the stone roof to the stone floor, near the walls. Then the centre judge spoke in a bored, drawling voice.

'Take Peter Mulligan's statement, Comrade Gallagher,' he said.

As soon as Mulligan heard his name mentioned he tried to jump to his feet, but the man standing behind him held him down. At the same time Gypo put his hand on Mulligan's thigh and made a threatening gesture with his head.

'Keep quiet, will ye? Ye rat!' he growled.

'Peter Mulligan,' said Gallagher, 'give an account of your whereabouts from noon today until midnight when you were brought in here.'

Mulligan looked at Gallagher for some time before replying. He was obviously trying to speak. His lips moved. But terror held the tip of his tongue against his upper teeth. He could only jabber inaudibly. Then at last the tongue sprang loose and the words rushed out in a flood, incoherent, almost inarticulate, like the barking of a dog. Then he gasped. He paused. When he continued, his speech was regular and almost calm. He had become possessed of that meaningless courage that comes to nervous and timorous people, when they find themselves in a position where it is useless to be careful, or to exercise any control over themselves.

'What's the meaning of this treatment of a working-man?' he cried. 'By you men that are supposed to be out for the freedom of the working class. Can ye find no better man to arrest an' carry off in the middle o' the night than me, that's dyin' on me feet o' consumption? An' havin', still an' all, to work me hands off at me trade, tailorin' an' stitchin' in a basement, that's more like the cave of a wild animal than a room. Me that's —'

'Mulligan,' interrupted Gallagher impassively but sharply, 'I asked you for a statement of your where — abouts between noon today and midnight tonight. You better be quick about your statement. We have no time to waste.'

Suddenly Mulligan's short-lived arrogance vanished. He looked around him on all sides pathetically. He saw only stern, unsympathetic faces. He sighed and dug his hands deep into his overcoat pockets. Then he drew the pockets closely about his body and crouched low on his seat. He began to speak in a meek, timorous voice.

'Lemme see,' he said, looking at the ground. 'At noon today, or let us say dinner-time, if it's the same to you, I was lyin' in me bed. I had a bad pain in me right side from bronchitis all the mornin' an' I had to stay in bed with it. At one o'clock about, the old woman gev me a cup o' tay an' an egg. I remember I couldn't ate the egg. Well, that's no matter. I had to get up then, on account of a suit that has to be made for Mick Foley the carter. It's got to be finished be Friday. His daughter is gettin' married next Monday to —'

'Don't mind Foley's daughter,' snapped Gallagher. 'What had she got to do with your movements? Tell us about yourself.'

Mulligan began to cough furiously. His body shook and he almost fell off the form. Then the fit subsided. He sat shivering and unable to speak.

'Come on, Rat,' growled Gypo, nudging him with his elbow in the ribs. 'Ye might as well come out with it now as another time. Go ahead an' tell 'em all about it.'

Mulligan looked at Gypo. His lips trembled. His great dark eyes filled with tears. The terrific, massive countenance of Gypo, cunning with drunkenness, did not inspire him at that moment with fear. For some peculiar reason, his poor, shattered soul had gathered to itself just then a great courage. His withered face shone with a spiritual power. He spoke softly, tenderly, with pity.

'It's not for me to condemn ye,' he said; 'maybe yer not responsible.'

'Blast ye,' yelled Gypo, jumping to his feet. 'What does he mean, Commandant Gallagher, about me not bein' res-re-prosible? What does he mean by it? I want to know what he's drivin' at.'

'Sit down, Nolan,' cried Gallagher. 'Sit down immediately and keep quiet. Sit down, I say.'

Gypo sat down with a clutter. He stared at Gallagher, with the strange, bewildered look of a dog that has been reprimanded by his master and is wondering why he has been reprimanded. For the first time he realised that there was a cold, dangerous ring in Gallagher's voice. He sat immovable for two moments, without drawing breath, meditating on this hostile ring which he had heard in Gallagher's voice.

Unconsciously he took off his little, tattered, round, slouch hat. He pushed it, without looking at it, into his right-hand trousers pocket.

Mulligan began again to talk.

'Lemme see,' he said, 'where was I? Oh, yes. I worked on till about half-past three, or maybe a quarter to four, when Charlie Corrigan came in an' said that his brother Dave had just come outa jail, after been on hungerstrike for eighteen days. Ye remember he was thrown in on account of the Slum Rents Agitation. "He's upstairs," says Charlie. Well, I went up an' we talked over a cup o' tay until about six o'clock. It was just six when I left, because I heard the Angelus beginnin' to strike an' I on me way down the stairs, because I stopped to cross mesel'. Then I ran down home an' put on me overcoat and went out to the chapel. I'm makin' the Stations o' the Cross for ...' He stopped and flushed ... 'Well, it's no matter to no man why I'm makin' 'em.'

'All right, then,' snapped Gallagher. 'We don't want to know why you are making them. We merely want facts, not superstitions. You went into the chapel at six o'clock, or a few minutes afterwards to be precise. How far is the chapel from your house?'

'Maybe it's a hundred yards, maybe it's more. If ye go around the corner be Kane's it's less, but be goin' the other road around —'

'Oh damn the other road. Pardon me, Miss McPhillip.

Let us say it's one hundred yards. You arrived at the chapel, then, at about three minutes past six. That correct?'

'Uh … that ud be right … about that.'

'Well? How long did you stay there?'

'I stayed there until about half-past six. An' then I stayed talkin' outside the door to Fr Conroy for maybe ten minutes. He wanted to know —'

'Did you talk to anybody other than the priest you mention?'

'I'm comin' to that. After I left Fr Conroy I met Barney Kerrigan.'

'Where? Near the chapel?'

'Yes. It must have been within fifty yards of it, as yer goin' be measurements, although we never —'

'Just a moment. Were you ever a member of the Revolutionary Organisation?'

'What makes ye ask me that? Does any man know better than yersel' whether I was or not?'

'WERE YOU A MEMBER?'

'Sure I was.'

'That's better. Why did you leave it?'

'I left it, Commandant Gallagher, for reasons that are known to yersel' as well as they are to me.' His voice became passionate and shrill. 'I left it because the only one I cared for in this world, outside me old woman, that's me sister, came to her doom through it. But it's not for me to judge. It's not for me …'

'Very well,' interrupted Gallagher. 'You left the Organisation owing to a personal grievance. Was that grievance against any particular member of the Organisation?'

'I bear no fellow-man a grudge,' cried Mulligan solemnly.

'You had no grievance against Francis Joseph McPhillip?'

'Lord have mercy on his soul,' cried Mulligan, crossing himself with his eyes on the ceiling. 'I hope his sorrows are over him.' He turned to Miss McPhillip. 'I swear on me immortal soul, Miss McPhillip, that I bore no grudge agin yer brother.'

'All right,' said Gallagher. 'Well. Tell us what you did after leaving Barney Kerrigan.'

'I went back to the house after that. I did another bit o' work until about eight o'clock. I didn't do much because fellahs kept comin' in an' out, an' me eyes are not as good as they used to be an' the gas now is a disgrace to the city. But anyhow, I finished the waistcoat. Then I went upstairs to Jim Daly's room on the third floor. Poor man, he's sick this three years with bad kidneys. Only for a pension he has outa the British Navy, there's no knowin' what ud happen to him, an' he havin' no one to look after him but himself, an' he that delicate. We had a smoke an' a talk until about ten o'clock. Then I came down again. The old woman had just come in, so we had another cup o' tay an' a herring. Then I sat be the fire readin' a newspaper until about half-past eleven. Then I began to pouch about makin' ready to go to bed, when three men under Tommy Connor came in an' put a mask over me face an' bundled me into a car, without by yer leave, as if I was a criminal. That's all.'

There was a slight pause. Everybody sighed for some reason.

'Very good, Mulligan,' said Gallagher. 'That will do.'

He got up and went over to the judges' table. The four

of them talked for about two minutes. The centre judge took notes, scratching loudly with his pen. There was a pause. Then another discussion in whispers began. Then Gallagher came back to his seat.

'Nolan,' he said, quite suddenly, 'repeat the statement concerning Peter Mulligan that you made to me in Ryan's public-house in Titt Street at ten-forty-five this night.'

'Yes, Commandant,' said Gypo immediately.

He cleared his throat aggressively and rattled off the story about his having seen Mulligan track Francis Joseph McPhillip out of the Dunboy Lodging House. He spoke in a clear, loud and distinct voice, making arrogant gestures and looking straight into Gallagher's eyes as he spoke.

Mulligan kept trembling while Gypo spoke. He seemed all the time trying to interrupt, but although his lips twitched and his hands trembled he neither moved nor spoke.

Gypo finished speaking. His loud, strong voice died out, leaving a sudden silence behind it. There was another slight pause.

'What time exactly did you see Mulligan leave the lodging-house?' said Gallagher.

'Just half-past six,' replied Gypo immediately. 'I know because I looked at the clock in the hall.'

'Very well,' said Gallagher. 'That will do you, Nolan. Miss McPhillip, what time did your brother arrive at your father's house?'

'He arrived at ten minutes to seven,' said Mary, after a little pause, during which she blushed slightly, glanced at Gallagher and then looked at the ground. 'It might be a little earlier than that, but not more than a minute or so. I had just come in from business.'

'Did he say anything about being followed when he came?'

'No. On the contrary, he said that he was certain that he was not noticed since he came into town at half-past five. Mother was very worried about his being in town, and she wanted to get him away immediately, but he was so confident about being safe that she thought it was all right his staying for the night. He said he met Nolan at the lodging-house. That was the only person he spoke to, he said. He came by back streets after leaving the lodging-house. He never stopped anywhere and he spoke to nobody. He crossed the river at the Metal Bridge. It was pitch black at that time on account of the rain and the fog. Anybody that knew Frankie's way of going along, listening to every sound, with ears as sharp as a fox, could hardly believe that he was followed without his knowing it. He came in suddenly by the back entrance through the yard. We thought it was his ghost,' she said with a little shiver of remembrance. She stopped and put her handkerchief to her face.

'Thank you, Miss McPhillip,' said Gallagher. 'Barney Kerrigan out there?'

'Kerrigan there?'

'Kerrigan'

'Yes. I'm coming,' came a voice from along the passage somewhere.

A tall man, wearing a black slouch hat and a new, though shabby, grey overcoat with a velvet collar, came into the room. He had a revolver strapped over his overcoat at the waist. He saluted and stood to attention.

'Did you meet Peter Mulligan at six-thirty this evening?' said Gallagher.

'Yes, Commandant,' replied Kerrigan. 'I saw him just about that time comin' down the street. He stopped me to know did I know anythin' for the Grand National.'

'Very well. You are quite sure about the time?'

'Well, I couldn't give ye the exact second, but it couldn't be more than a minute one way or the other. I knocked off work at six an' it takes me always just about twenty minutes to walk from the quays as far as Farelly's. Well, I had a pint in Farelly's an' I stopped for a few minutes to talk to the boys, an' then when I came out I met Peter Mulligan. Just about half-past six I'd say it was.'

'Very well,' said Gallagher, 'return to your post. Peter Mulligan, you can go now. You will be taken home in the car that brought you here and we'll see you right for any inconvenience that was caused to you.' He walked over to the judges and whispered something hurriedly. They all nodded and put their hands in their pockets. 'One moment, Mulligan,' he called. They all gave him money. He added some from his own pocket. He came over to Mulligan and handed him a fistful of silver. 'For the present this might help you. I'll see what can be done for you later on. I'll bring your case up before the Relief Committee. Good night, Comrade.'

Mulligan took the money with bowed head. He got up and moved to the door hurriedly without saying a word, with his hat crushed in his two hands and his overcoat flapping behind him. He disappeared out the door, head first, stooping, hauling his two flat feet after him as if he were dragging them against their will. Then, with a hard, biting cough he disappeared.

The sentries stood again across the door. Gallagher walked slowly back to his table. There was a deadly silence.

The silence lasted only about twelve seconds. During this pause Gallagher took out a notebook and turned over the pages, while Mulholland bent over his shoulder whispering something, and the three judges murmured with their heads close together. But to Gypo these twelve seconds were as long as twelve years to a man stricken with a painful and incurable disease. A succession of terrors flitted through his mind. They were not ideas or thoughts, but almost tangible terrors that seemed to materialise in his brain as the result of the reasoning of some foreign being. His cunning and his assurance were gripped suddenly by that amazing foreigner and hurled out of him, clean out of him into oblivion, like two bullets fired into the air.

Ha! They were hurled out of him by the amazing fact of Mulligan's disappearance, free, with money in his pocket given to him by Gallagher. They had given him money. They had called him comrade. They had promised to bring his case up before the Relief Committee. They sent him away free. He had gone … Jesus, Mary and Joseph! What was the meaning of it?

Then suddenly, as he sat there, bolt upright on his seat, massive, those unspeakable terrors crowded into his mind. They came ready-made, fully matured, nauseating like bilious attacks, sharp and biting like bayonet wounds, heavy and ponderous like palpitations of the heart. They came, one, two, three, four … scores of them, lining up in his brain, shoulder to shoulder, in a mass, standing there solidly and then immediately disappearing like ghosts without a sound and giving place to others. There was a mass of them, but each one was distinct. Each had its own peculiar silent screech. Each had its own peculiar demoniac grin. Each had its own peculiar ... damn them all! The curse of them was that he did not know what they were. It seemed that his personality was bound in chains and he was unable to grapple with the cursed things. He must sit still, bolt upright on his wooden form, and permit them to stand there unchallenged in his brain. He was helpless. A cold sweat came out through every pore of his body.

Four seconds passed. Then his mind began to grope about among the terrors, timorously, like a snail that had been touched and has gone into its shell feigning death and has come out again touching blades of grass suspiciously and wriggling its horns. Gypo opened his nostrils and his mouth. He drew in a deep breath through both organs simultaneously. The cold sweat suddenly became warm. His blood flooded his head with a surging movement. He became ferocious. At first his eyes narrowed and his eyebrows that were like snouts bent down. Then his eyes opened wide and his eyebrows lifted, like guns that are elevated in order to train them on a target. His lower lip dropped. His mind began to work methodically. The terrors vanished out of it and gave place to an iron determination to fight to the bitter end.

With his blood maddened by alcohol, he became conscious of the vast strength in his body. He almost experienced a feeling of happiness at this opportunity for using it. It was that savage joy that is always present in the Irish soul in time of danger, the great fighting spirit of our race, born of the mists and the mountains and the gurgling torrents and the endless clamour of the sea.

He looked around him, measuring those against whom he had to fight. To his left he saw Mary McPhillip sitting. She had her hands in her lap. She was leaning forward slightly, with a nervous, expectant look in her eyes, looking at Gallagher. She cast a terrified glance, occasionally, towards Gypo, but her eyes always came back to Gallagher's face as if they were fascinated by it. It was obvious that she was terrified and that her mind was trying to keep itself fixed on the object of the prayers which her moving lips were uttering. Gypo saw the terror in her quivering face and knew that he had nothing to fear from her. Then he looked at the three judges. He knew those masked men. They were merely puppets, politicians, figure-heads who would do Gallagher's bidding, afraid to contradict him. Ha! Gallagher was the man he had to fight. Gallagher and that rat Mulholland. He saw them over by the little table with their heads together. He fixed his eyes on them.

Feverishly he set himself to form a plan, not that he hoped anything at this hour from the formation of a plan, but merely because making a plan was an end in itself to his peculiar reason. But he could not even think of a plan. All his energies were concentrated on maintaining his anger at fever heat. He struggled feebly with threads of ideas and then dropped them hopelessly. He doubled up his fists and held them, knuckles downwards, one on each hip. The two armed men who stood behind him, saw his back muscles rise and strain against his dungaree jacket.

Then the silence broke. Gallagher got up with his open notebook in his hand. He walked over to the judges' table. He placed the notebook in front of the judges, pointing out something with his finger. The centre judge nodded. Gallagher walked back again to his table and sat down. Gypo followed every movement with frenzied excitement. He seemed to be on the point of jumping to his feet and rushing at Gallagher. The two sentries in the doorway and the two armed men standing behind Gypo's back slipped their fingers over their revolver triggers. They leaned forward slightly. There was a tense moment. Then Gallagher looked at Gypo and began to speak sharply, in a low, restrained voice.

'Now Gypo,' he began, 'tell us how you spent your time from six o'clock this evening until you came in here at half-past one. Hurry up. Don't waste any time. We are in a hurry.'

Gypo's eyes almost shut. Then his face seemed to swell. His mouth contorted.

'What's it got to do with you where I ben?' he thundered in a queer, hollow voice. It seemed his mouth had gone dry.

'You never know,' said Gallagher carelessly. 'It might be interesting for us to know. Don't you feel like telling us how you've been amusing yourself from the time you met Francis Joseph McPhillip at six o'clock in the Dunboy Lodging House until you came in here?'

'An' supposin' I don't tell ye, what are ye goin' to do? Wha'?'

'Well, I'm not going to tell you that. But we can do a lot. You know that yourself, don't you? You have your choice in the matter. You either tell me or I'll go to the trouble of telling you and the court myself.' He paused for an instant and then added: 'with the help of Bartly Mulholland here.'

Then he stared at Gypo dispassionately, with the cold and indifferent look of a man examining a statue. Gypo's chest heaved in and out. He had not been prepared for this point-blank attack from Gallagher. He had expected that Gallagher would adopt his usual tactics of friendliness and cajolery, trusting to madden his prey into letting some chance important word slip unawares from his lips. Gypo felt himself actually cheated out of his rights by this insultingly crude and insolent attack. Gallagher was not even doing him the honour of playing with him. Then he must know everything already. Did he?

The last trace of his self-control left Gypo. He abandoned himself to a frenzy of passion. A delirious wave of ferocity mastered him. He clenched his fists so that the bones cracked. His right leg went so rigid that the boot rushed along the stone floor with a harsh scraping sound, until it brought up with a bang against the leg of the form. There it stayed. His knee was pointed and shivering. He opened his mouth and yelled, almost incoherently, a torrent of blasphemous and obscene oaths at Gallagher. He yelled them in an endless sentence, without a verb or pronoun or conjunction. He kept yelling until he had to stop for breath.

When Gypo stopped, Mary McPhillip's sobs became audible. She was trembling violently and sobbing. Gallagher got up, walked past Gypo without taking the slightest notice of him and took Mary by the arm. He led her up to the judges' table.

'I have no further need of this witness,' he said, 'so I suppose I may take her into another room.'

The judges nodded. He led Mary out of the room. Gypo's eyes followed him everywhere. He was staring wildly and he seemed to have lost all power of directing his bodily activities. He was shivering spasmodically in his legs. Gallagher came back into the room and sat down at his table.

Still Gypo's eyes were concentrated on Gallagher's face. His outburst had left him completely empty, like a shaken sack. There was a pain at the pit of the stomach. Mob orators know that pain, when they have spoken for over an hour under a perfect hail of frenzied interruptions. His eyes were dazed. Some machinal force kept his eyes concentrated on Gallagher's face. He responded to every movement of Gallagher's face in a half-conscious way. Every time Gallagher moved a limb he felt a sharp stab in the pit of the stomach. He was conscious of even the most minute movements. A thing that terrified him especially was Gallagher's chronic habit of twitching his cheeks by grinding his back teeth at intervals.

As before, this agony lasted during a few moments only, during the time that Gallagher was looking at some notes on his table, with furrowed forehead. But the moments seemed years, the agony was so concentrated. Gallagher spoke again.

Then again a strange change came over Gypo. For as soon as Gallagher spoke he felt an instantaneous relief. He breathed deeply. He sighed. A delicious tremor swept over his body like a cool breeze sweeping the back of a sultry sea in summer. His jaws set again. Gallagher's voice had a different ring in it. It was softer. It was friendly. It was ... honour bright ... it was argumentative. Then there was a chance ... There must be a chance yet ...

'What did you mean, Gypo?' cried Gallagher. 'What did you mean by telling us all those lies about the Rat Mulligan? You should be ashamed of yourself. Even if you got a grudge against a man, that's no reason why you should try to get a thing like that slung on to him. Good Lord! You're a funny man, Gypo. What put it into your head to tell me that you saw him this evening at the Dunboy Lodging House, when we know very well that he was within one hundred yards of his own home at that very minute, three miles away or more? Were you drunk or what?'

'I know I was drunk,' cried Gypo, responding joyfully to this friendly overture from Gallagher. His anger vanished. His whole soul leaned out eagerly towards Gallagher, craving support. He paused momentarily after uttering the first sentence. He remained silent, leaning forward, looking at Gallagher, intently, as if he expected Gallagher to finish the statement for him. But when Gallagher's thin lips remained sealed, he hurtled on excitedly, as if he were stumbling recklessly through dangerous obstacles. His voice was uneven and flurried. 'But I'd swear be Almighty God that it was him I saw goin' out the door and runnin' up the lane after Frankie. An' if it wasn't him it must have been somebody else like him, for I'd know the cut of his shoulders anywhere. I would if ye put my head in a bag.'

'You told me,' continued Gallagher in the same

friendly scolding tone, 'that you followed the Rat across town until you came to … Where was that you said you lost sight of him? I forgot now.'

Gypo started and stuttered. Good Lord, what had he said? He must say the same thing he had said before. But he could not remember saying that he followed the Rat across town. Did he say it in the public-house or did he not? His forehead was burning. The hammering at the top of his skull was blinding his eyes with pain. Almost unconsciously he put his hands to his forehead and blurted out, pathetically, on a peculiar high note, an amazingly childish and hysterical sentence.

'Commandant, I'm all mixed up an' I can remember nothin'.'

It was horrid, that pitiful, forlorn cry of pain and of absolute despair coming from such a giant.

'All right then,' said Gallagher, 'don't worry yourself. We have to get to the bottom of this business, so we'll just set to work, the two of us, and maybe we can piece the whole thing together. Now the best thing we can do is to begin at the end and go backwards. We'll work backwards until we come to the point where you lost that man you saw tracking Frankie McPhillip out of the Dunboy Lodging House. In that case we'll begin with where you were before you came in here. Bartly Mulholland tells us that you were at Aunt Betty's, with a woman called Connemara Maggie. You must have been with her, because Bartly saw you with his own eyes giving her two pound notes. There were three empty whiskey bottles in the room. They had been bought by you, I suppose. Well? A man is entitled to drink his own whiskey that he had bought with his OWN money, I suppose. That has got nothing to do with OUR business, has it, Gypo? None whatsoever. We merely want to trace that man that tracked Francis Joseph McPhillip out of the Dunboy Lodging House. Well! What do we find next? A friend of yours called Katie Fox, once upon a time a comrade of ours, they are all to the front in this business, all those people that were once comrades of ours, she told Bartly Mulholland that you gave three pounds to an English woman at Aunt Betty's and two pounds to Aunt Betty to pay a debt for this woman. You wanted to send her back to London. A kind of Barnardo's Home or something, this Aunt Betty's, for stray women. Well, of course, that again has nothing to do with us. A man is entitled to do what he likes with his OWN money. But ... Good Lord, Gypo,' he cried, striking the table and bursting out into a strange hilarious laugh, 'you were having a time of it. Where did you get all the money? Ha! Now don't get excited. I know it's no business of mine. But if you're going to be taken back into the Organisation ... Well! There are ugly rumours flying about ... You know the way silly rumours fly around Dublin. It's awful. But the fact is, that people are talking about sailors, American sailors, being robbed at the back of Cassidy's public-house. It's only a rumour, of course, and again, that friend of yours, Katie Fox, shall we call her one of our ex-comrades, she is responsible for the rumour, according to Bartly Mulholland. Of course, it's obviously originated with her. She has very probably invented that story out of spite, simply because you went with the other girl. Or ... Tell me, is there any truth in it, Gypo? I mean in the rumour of your having robbed a sailor?'

Chapter Eleven

Gypo started, as if out of a heavy sleep. His brain went 'thud, thud, thud', trying to think whether he should say 'yes', or 'no'. If he said 'yes', would he be caught in the act of telling a lie? If he said 'no', would he be able to find any other means of explaining how he got the money? Several other questions and problems also crowded into his mind simultaneously, in confusion. There were doubts, uncertainties and suspicions. He was completely in a mesh. His mind was like a refuse-heap. There was no beginning or end to any chain of reasoning. He gave it up in despair.

'Commandant,' he said, again touching his forehead, 'I can make out nothin'. My head is sore. I must be drunk.'

Again it was the same bewildered, agonising cry of a lost human soul. A weak, thin, childish voice, coming from a giant.

'Well, never mind,' said Gallagher cheerfully, 'we'll leave it at that. We'll carry on. Before you went down to Aunt Betty's, Mulholland saw you in a fish-and-chip shop, treating a crowd of people to a free meal. He said you spent about a pound there. Two pounds, three pounds, two pounds, one pound … Well! You certainly were in a generous mood. American sailors are paid well, of course. Throwing money about in all directions, eh? Like a millionaire! But of course that's your own business. We are simply trying to get at the bottom of the business we have in hand. That business is simply this: WHO INFORMED ON YOUR PAL FRANCIS JOSEPH MCPHILLIP?'

Gallagher uttered the sentence slowly and in a loud voice, looking closely at Gypo as he did so. Gypo started.

His lips opened wide. But he remained silent. His lips moved, forming the words Gallagher had uttered, silently.

Gallagher watched the movement of Gypo's lips with curious detachment. Then he smiled slightly before continuing.

'Before that, of course,' he continued, 'I met you myself in the public-house, in—er—Ryan's public-house in Titt Street. There was where you told me that funny story about the Rat Mulligan. Ha, ha, ha! Ha, ha, ha! ...'

Gallagher suddenly roared with laughter, holding his sides, with his head in the air. Gypo almost leaped from his form. He trembled.

'Well, of all the stories!' continued Gallagher, pretending to gasp with laughter. 'I can't make out why you told me that story, Gypo. I can't make it out. Well, there's no knowing ... But we must get on with our own work. Time's running short and we have some stiff work to do before the night's over. Some stiff work, Gypo. Well? Before you came into the public-house you were in Francis McPhillip's house in 44 Titt Street. There again, you seemed to be acting in a very funny way, according to Bartly Mulholland. Of course, I can understand your being stirred up and excited on account of the death of your pal. But still ... Do you remember giving Mrs McPhillip the money that fell out of your pocket on to the kitchen floor? What did you do that for? Eh? Good Lord! You have left a trail of gold after you all the evening. I wish it were as easy to track the man you saw coming out of the Dunboy Lodging House after Frankie. But why did you give that few shillings to Mrs McPhillip and say it was all the money you had when you knew very well you had a lot more in your pocket at that very moment?'

'I don't know,' growled Gypo.

His voice was no longer weak and childish. He was stiffening again.

'Maybe you were drunk even then,' suggested Gallagher, almost excitedly, as if he were deliberately trying to apologise for Gypo's absurdities.

'Maybe you were drunk. What?'

'Didn't I tell ye before I was drunk,' grunted Gypo.

'Ha! I knew ye were drunk. Where had you been drinking?'

'Couldn't tell ye where, but I know I was drinkin' with Katie Fox.'

'Ha! Now we have it,' cried Gallagher, striking the table.

'Now you got what?' yelled Gypo, panting and leaning forward savagely. He opened his fists out like claws. He spread his feet out ready to spring. 'What have ye got, Commandant?' he yelled hoarsely.

Gallagher took his pistol by the butt and tapped the muzzle slightly on the table three times. The two armed men pointed their revolvers at Gypo's back. The three judges who had been calmly smoking cigarettes started. Mulholland made a slight movement towards the door.

Then Gypo subsided into his seat loosely. The dreadful fascination of Gallagher's cold eyes sucked his passion clean out of him. Breathing in a tired way, he sat still. The tension relaxed again. Gallagher laid his pistol on the table and smiled.

'No need to have got excited, Gypo,' he said. 'I was just saying that it was when you were drinking with Katie

Fox you said you robbed a sailor at the back of Cassidy's public-house. Maybe she asked you where you got the money out of pure idle curiosity and you told her that as a joke. We all know what curious creatures women are. That doesn't matter, though. What does matter is this. Could you remember what time that was? When you were drinking with Katie Fox? What time was it?'

'I can't say,' mumbled Gypo stolidly. 'I'm drunk. I can't remember.'

'Well, now that's a pity,' said Gallagher. 'For it's very important for us to find out what that time was. If we were able to find out what time that was, then we would surely be able to find out lots more. Let us say it was nine o'clock at that time. Let us say nine. That wouldn't be far out? Would it be far out, Gypo?'

'How do I know what time it was?' roared Gypo. 'Amn't I tellin' ye that I was drunk?'

'Well, now,' continued Gallagher, getting a little more excited, 'we have got as far as nine o'clock. We are as far back as nine o'clock.'

He paused. His face began to light up and his forehead began to wrinkle. His eyes were no longer steely and cold. They became restless points, fiery and full of turbulent activity. They kept roaming over Gypo's face. His lips, on the contrary, were creased at the corners in a strange, dry smile. His voice was laughing and at a slightly higher and sweeter pitch.

'Now we have arrived at nine o'clock,' he continued, 'travelling backwards. Great way this for travelling, Gypo. You never know what you are going to bump against without knowing. Any minute now we are liable to find something, Gypo. We might in a few moments, even jump on the man that informed on Frankie McPhillip. WE MIGHT JUMP ON HIM. Now! Easy there, Gypo. I mean the man you saw tracking Frankie McPhillip out of the Dunboy Lodging House. Could you give the court any idea of the description of that man you saw? You say he was like Mulligan? Do you say he was like Mulligan? Speak, man. SPEAK, I SAY,' he roared.

But Gypo was no longer able to speak.

A sudden transformation had come over him. As a thunder-storm bursts over a calm sea on a sultry day, rending the oily ocean back and covering it with cavorting, black ridges and white, churning froth, so his body and soul responded to the sudden lightning in Gallagher's eyes and the ominous crackle of his voice, uttering sugared threats, gambolling devilishly with words. He crumbled away into an immense, flabby, supine mass, that writhed on a wooden form, a tangled heap of limbs lying piled helplessly. His head dropped forward on his chest, swaying from side to side on the pivot of his chin. His eyes sank into their sockets. His face went ashen and still. His stomach wrinkled up like an unpropped wall collapsing on its own foundations. His whole body shivered and started into awe-inspiring movement, monstrous and inhuman, revolting as a spectacle of degrading vice and yet pitiful in its helplessness.

All the countless centuries of human development that had left their impression on that body, to make it into the glorious image of a God-like human being, withered away during that time of agony, leaving only a chaotic collection of limbs writhing and strange visions racing over his convulsing features.

The sight was fearsome even to the callous men that surrounded him. Even THEIR hardened souls saw a vision of a strange life just then, an unknown and unexpected phantom that comes to some once in their lives and that never comes to many, the phantom of a human soul stripped naked of the covering of civilisation, lying naked and horror-stricken, without help, without hope of mercy. They forgot for the moment their hatred of him. They forgot that this helpless, shapeless mass of humanity was a menace to their lives. They forgot that he was a viper they must crush. They only knew at that moment, that he was a poor, weak human being like themselves, a human soul, weak and helpless in suffering, shivering in the toils of the eternal struggle of the human soul with pain.

Their mouths opened wide. Their eyes grew soft. Some made unconscious movements with their hands, others with their feet, unconscious movements of which their minds were not aware. For their minds, disciplined by the corroding influence of hatred, sat still and indifferent.

One man alone revelled in Gypo's agony. He revelled in it unconsciously. He was no longer conscious of his emotions. He had become demented, drunk with the fury of his hatred. That man was Gallagher.

He rose lightly from the table, without a word, pawing the table softly with his hands for support, like a panther finding foothold for a spring. His lean, glossy, sallow face was lit with a glow of passionate eagerness, like a lover approaching his beloved. But it was not the pure, resplendent eagerness of love. It was the eagerness of the preying beast about to spring. The lips laughed, thin,

wrinkled, red lips drawn upwards and downwards from
the set, white teeth. The eyes glittered. The forehead
twitched. The hands trembled. The whole body shivered
slightly, with those minute shivers that pass down the
side of a setter when he stands poised over his prey. He
rose gradually from the table. He stepped over his chair
with his right foot, to avoid moving the chair. He released
his body from contact with the table and the chair. His
eyes were fixed on Gypo's face. He stood crouching. His
head was swung forward, almost on a level with his
stooping shoulders. He groped with his right hand on the
table for his pistol. His fingers found the butt. Slowly they
embraced it. The forefinger sought the trigger and found
it. He lifted the pistol from the table. He brought it with a
sharp movement to his hip. Its muzzle pointed at Gypo's
chest. He took one short pace forward.

Gypo uttered a sharp yell and put his two hands to his
face, shielding his eyes. But he took them away again
almost immediately. They dropped to his sides. He must
look at Gallagher's eyes. He could not remain hidden
from those eyes. They burned into his flesh unless he
looked at them with his own.

Gallagher spoke. His voice was almost inaudible. It
was soft and sweet like a girl's voice.

'As you seem to have lost your voice,' he whispered, 'I
had better tell you myself who that man was. There's no
need to describe him for the court. The court can see the
man for themselves. I'm going to tell the court the very
name of the informer that betrayed his comrade, Francis
Joseph McPhillip. I'm going to point out the informer
with my own hand. That is the man,' he cried suddenly,

with terrific force, turning to the judges and pointing his pistol at Gypo. 'Comrades, the informer is Gypo Nolan, who is sitting there on that form.'

He had scarcely finished when Gypo uttered a muffled scream like a dumb animal in mortal agony. He tumbled forward to the stone floor. He frothed at the mouth. He reached out his trembling hands towards Gallagher.

'Commandant,' he cried, 'I didn't know what I was doin'. I declare to God I didn't know what I was doin'. Can't ye see what I mane?' He raised his voice to a scream and he kept dragging himself forward over the floor towards Gallagher's feet. Then he struggled to his hands and knees. He stretched out his hands on either side, panting: 'Is there no man here to tell him why I did it? I can't tell him. My head is sore. I can't tell him. Commandant, Commandant, you an' me, Commandant. We'll make a plan, the two of us ... uh-r-r-r ...'

His voice sank into an inarticulate jabber as his hands clutched Gallagher's boots and he sank again prone to the ground. His thick lips that tried to kiss Gallagher's boots were imprinting kisses on the stone flags. Gallagher kicked away the clutching hands and called out sharply:

'Take him to the cell and place him under close guard.'

Immediately the four armed men rushed forward and bent down to seize Gypo. But as soon as they touched him, he stiffened. He immediately rose with them to his feet, with an accession of unaccountable strength. He shook the four men off with a shrug of his whole body. Then he was about to crouch to rush at Gallagher, when the four of them flung themselves upon him again with a simultaneous cry. He swayed for a moment on bent thighs, reeling under the impact of the four bodies, two of them on his back, two gripping him about the waist. Then he took a fierce, taut step forward with his right foot, gasping as he did so. He planted the boot on the floor with a ringing sound and then jerked himself backwards. The two men who had landed on his back, flung their arms around his neck and swayed, banging their heads together, their legs flying adrift. A cry arose: 'Overpower him. Help! Help!'

The three judges moved back from the table and stood against the wall, undecided whether to run for safety, or to rush to the attack.

Mulholland pulled at Gallagher's arm excitedly.

'Will I fire, Commandant?' he whispered.

'Don't shoot,' murmured Gallagher in a dazed, sleepy voice. He was staring at the struggling men with a sad smile on his face, as if he were dreaming. 'Don't shoot. He's not sentenced yet. Don't fire, I tell you.'

Then Mulholland ran crouching and threw himself at Gypo's legs, trying to encompass them with his arms. There were now five men hanging on to Gypo. He was like Laocoon, entwined with snakes. He stood bolt upright, with every muscle on his body knotted.

Then he lurched away to the right towards the door, with that human cargo, unmoored and swinging by the sudden lurch, clashing with soft thuds, in a panting mass. He was brought within three paces of the door by the lurch. He saw the door. With an immense wrench that made his biceps crack, he shook the men from off his back and neck. They slithered downwards with a scratching sound of their nails clawing his clothes. They clung around his hips. Then he growled and stooped down to man-handle the men that clung to his legs. His groping hands clutched Mulholland's hair. His fingers groped downwards, seeking the throat to garrotte him, when a mad rush of feet startled him. He looked up.

They were rushing at him through the doorway. He saw them for a moment, a number of flashing eyes, and set lips and clawing hands, rushing at him. Then he dived headlong at his new enemies. He forced them backwards in a mass into the doorway. There they all fell, amid yells and hissing curses and shrieks of pain. Then Gypo's great boots stuck out of the pile in the centre, while Mulholland's grinning, sallow face peered up between them.

When they cleared away the jam of human bodies from him he was exhausted. Four men pinioned his arms behind his back. Then he was dragged along the passage into the prison cell. They loosed him and threw him in. They bolted the door.

CHAPTER TWELVE

At eleven minutes past three Gypo was condemned to death. The three judges went away, leaving Gallagher in charge of the execution of the sentence.

At eighteen minutes past three Mulholland entered the inquiry room, with the three men who had been detailed to carry out the sentence passed on the prisoner. They stood to attention in front of the table at which Gallagher was sitting. Gallagher read to them the decision of the court. Then he gave them their orders.

'Comrade Mulholland,' he said, 'will be in charge. When I leave this room you will cast lots in the usual manner. You will then take the prisoner in the motor-van to any part of the mountain road, about half-way between Killakee and Glencree. There is bog on either side of the road. At any spot in that locality, you will be at least two miles from the nearest house. Execute the sentence there. Bury the body some distance from the road. Just drop it into a pool of bog water. When you have finished the job go straight ahead across the mountain to Enniskerry and come back to the city by another route. There are several.

You can choose the most convenient. Report to me at headquarters as soon as you come back, Bartly. I will wait for you there. Carry on, comrades. Get the prisoner away as quickly as possible. Use force if necessary to prevent him from creating a disturbance, but you must on no account execute the sentence until you get to the mountains.'

Gallagher left the room. He went across the passage to the room where Mary McPhillip was sitting alone. All the armed men were gathered in the guard-room at the foot of the stairs. Tommy Connor had come in now. He was explaining something to them in a hoarse voice. Two men were stationed outside the door of the cell. The sentry paced up and down the passage again.

Gallagher sat down on the wooden form beside Mary McPhillip. He did not look at her. He stared at the floor. His forehead twitched. His face was very drawn.

'We have discovered the informer, Mary,' he said in a low voice. 'Your brother will be shortly avenged. It was Gypo Nolan who betrayed him.'

There was silence. Gallagher had uttered the last sentence dramatically, like a tremendous revelation. But Mary did not speak. He looked at her.

'Mary,' he said again, a little louder. 'It was Gypo Nolan who informed on your brother.'

She shuddered and looked at him sadly in the gloom.

'I knew that,' she said, 'all along. Poor fellow.'

'What?' he grasped, staring at her.

'What are you going to do with him, Dan?' she asked, almost inaudibly. 'I hope you're not …' She stopped.

Gallagher looked at her sharply, in wonder, suspiciously,

as if he had suddenly proved to himself that all his calculations had been wrong about something.

'Surely what, Mary?' he said at length, almost timorously.

'You're not going to kill him,' she said. 'That would only be another murder, added to … to the other. It wouldn't help the dead. Lord, have mercy on him.'

'Murder!' ejaculated Gallagher dreamily, as if he had heard the word for the first time in his life and he were reflecting on its significance, incredulously like a philosopher confronted unexpectedly by a stupendous superstition. Then his nostrils expanded and his face hardened into anger, as he realised her meaning and her attitude towards the sentence that was about to be passed on Gypo. 'Murder, did you say? Great Scott! Do you call it murder to wipe out a serpent that has betrayed your brother? Where is your …? Do you call yourself an Irishwoman? What? Good Lord! I don't know what to make of it. What …? Good Heavens!'

'Listen to me, Dan,' she said, sobbing; 'for God's sake, listen to me before you do this. Listen. I didn't know until now how awful it is. I was foolish the way I talked at home this evening when all the people were there. I was so mad the way father was talking that I thought I could shoot the man that informed on Frankie myself. But it would be murder, Dan, just the same as any other murder. And —'

'Oh, hang it!' snapped Gallagher.

'Dan,' she whispered, 'don't do it, for my sake. I love you. Don't do it, for my sake, and I'll do anything you want me. I feel I'm the cause of this.'

'Mary, do you love me?' whispered Gallagher

excitedly, panting as he seized her right hand in both of his. He bent towards her. 'Say it again. Say you love me.'

But he drew back immediately, with a strange and unnatural presence of mind. He was afraid that the passing sentry might see him.

Tears were rolling down Mary's cheeks. She looked away towards the doorway. She kept silent. Gallagher leaned back from her, watching her face intently. He looked at her from under his bunched eyebrows. His lips were set firmly. His forehead convulsed. He appeared to be struggling with a savage passion and at the same time struggling to think coherently on the intellectual plane. He was trying to probe the movements of her mind, so that he might conquer it with his mind. He wanted to conquer her mind and make her subject to him, to make her his mate on his own terms. He told himself that he was doing this, so that she might help him for the conquest of power. He refused to admit to himself that he was inspired by passion. He despised passion.

The silence was very peculiar and tense. Mary was conscious of it. But Gallagher was not conscious of it. Then Mary spoke. She talked rapidly without looking at him. She talked in an irritated tone.

'Take me out of this place immediately, Dan,' she said. 'I was mad to come here with you. I had no business to come here atall. Also, if you were a gentleman you wouldn't ask me to come. What I said just now about loving you was not true. I only said it trying to persuade you not to murder that man. Before, when I used to read in the papers about a man being shot, I used to think it was right, but it's a different thing when a man you know does a thing like that. Frankie killed a man too, Lord have Mercy on him. Oh, God, have pity on us all.' She became slightly hysterical. 'Why can't we have peace? Why must we be killing one another? Why —'

'Hush! Keep quiet. Keep quiet.'

'Isn't it cruel, Dan?'

She let her head fall on her hands. Her body shook with silent sobs.

Gallagher stared at her dreamily.

'I will let her alone now,' he thought. 'The logical sequence of this outburst will be this. Her mind will wheel around to the other extreme if I keep quiet and don't irritate her by attempting to convince her that I am right. Her terror and her moral excitement will exhaust themselves and go to sleep. Then she will become aware of her strange surroundings, mentally, in a different way. When her mind becomes awake and normally acute again, she will see me, this place, and what's going to be done with Gypo, in an opposite light. When her mind is groping about in this new attitude it will be easy for me to influence her. I think I'm right. At least it always held good, that rule. I remember the struggle I had with Sean Conroy. But women are supposed to be different from men a lot psychologically. But I have to chance that. It would be suicidal to interfere with her now. That's certain. Still ... I'm not sure of myself with her somehow ... It's not like the others. And ...'

Again his passion surged upwards. He sat without thought, fighting it, squeezing his palms together, with his eyes on her bent neck.

CHAPTER THIRTEEN

When Gallagher left the inquiry room, Mulholland went silently to a form and sat down. The three men stood nervously in front of the table watching him. They watched him intently, in silence, as if each movement he made was fraught with grave consequences to themselves.

He took three matches from a box and placed them beside him on the form. He handled them slowly and deliberately, with a serious, contemplative expression on his face, like an old fisherman baiting his hooks under the admiring glances of a party of tourists. Then he took out a clasp knife and opened it. He cut a piece off one match. He put the knife back into his pocket.

Then, suddenly, he cleared his throat with a noise that sounded enormous in the silence. The three men started. They looked at one another fearfully, as if each had been caught by the others in the commission of an indecency.

Mulholland rose calmly and approached them, holding the three matches on his open palm. Without speaking he pointed to them. Two long and one short. They all examined them. Right. Each nodded his head solemnly. Not a word. Mulholland nodded and marched away to the far end of the room. They did not follow him now with their eyes. They stared painfully at the floor.

The tallest of them was a docker called Peter Hackett. He was a fair-haired young giant, slim and lean-faced, with sleepy blue eyes and a gentle mouth. His great bony hands were thickly covered with long white hairs. He stood with his arms folded on his chest, one leg thrust forward, his eyes wide open and strained, his forehead wrinkled. He was only twenty-two. This was the first time he had been chosen for an affair of this sort. It was particularly strange and odious to him, because he was a good-natured soul, loved by all on the quays where he worked. He had no conception of politics or of any problem other than hurling, football, horse-racing and pitch and toss, which he played all Sunday afternoon on the Canal bank with his cronies. He often lost his whole week's wages playing pitch and toss. On these occasions, when he went home to his young wife penniless, he would first of all dance around the kitchen in a fit of rage and perhaps break a thing or two, threatening to blow Kitty's brains out if she said a word. Then his anger would suddenly evaporate, to be followed by a fit of sobbing. During this fit he sat by the fire with his head in his hands, moaning and begging Kitty to forgive him. His wife always felt exalted when these outbursts occurred, because the excitement of the quarrel and Peter's kisses, which lasted far into the night afterwards, were a welcome break in the dreary monotony of everyday life as a docker's wife, scouring, cooking, washing, with two children to look after on a docker's wages.

Peter had no imagination. He lacked the refined conscience and sense of injustice that attracts most gentle natures like his towards a revolutionary movement. He was not the stuff of which the other sort of revolutionary is made either. He belonged to the Organisation simply because the rest of 'the boys' belonged to it, and out of fanatical hero-worship for Commandant Dan Gallagher.

Dart Flynn, on the other hand, was designed by nature as a revolutionary, a man to stalk ahead of the bulk of humanity, grimly destroying obstacles, disturbing the sluggish existence of the herd, terrifying the contented ones into activity, born with a curse upon his brow, anathema to the mass of beings who always seek tranquillity and peace at any price. He was dour, dark-visaged, built like the base of an oak tree, almost square. His body and face were fleshy and jealous of movement. His eyes were small. They moved horizontally. He was clean-shaven, with a pink and white complexion, in spite of the fact that he was thirty-five and lived a hard life as a carter. In company, he hardly ever expressed an opinion on politics, religion, or on any other of the fundamental things that are discussed with avidity by revolutionaries who carry their lives in their hands. But in the secrecy of his own soul he thought deeply on these matters. In his little bare room in a lodging-house in Capel Street, he had several works on philosophy and economics. He had also worked out an amazing system of philosophy, based on the premise that each human being shares his soul with several different animals. The man who could discover and have constant intercourse with these animals would be supremely happy and immortal.

Flynn had no moral sense. He hated all human beings who were not Communists. He loved all children and animals. He gave most of his wages to the hungry little ruffians in his street. He had no relatives or dependants. He was an old member of the Organisation, highly respected for his courage, his fidelity and his taciturn habits.

The third man, Laurence Curley, was of a totally different type from both his companions. He was also the most nervous and timorous. He was twenty-eight, pale-faced, red-haired, with a tall, thin frame, slightly consumptive-looking, on account of his hollow chest and stooping shoulders. His father had been a doctor in a country dispensary district. He had received a good education, but he early grew dissatisfied with life and refused to study for the Bar as his father wished. Instead he took a job in Dublin as a clerk, in order that he might plunge into the revolutionary movement.

The theory of revolutionary Communism interested him far more than working for a revolution. He gradually became a crank, hated by everybody. He was always finding fault and reading or discussing dull works on Socialism. His views were always the most extreme and blood-thirsty. He used to whisper excitedly, whenever he met a stranger who did not know him yet, or when the least industrial disturbance occurred:

'The red flag will be hoisted any minute. Wait till you see. Then blood will spill. Wait till you see. Justice and liberty are bourgeois watchwords. The proletarian watch-words are revenge and bread. The proletariat knows how to deal out their deserts to the oppressors.'

He had always this sort of patter.

Now, however, the three of them, so different in essential characteristics, had reached a common level of emotion. The silence of the night, the phantom-filled cellars, the illegality and danger of the contemplated act, the torturing uncertainty of the choice, filled them with such delirious emotions that they were beside themselves. They were not afraid. They were beyond fear, on to a distant level of emotion, where the common impulses, that agitate the hearts of men, are unknown.

Then Mulholland approached with the matches arranged in his hand, so that their red heads alone were visible.

'Who'll draw first?' he said carelessly, standing in front of the group.

After a moment's pause Flynn came forward hurriedly. He stretched out a fleshy hand, fumbled awkwardly with the matches, and then pulled one.

They all strained eagerly to look. It was a long match. Everybody sighed.

'Next,' said Mulholland.

Curley and Hackett looked at one another excitedly. Then each spoke.

'You go first.'

'No, you go first.'

'Go ahead. I don't mind drawing the last.'

'What's the difference? Your nearest. Draw.'

'Why should I? It's your turn. You draw.'

'Come on,' snarled Mulholland, 'one of you draw. We have no time.'

They both made a movement towards the matches. Then each stopped to let the other advance. Their hands and legs were jerky. They stared at one another with hatred.

'Come on,' hissed Mulholland again. 'Didn't ye hear the Commandant's orders, that we were to get outa the place as soon as possible? Are ye afraid or what?'

'Oh no,' cried both men together in an off-hand tone.

They both rushed at the matches. They tussled for them.

'Keep back now. It's my turn.'

'Keep back, you. You weren't so quick before. Let me draw.'

'No, I won't. I was here first.'

'For goodness' sake,' cried Mulholland, 'ye pair o' babies. Will I have to pull me gat on ye?'

The two of them stood still, looking at Mulholland dazedly.

'It's against the rules,' continued Mulholland with a great sense of importance, 'but I'm goin' to call ye in the order o' yer rank. You draw first, Comrade Curley.'

Curley's thin fingers shot out instantly. He drew the match. It was a long one. He gasped. Then he burst into a thin laugh.

'Comrade Hackett.'

Hackett stumbled forward. He reached for the short match that Mulholland held out to him with a strange smile.

'It's your shot, comrade,' whispered Mulholland.

Hackett grasped the match and crushed it into fragments immediately. He threw the little bundle away in terror. He rubbed his palms slowly. Then he struck his right coat pocket suddenly with his hand. He laughed.

'Good Lord!' he blubbered, 'I thought I'd lost me penknife.'

CHAPTER FOURTEEN

For ten minutes Gypo lay perfectly still in the cell, after the door was bolted. He lay on his back. His head and neck were buttressed into an upright position by a square block of stone that jutted from the floor, by the wall farthest from the door. His feet were stretched out, wide apart. One hand lay on his right hip, palm upwards, with the fingers bent inwards, as if he had fallen asleep clawing something. The other hand lay across his eyes. He drew very deep breaths at long intervals. His face was perfectly at peace. It was bruised slightly around the mouth and on the cheek-bones. Each feature was impassive, like the features of a carved image. The glossy skin, the humps, the eyebrows that were like snouts, the thick Ethiopian lips, attained a majesty during that ten minutes of abnormal rest, a majesty that was not so apparent while they were in movement, responding to the strange impulses of his mind.

Gypo rested, exhausted, while he was being condemned to death. It was a dead rest, like the rest of a child in the womb before birth, sucking strength all round for the savage struggle with life that will soon commence. Every organ and tissue and muscle was straining for a renewal of strength.

When blundering reason flees, instinct, that is fundamental and unerring, rushes to the defence of life.

At twelve minutes past three, one minute after he had been condemned to death, Gypo moved. He opened his eyes and closed the right hand that lay palm upwards on the ground. He clenched the hand rigidly until the wrist joint snapped with the tension. Then he took the other hand away from his eyes and dropped it to his bosom. He moved his eyes around from side to side, slowly, suspiciously, blinking and listening intently.

The cell was pitch black. Only at one point was there a speck of light. There was a dim, oblong patch of light hanging slantwise in the darkness some distance to his left front. That was the aperture near the top of the door. It did not penetrate the darkness of the cell. It merely hung there, obscurely and uselessly, like a foolish suggestion. All round was pitch dark. Gypo shivered.

He was not afraid. No. He did not feel at all in the ordinary sense of the word. But he was immediately fully conscious, as soon as he moved, of all that had happened before he had been thrown into the cell. Still more peculiar, he was quite calm and collected about everything. The darkness consoled him. He felt at home in it. It concealed him. He felt immensely big and strong in the darkness. There was nothing in his immediate neighbourhood but a darksome void that his personality overpowered. He could bellow and his voice would resound through that darkness indefinitely. There would be no resistance. There was no limit to the darkness, no wall, no horizon, no end. He was encompassed by it, sheathed in it. It wound round and round him. It was an impenetrable coat of mail, without weight, without thickness, intangible.

Beyond it somewhere were his enemies. It came between him and them. Ha!

He gathered himself up with a sudden spring. He got to his hands and knees. Several joints snapped as he did so. His bruised body had grown stiff, lying motionless on the stone floor. Just as he lay that way on his hands and knees, he heard a rattle at the door. Immediately he threw himself down again and pretended to be asleep. But he fell so that his eyes were toward the oblong patch of light. He knew what had rattled. It was the sentry having a look at him. An electric torch was thrust through the aperture. It rested on him for a moment or two. Then it was withdrawn.

During the couple of moments that the torch-light had flooded the cell Gypo's eyes were busy. They had darted around. Yes. The walls were hopeless. He knew that, of course. He had himself guarded a prisoner in the same cell, a condemned prisoner whom he and McPhillip and Jem Linnet, the bookmaker's clerk, had afterwards brought out in a car. He knew the whole routine. Perhaps that knowledge was responsible for his calm, partly responsible. Nothing was uncertain in the near future. In a few minutes they would come for him. Once in the car it would be impossible to escape.

All right. His only chance was in the cell. Ha! That was why he was calm and collected. After all, it was neither the darkness nor his knowledge of what was destined to happen that made him calm. McPhillip had at last made a plan. The door ... the door ... the door!

'Gypo,' he had said one night in Cassidy's when he was drunk, 'if we ever get ... ye know what I mean, Gyp ... click ... you know ... ye needn't worry. I can manage that cell easy. Only I'd need you. I'm too small. Listen.'

'I'll do it, Frankie,' mumbled Gypo to himself excitedly, as he crawled along the floor towards the door.

He moved like a bear on his hands and knees, with his head down and his haunches high in the air. He moved noiselessly until he reached the door. He felt along the edge of the wall and then drew himself gradually to his feet. For a moment he toyed with the idea of taking off his boots, but he could not remember that Frankie had said anything about that. He decided to leave them on. He reached up with his hands. He strained them to their full length before he reached the top of the stone ledge over the door.

Drawing a deep breath, he hoisted up his body, using his biceps as levers ... His biceps swelled and knotted and snapped ... His body rose smartly and without apparent effort. In an amazing way he swung around his legs from the hips and landed his body gently on the ledge, resting on the right side of his chest and stomach. The stone ledge was no more than six inches wide. More than half his body rested on the empty air, as it lay along the ledge. But he was as cool as if he were standing loosely on the broad, firm earth. He was acting on the plan he and McPhillip had rehearsed. His body performed the movements without his mind exercising any control, either of guidance or of warning, warning against danger that is called fear.

After a slight pause, he leaned his weight on his hands and rolled his body around in a reckless movement. His legs shot into the air about two feet. He stood poised on his hands for two seconds, as if he were going to stand on his head. Then he lowered his right leg. He brought it up to his hands. Slowly, with snapping gasps, he balanced himself on the right leg and stood up straight.

He stood straight in the solid darkness for a moment. He breathed twice rapidly. Then he groped upwards for the roof. He found it about three inches above his head. He pawed the stones hurriedly, searching. He couldn't find what he wanted. It should be there. Mother of Mercy! He pawed out farther. Nothing yet. Sweat stood out on his forehead, suddenly, as if his body had been wrung. Savage anger gained control of him. He bared his lips and distended his eyes. His last hope gone? Had they taken it away during the last six months? He reached out one inch farther. Too far.

With a muffled gasp, he hurtled forward from the ledge. His hands scraped along the roof with a rasping sound. Then, just as they fell in pursuit of the falling body, the fingers of the right hand closed on an iron ring. They closed on it like a vice. The shoulder muscles snapped. Gypo swung across the floor, brought up with a grunt, jerked and swung back again, suspended from the iron ring by his right hand.

When he steadied himself, he changed hands on the ring and groped about with his right hand, until he found a hole in the roof about three inches away from the ring.

That was the hole of the trap-door, through which the wine had been let down into the cellar from the garden. He gripped the ring with both hands and swung up his legs, until they found the far side of the hole. He jammed both feet against the side of the hole and rested for four seconds, breathing deeply. His knees were bent upwards.

He reached up into the hole with his right foot. The foot reached the oaken door that lay across the mouth. It had been fastened with leather hinges, but these had worn away and they had not been renewed since the house became deserted. Several inches of earth had collected on it. Gypo pushed against it and made no impression on this mass of earth and rubbish that covered it. He took another rest and then pushed with all his might. He raised it suddenly, with a sucking sound, about three inches. A mass of dirt and earth fell down with a swish. It landed on the floor beneath with a showery thud. The noise terrified Gypo. The sentries outside the door would hear it.

In a furious rage, he kicked with all his might and sent the door flying away from the hole. A whole load of earth fell with a rush and a gust of cold night air came with it, with equal rapidity, ferociously, as if it had been waiting a long time to attack.

In spite of the blinding dirt and the freezing air, Gypo stuck his legs through the hole immediately and clutched the garden surface with his heels. Then he let go one hand off the ring and gripped the side of the hole. He hurt his collar-bone badly as he did so. Now his body was secure in the hole. He let go the other hand, supporting himself on the thigh muscles that gripped the sides of the hole until the second hand and his head came into the hole. Then he scrambled through on to the garden. He bounded to his feet and hurtled forward on his face.

Two shots had thundered through the hole as he cleared it. They were after him. He snorted with fright. For a moment he stood still, confused by the din of voices and the rushing feet. Then he darted away headlong through the rubbish towards the house, ten yards away. His only escape lay that way. He entered the house at a bound, through a hole in the kitchen wall. He cleared the kitchen in two strides. He was in the hallway. Flash, flash, bang, bang. Two more shots. His fist floored a tall man. He rammed a second with his head. He floundered through the hall. Bang, bang. They whizzed closely past his right side. He slipped on the flags of the hall as he tried to wheel towards the right wall. He came to his hands and knees. As he rose again a man threw himself upon him, firing as he did so, so closely that Gypo smelt the explosion that flashed blindingly by his ear. Missed again. They closed, grappling one another's bodies, with groping, shifting paws. They tumbled in the doorway. They both rose. Gypo loosed one arm and struck. The other man collapsed without a sound. Gypo dropped him. He fell on his back. It was Dart Flynn.

Gypo grunted, bounded to his feet and wheeled to the right, into the open air. With a gurgling laugh, he bounded away into the darkness. He was away, swallowed by the night.

CHAPTER FIFTEEN

When Gallagher heard the first shot, he started to his feet angrily. He thought that his orders had been disobeyed and that they had shot the prisoner before taking him to the mountains. But even as he stood up, his anger changed to terror. He heard the rushing of feet and the babble of shouting voices, calling excitedly, in a panic:

'He's escaped. He's escaped.'

'The stairs. The stairs. Up the stairs, quick.'

Mary McPhillip screamed. Gallagher did not heed her. For three seconds his body was numbed with fear. He could not move a muscle. His lips blubbered. He was like an exhausted man, about to have a heart attack. He stood unstably, like an uprooted tree, balancing for its fall. Mary jumped up and clung to him. He did not look at her. Then Mulholland rushed in. He was livid with fear.

'He's escaped, Commandant,' he gasped; 'he's gone.'

Then Gallagher shook himself violently, thrusting Mary from him rudely. Uttering a volley of almost inarticulate oaths, he drew his pistol and grasped Mulholland by the throat. Mulholland yelled and struggled downwards to his knees.

'Don't shoot me, Commandant,' he whined. 'It wasn't my fault. That man is a devil out of hell. There's a spell on him. Don't fire for the love of God.'

'Damn you and God,' snarled Gallagher, hurling him away.

He rushed out into the hall.

'After him,' he yelled. 'After him. After him.'

There was nobody to take any notice of him. Everybody was on the street in pursuit of Gypo, except the sentry, who stood uncertainly in the doorway of the empty cell, with his pistol in his hand and his cap turned backwards, terrified, gaping at Gallagher.

Then a rush of feet came on the stairs. Four men were coming down carrying Flynn between them.

'Who is that?' cried Gallagher.

'It's Flynn, Commandant,' whispered one.

'His jaw is broken in a jelly,' whispered another.

They arrived at the bottom of the stairs. Gallagher glanced at the prostrate, sagging body of Flynn. 'Throw him in there on a form at once,' he said. 'Mulholland. Come here. Where are those others?'

'Here they come, Commandant.'

'There's no sight of him, Commandant,' gasped Tommy Connor, leaping down the stairs. 'We thought we had better come back.'

'All right,' said Gallagher. 'Are you all here now?'

He spoke in a terribly calm voice now. It was terrifying. Nobody answered for a moment.

'Hurry on, Peter,' said Connor to somebody that

appeared at the top of the stairs.

It was Hackett. He rushed down, panting, with wild eyes. They were all back again.

'Who's responsible for this?' cried Gallagher.

Nobody answered. He swore and strode away down the passage to the cell. Connor and Mulholland followed him. The others stood spellbound. Gallagher pushed the sentry out of the way with a curse and entered the cell. He flashed his torch. He saw everything. A cold perspiration started gently around his temples. He shivered. He left the cell followed by the two men. Nobody spoke. They returned to the men at the foot of the stairway. As Connor passed the room where Mary McPhillip was, he ran in, picked her up from the floor and put her sitting on the form. Then he rushed away to Gallagher.

Gallagher stood looking at the ground for a few moments, with the men standing around him in silence. Then he looked around fiercely at every one. He spoke gently and in a friendly tone.

'Comrades,' he said, 'our lives are at stake. What's more, the Organisation is in danger. The cause is in danger. Comrades, that — man — must — be — found. That man must be found if it costs a hundred men. Do you understand?'

'Yes, Commandant,' cried they all eagerly.

'Finnigan and Murphy stay here on guard. Do you hear?'

They clicked their heels in silence.

'Mulholland, you take the rest with you in the van and try and cut him off from the bridges. He will try and cross the river to the south to get away to the mountains. Get away immediately. Place your men and take up position yourself at the Butt Bridge. I'll send reinforcements to you there and another officer. Slattery, you get reinforcements. Mobilise ten men from this district. Take them off your own list. Beat it. Quick. Off you go, Bartly. Remember the Cause is at stake. We are lost if that man gets away. He may be making for the police already. Run for your lives.'

They went up the stairs, rushing with fanatical enthusiasm. In three seconds Gallagher was alone at the foot of the stairs. One sentry took up position at the top of the stairway. The other man went into the guard-room with Flynn. Mary McPhillip was standing in the doorway of the witnesses' room, shivering, almost hysterical with fright.

Gallagher stood for almost a minute, motionless, looking at the stairs, with his eyes almost shut. Then he shuddered and went into the guard-room. The sentry, a red-faced, young grocer's assistant, was tying a red silk handkerchief around Flynn's jaws. The only part of Flynn's face that was visible was his eyes. Gallagher watched the sentry tying the knot at the back of Flynn's skull. Then he looked into Flynn's eyes.

Flynn stared back coldly. Although he was suffering agonies of pain from his broken jaw, his eyes betrayed no sign of pain.

'Did you fire at him, Dart?' said Gallagher in a whisper.

Flynn made a slight nodding movement.

'Did you hit him?'

Flynn raised his right hand and waved it from side to side, like a marker giving the signal for a washout. Gallagher sighed.

'Stick it out,' he said coldly. 'We'll get a doctor as soon as the reinforcements come. Can you swallow a drop of brandy?'

Flynn nodded.

'Here's my flask. Use it.'

He put the flask into Flynn's hand. He pressed the hand as he did so. Then he left the guard-room and walked over to Mary McPhillip.

She left the doorway when she saw him coming. He found her sitting on the form. He stood beside her, looking at the ground, wrapped in thought, gripping her shoulder with his right hand. She became terrified at his attitude, at his silence and the look on his face, which she could see dimly in the gloom. His face had become ashen pale. His eyes had sunk and grown glassy. The blood had left his lips. He was continually grinding his teeth, slowly.

'Dan,' she whispered at length, 'what's the matter with you?'

He did not answer for several seconds. Then he started, gasped, and let go her shoulder. He took two paces rapidly towards the door. He halted and put his hand to his forehead. He wheeled about and looked at her curiously.

'Oh yes,' he said calmly. 'I forgot. Excuse me. I was thinking of something and I didn't hear what you said. Let me see. Yes.'

He sat down beside her. He took her right hand gently

into both his own and began to fondle it, with the soft gentle movements of a cat. He began to speak gently, in a soft, sad voice, looking at the floor in front of him.

'You'll have to stay here with me now, Mary,' he said, 'until I'm leaving here. Maybe we'll have to stay here two hours, maybe more. Gypo has escaped. I can't move until I get news of him. The prisoner has escaped,' he repeated almost inaudibly. 'If he can't be found it will be the end of me, Mary. He knows so much.'

Mary turned towards him eagerly and swallowed her breath. Her eyes grew moist and her lips quivered. The gentle tone of his voice went straight to her heart. It drew her towards him, not with the dreadful fascination with which she was drawn towards him before, but with a soft, gentle attraction, like what she had imagined love would be. Not the calm, calculating, respectable affection she experienced for the man she intended to marry, Joseph Augustine Short, but that tumultuous, devouring passion which she had expected real love to be, the love that was written of in books and poems. Ah! How she could love him like this! Soft and gentle like this! She could approach him and touch him, touch something in him that was soft and gentle and sympathetic and human. He was in danger. Good God! It was good that he was in danger, if it helped to disclose to her his real self. It had made him weak, this danger, ridding him of the horrid, impenetrable strength, that kept him cruel and cold. If she could have him to herself like this, she would sacrifice even her religion for his love. Aye! She would even forsake God for him like this.

So she thought, looking at him with tears in her eyes.

She smoothed his shoulder gently with her hand and whispered to him:

'Dan,' she said, 'you are in danger. Can I help you, Dan? Dan, you know I'd give my life for you.'

Gallagher turned towards her slowly.

'You would, Mary,' he said softly.

She nodded. He took her suddenly in his arms.

'You love me, Mary. Say you love me, Mary.'

'I love you, Dan,' she breathed on his lips.

They kissed passionately, with strange abandonment. Then they sat for a minute, with their cheeks together, hardly conscious of anything but of a strange exaltation that was undefinable. A hot feeling of joyous exaltation pervaded their bodies. But it was not the exaltation of love. It was an abandoned sadness born of grief. The grief of two human souls clinging together for solace. It was beautiful and pure like love, that exaltation, born of fear, and of the eternal melancholy of the entrammelled Irish soul, struggling in bondage.

For Mary, perhaps, it was almost pure mating love. For she loved that gentle voice, the last remnant of the gentle nature, that had been devoured in the struggle of life and replaced by a cold, callous, ambitious nature. She loved, but she only loved a phantom, a shy ghost come for an hour of the night, to fly from the dawn.

But for Gallagher, his caresses were a mask. He had hidden behind his gentle nature for the moment, as behind a mask, to rest and plot. Men like him always lean on women for support in moments of extreme danger.

Even as he sat with her arms about him, with her breathing words of love on his lips, he was thinking, not of her, but of the great danger that confronted him. Would Gypo inform again before he was caught?

At length, with a low exclamation he got to his feet, releasing himself hurriedly from her embrace. He clenched his fists.

'Mary,' he said without looking at her, 'you see how I need you. I need somebody to talk to, somebody to trust. There is nobody else but you I can trust, Mary. And I don't know why I trust you.'

He paused. She was not listening. She was suffering a reaction from her exaltation. Why was he talking like this? A lover did not talk like this. He was only thinking of himself.

'But since the first time I saw you, standing in the crowd with another girl, while I was addressing a strike meeting, I knew I could trust you. I remember thinking as I saw your face, that you were the woman for me. It was queer and I can't explain it. Something in your face told me that you were my woman. It's very queer that. You see thousands of faces every day. There is something queer and mysterious in them all, something suspicious and hostile. Then you see one face that you have been looking for all your life as it were. There is nothing hidden or mysterious in that face. It can hold nothing hidden from you. It's queer. I haven't worked it out yet. It's in the eyes, I think. The eyes are the doors of the mind. But I haven't worked it out yet. But what am I talking about? It's a sure sign that I'm worried when I ramble off like this. I talk to myself in my room, for want of a listener, when I'm up against it. I talk all night, sitting up in bed, with a pistol in my hand.' He lowered his voice and smiled with his lips, while his eyes glittered. He looked at her for a moment. 'If the boys knew that I get the wind up now and again, they wouldn't be afraid of me. And then ...' He drew his hand across his windpipe. 'Sure. That's what keeps me safe. They are afraid of me. That's all it is. It's not love. Oh no. I wouldn't have it, anyway. There's nothing like fear. Nobody loves me. Not even that slobber of a fellow Hackett, who stooped down one day on the quays to tie my shoelace. He'd die for me, but only because he believes I'm cold and hard and callous and that I could shoot him dead without a quiver of an eyelid. You see ... he's the opposite from ... There you are, Mary. Good God! I must be very bad tonight. I'm wandering. Mary, does your right knee tremble and you can't stop it?'

'Dan, Dan,' cried, Mary, seizing his right knee in both her hands, 'don't worry. Don't worry, Dan.' She began to rub the knee. 'That's nothing. My father often gets it. It's only nerve tension. A nurse out of the Mater Hospital told me all about it. You can live to be a hundred with it. She says it's due to tea-drinking. But ... Dan, why are you so hard and cynical all of a sudden about everything? Can't you give it all up and settle down? You said you —'

'Settle down?' cried Gallagher, jumping to his feet and looking at her fiercely, as if she had suggested a heinous crime. 'Give it up! How do you mean? Pooh! Women, women, women! You don't understand that it's my life. It's my life, I say. You might as well tell me stop breathing and ... After all ...' He seemed to think of something startlingly unexpected, for he looked at her with open lips. He continued, shyly almost, in a scarcely audible voice, as if he were soliloquising. 'After all, you weren't affected the way I expected you would be. You would never understand. You would never join me in the way … Hm! I see.'

'Now what have I said, Dan?' she whispered nervously, biting her fingers.

She was terrified that she had lost him … yes, in a way, strangely enough, she was terrified at losing his love, as if she had him securely in her possession, as a loving husband for a long time … that she had lost him by some foolish phrase.

'Nothing,' he muttered stolidly.

He crossed his hands on his chest and began to pace up and down once more. It was a long time until he spoke. She tried to get enraged with him and could not do so. She began to pity herself.

'It's waiting like this that's hard,' he said suddenly in a whisper. 'I don't mind dying. It's not that I mind. It's waiting without a chance of knowing what's going to happen. They talk of the bravery of those louts that get the V.C. What are they but stupid carrot heads? Theirs is the bravery of the dull-witted ox. A man must be intelligent to be brave. It's only the intelligent man that can visualise danger. If he is brave he never seeks danger, but he seeks dangerous methods of life. You see the difference? Well, it doesn't matter, anyway. I have this all worked out a long time ago, so I don't need to discuss it very much. But this is the point I have to explain now. There is no danger in open warfare. There's merely death, and death is not dangerous. The Russians proved that. Not recently, but in Bielinsky's time. That is, of course, they proved it in relation to their own needs. But according to my own calculations and discoveries, death brings us back into the great consciousness of the Universe, which is eternal. Therefore death, properly speaking, is not death. It is a second stage of birth. No, that's quite wrong. I can see where that would lead me. There is neither birth nor death. But ... All that's out of the count. We have to tackle a minor question. Obviously it's a minor question. Now that's better. Now we see death is not a danger. But defeat is a danger. Defeat by one's enemies. Not defeat by one's friends. But of course there are no friends. Friend is a bourgeois word. It has no longer any meaning. So defeat in the true sense means defeat by one's enemies. It's synonymous. Well, I face defeat. Therefore ...' Suddenly he waved his right hand in a circular fashion above his head and then pointed it fiercely at the wall to his left. 'It's waiting like this that's hard,' he cried fiercely. 'I've been out with a gun many a time. I've been shot at. I have two holes in me. That's nothing. You don't know what's happening because you become an animal. But waiting is different. You are in command. That's different. A brain, a mind, a great eye, probing the unknown. But ...' He stopped suddenly and tittered audibly in his throat.

'Jesus, Mary and Joseph protect me,' Mary began to murmur rapidly to herself. She shut her eyes and tried to think of Heaven. Her mind had suddenly become void of all sense of knowledge and emotion. She felt an intense cold in every pore of her flesh. As she rambled through the prayer over and over again with her lips, a ridiculous rigmarole of a song went through her mind with a tintillating sound, about 'Piping Tim of Galway'.

He sat down beside her on the form, bent towards her and kissed her coldly on the forehead. His cold lips remained on her forehead for three seconds. Then he sighed and got to his feet again. He must keep in movement. He must keep talking. He could not stop his brain from thinking at an enormous rate, and the only way to relieve the congestion was by talking aloud. The formation and enunciation of the words deflected a fraction of the brain-forces and liquidated them. Faster, faster, wilder, wilder he must talk, to keep pace with the tremendous speed of his heated brain.

'Where is he now?' he whispered with a kind of cackle in his throat that was like a laugh. 'Where is he now? Why can't we see with the mind, long distances? How very stupid I am, after all, in spite of my philosophy. He might be in the police-station at this very moment, with a big, fat sergeant taking down his statement.' He shuddered and bit his lip. 'Good Lord, Mary! If you only knew what a statement he could make. Ha, ha! He and Francis are the only two men in the Organisation who could tell anything worth while. And Francis is dead.'

He paused. Mary bit her teeth, dispelled the tintillating rigmarole of a song and began another prayer, one to Our Lady of Perpetual Succour.

'Ye see, Gypo was so useful. There were things he could do that no other man could do. Not so much by his immense strength, as on account of his particular mental qualities. It's easy to get as strong a man, but a mind like that is hard to find. I doubt if there is another. He was priceless. Damn him. He's a superhuman monster. Why did I say *was* before? He is. He is. That's the worst of it. I wish he … The government would give a million pounds for that statement. Good Lord! I never thought Gypo could turn informer. It must have been a mistake. I couldn't be wrong about him. Some mistake. Sure. He isn't the type. Sure. I swear he isn't. How could he be? He responds to me like, like a needle to a magnet. Then how did he inform? On his own pal too! That's the strange thing about it. I've been studying him for eight years and he never showed any signs of personal initiative. Never once. I shouldn't have dropped him for six months. But of course I had to keep up respect for the rules of the Organisation. Good Lord!' he cried pathetically, looking at the ceiling and wringing his hands almost in despair, 'I'm alone with nobody to help me. Mary, there's nobody to give me advice. Why did nobody warn me against expelling Gypo? What?'

He paused. She did not reply. She shuddered and did not look. It was difficult to pray. She was so tired. And it was terrifying not to pray. Then she might have to listen to him.

Then suddenly she was startled into an upright position, with her eyes staring and her mouth wide open. Gallagher had uttered a strange sound. Then he ran crouching to the form. He hurled himself upon it. He clutched at her knees. He was looking with wild, strained eyes at a point on the wall. He jabbered in a dry parched voice.

'There he is, Mary. I see him. I see him. I see the sergeant writing it down. They are giving him a drink. D'ye see him, Mary, with his little hat perched at the back of his head, making the statement? D'ye hear him say my name? D'ye hear him?'

She drew his head towards her with both hands, trying to make him look at her face, trying to get his staring eyes away from the wall, but he struggled against her. His eyes were fixed wildly on some point in the wall. He writhed.

Then suddenly he sighed, turned towards her and smiled. It was a natural, healthy smile. His eyes danced humorously as he smiled. His terror had passed away, giving place to a momentary joy. He felt hilarious, like a woman drunk with wine. He took Mary suddenly into his arms and kissed her. He tickled her neck playfully with his fingers, laughing all the time.

But she struggled to free herself, panting. He loosed her and stopped laughing, looking at her in surprise.

'Did I frighten you, Mary?' he said casually. 'That's all right. I often get a fit of the blues like that. Don't worry. Did you think I was mad?' he added with a little laugh.

'Oh, you're all right now, Dan. Ha, ha!'

She was trying to laugh to cheer herself, but she made a poor job of it.

'Sure I am, Mary. As right as rain. Everything will be all right. Of course it will. Don't worry.'

There was a long silence. They sat close together, looking at the ground.

'Tell me, Dan,' whispered Mary awkwardly, 'did you see anything that time? When you were looking at the wall? Did you see anything? Tell me, quick. It's such a queer place, this. I think there are devils in it.'

'Damn it!' snapped Gallagher. 'Why did you bring the

subject up again, when I want to forget it? Devils! Huh! Devils!'

He jumped to his feet and took two paces forward, stretching his hands out over his head with peculiar intensity, like a man with a rheumatic twinge in his shoulder-blades. Then he shrugged himself and rattled off with startling suddenness, in a quite calm voice, cheerful and debonair.

'You are right,' he said, 'after all, in asking the question. I should have explained at the time,' he yawned, 'what I meant by seeing him. Of course I was speaking figuratively. There are no such things as devils, at least not supernatural creations, as the current superstition understands them to be. The only devils to be afraid of are human devils. I know numbers of them. They are real enough. But they wear sheep's clothing. Respectable, law-abiding fellows. I'll see them again in a few hours, if Gypo gets to the police-station with his story. They'll drawl out slowly their sentence on me. Ha! Pretty boys. And here I am doing nothing while they are ...'

He moved rapidly up and down again, clutching his hands behind his back, jerking his body about and crunching his teeth.

'I am alone,' he continued. 'Alone. I stand alone. They can easily buy off the rest of the Executive Committee. They'll be only too glad to get away free, with their lives, at any cost, if it comes to a fight. If evidence is found against me, sufficient to prove certain things, they can strike at me with impunity. My own rank and file would be the first to stone me to death. Their damn superstitions always stand in the way of

revolutionary beliefs. They talk at International Headquarters about romanticism and leftism and all sorts of freak
notions. What do they know about the peculiar type of hog
mind that constitutes an Irish peasant?'

'How dare you?' cried Mary indignantly.

He looked at her. Her eyes were flashing. She sat erect
on the form. He had never seen a woman wild and
imperious like that. He smiled weakly.

'Sorry to hurt your feelings,' he said cynically. 'But I'm
beyond that. Pish! I've got the whole country in a fine net
and I'm within the law until they find something definite
to go upon. I can snap my fingers at the lot of you.' He
grew fierce and arrogant. 'You and your patriotic ideas! I
was wrong about you. I don't want you. I never wanted
you. Do you hear? I snap my fingers at the whole world.
That hulking swine can do his best. I will drain his blood
before dawn. Mark my words. He'll never reach the
police-station. My destiny stands against him. And —'

Just them the sentry's challenge rang out. Gallagher
immediately stood stock-still and listened. Then he
rushed into the passage, drawing his pistol and
muttering something. Two men were hurrying down
the stairs. The first of them came up smartly to Gallagher
and clicked his heels.

He was a small, slight man, with hawk's eyes and a
long, pointed, curved nose. He wore a loose raincoat and
a check cap. He was Billy Burton, an Insurance Agent, a
captain in the Revolutionary Organisation. Gallagher
shook hands with him eagerly.

'Glad they found you in, Billy,' he said. 'You're the
very man I want.'

He led Burton into the guard-room and rapidly explained the situation. Then he detailed a plan. He detailed the plan coolly and minutely as if he had spent weeks at it.

Burton listened, blinking his little eyes, sniffling, biting his nails, fondling the butt of his automatic pistol in his breast pocket.

Over on the form, Flynn was sitting, with his broken jaw swathed in a red silk handkerchief. He sat impassively, inscrutably communing with himself. He seemed to be unconscious of his surroundings, with his mind fixed immutably on some infinite problem.

The only sounds in the room was the drip, drip of the water from the many roofs and the patter of Gallagher's voice.

His voice was again cold, hard, dominating, vital.

CHAPTER SIXTEEN

At a quarter to four the drizzling rain ceased. A sharp bustling wind arose. It came screaming down from the mountains upon Dublin. It was a hard, mountainous wind, a lean, sulky, snowy wind, that rushed through the sleeping city savagely, so that even the drops of rain on the muddy sidewalks leaned over before it, with frills on them.

The clouds arose, their hanging rumps cut away by the newborn wind. They hung high up in the heavens, gashed and torn, with a sour expression on their grey, slattern bodies. Here and there a rent came in the dishevelled panorama of cloud and the sky appeared, blue and chaste and a long way off.

This change in the mood of nature occurred when Gypo was bounding away from the Bogey Hole, trembling shakily with excess of energy. He ran through a short, narrow lane, so narrow that his shoulders grazed either side as he dashed through. He crossed a thoroughfare in four strides, casting a look on either side as he leaped across. He saw a sloppy roadway on one side, with a watchman's glowing brazier at the far end and on the other side a hill. Tall tenement houses lined the thoroughfare, their battered old walls rambling up towards the sky, their squalor hidden by the majesty of the night.

He fled across the road and entered a dark archway. Then he bumped suddenly against an old cart and went head-over-heels with a smothered exclamation. The concussion and weight of his body propelled the cart a distance of three yards on its crazy wheels, with the shafts scraping along the ground. He struggled to his feet and was about to rush away again, when a human voice, coming from beneath him, made him stand still. He looked down fiercely. It was only some homeless derelict, who used the archway and the cart as a house and a bed.

'The curse of —' began a cracked, shivering voice.

Gypo was gone, with a clatter of boots, over the cobblestones of the archway. He debouched into a wide street of new red-brick houses. He gripped a wall and peered around him, panting for breath, wild with the excitement of his escape.

It was then that he noticed the wind, the lifting clouds, and the far-away sky. He smelt the wind as he breathed in great gasps through his nostrils, to ease the pressure on his heart and lungs. Then suddenly, he longed for the mountains and the wide undulating plains and the rocky passes and the swift-flowing rivers, away to the south in his own country. Freedom and solitude and quiet, with only the wind coming through the bog heather! Hiding in some rocky fastness of the mountains, listening to the wind! Away, away, where nobody could catch him! To the mountains! To the mountains! Dark blue mountains with bulging sides and little sheep roaming over them, that he could catch and kill!

A wild ferocity of joy overcame him. He stared with dilated nostrils ahead into the rim of the sky above the houses, towards the south. He gazed, as if he were measuring the distance between him and the mountains, so as to take a giant leap, that would carry him at once into the heart of their solitude.

Then he bent down, looking ahead intently. He spat on his hands. He put his hand to his head to settle his hat. But his hat was not there. His skull was bare and damp. He felt all over it and found a patch of clotted blood at the rear base, where it had been kicked during the struggle in the inquiry room. He took no notice of the blood, but kept feeling all over the skull, with a dazed look in his eyes, muttering:

'What am I to do without a hat? I had it this two years.'

In the same dazed way he felt all over his body. He uttered a little shout. He had found it in his trousers pocket, where he had stuffed it, during the inquiry, when he heard that ominous ring in Gallagher's voice. He clapped it on to his skull, all wrinkled and tattered and tiny. He beat it with his palms, as if it were a mattress. Then, with a gentle sigh, he darted away, headed due south for the mountains.

He ran recklessly, without thinking of the way, or taking any precautions. It was the slum district which he knew so well, the district that enclosed Titt Street, the brothels, the Bogey Hole, tenement houses, churches, pawnshops, public-houses, ruins, filth, crime, beautiful women, resplendent idealism in damp cellars, saints starving in garrets, the most lurid examples of debauchery and vice, all living thigh to thigh, breast to breast, in that foetid morass on the north bank of the Liffey. He ran through narrow streets and great, wide, yawning streets, lanes and archways, streets patched and buttressed, with banks of earth from fallen houses almost damming them in places, pavements strewn with offal, soddened by the rain.

He never made a mistake. He was headed for the mountains. The smell of the mountains was in his nostrils, flooding his lungs, making his heart pant with longing.

At last he entered Beresford Place and saw the river. Instinctively he paused, leaning against a wall, to examine the Bridge. He gasped and trembled.

Two men were standing at the near side of the Butt Bridge. They had already forestalled him. He listened. He toyed with a last hope. He moved cautiously across the open space, to reach the shelter of the ruins of the Custom House. He reached it. He peered closer at the men. They were still indistinct. After all, they might be robbers, workmen, homeless fellows trying to pass the night, students coming from the brothels and having a last drunken argument on their way home. He crawled nearer. Then his little eyes blinked and narrowed.

One of the men crouched against the biting wind. Gypo recognised the crouching figure silhouetted against the sky. It was Mulholland. And the other man, standing stiff, with his hands in his pockets, was Peter Hackett.

Gypo's head became hot and stuffy. His eyes closed, as a sudden pain struck him in the forehead. He had an impulse to rush forward at the two men and strangle them. But he did not move. He was not afraid of the two of them, in spite of their being armed. He did not fear their guns. But they were part of the Organisation. The Organisation was at the Bridge. It had got there before him. He could not pass. Gallagher's cold, glassy eyes were on the Bridge. He could not pass.

The smell of the mountains left his lungs and his nostrils. The wind still blew about his crouching body. But it had lost its odour. Now it was only sharp and biting, an enemy that drove him backwards, skulking and dumbfounded. Where was it driving him? Where was it driving him?

He crouched away before it, without taking counsel with himself, with his head hanging limply on his breast. He crouched across the open space and entered a roadway that led northwards. There was nothing within him with which he could take counsel. Within him he was blank and dark, like a bottomless abyss filled with thick fog. His hulking figure was driven by the wind to some boundless region where there was no shelter. He was driven by the wind to some boundless region where everything was coloured a dim grey, amorphous, terrible.

The vision of an abyss, grey, without shape, swayed before his eyes as he strode northwards, moving un-certainly, staggering slightly, without guidance. His footsteps became slower. He came to a halt and looked about him curiously. He was under a railway bridge that crossed the street sideways over his head, encased in a black covering. A little dark laneway opened to his right. He walked three paces up the laneway and leaned his shoulder against the damp wall.

There was shelter there. The wind did not come in. Only an odd gust swivelled around the corner and stirred the damp, musty air for a dying moment. It was quiet and dark, like the interior of a cave. He sighed.

Gradually he grew composed. He grew calm and very weary. He wanted to lie down and go to sleep for a long, long time. There was no use struggling any farther. He was alone. The darkness of the night enveloped him.

'There's nobody here,' he murmured aloud.

The ground was a puddle. The walls were blank. He felt with his feet, seeking a dry spot to lie down. Everywhere his boot sank into a puddle. He cursed and moved on a pace. He felt again with his feet. Still more puddles. He moved along still farther and tried again. No use. Then he began to walk along mechanically, feeling the ground at intervals. Then he kept walking slowly without feeling the ground. He had forgotten about lying down.

He came to the end of the lane and saw a wide street in front of him. He halted excitedly.

'Where am I going?' he cried aloud.

He started at the sound of his voice and peered suspiciously over his shoulder. Of course there was nobody there. Then he steadied himself and tried to think of where he was and what had happened. It was a terrific struggle.

Slowly he began to remember recent events. Fact after fact came prowling into his brain. Soon the whole series of events stood piled there in a crazy heap. Everything rushed towards that heap with increasing rapidity, but nothing could be abstracted from it. It was just as if the facts were sinking in a puddle and disappearing. It was utterly impossible for him to reason out a plan of action.

'I must make a plan,' he murmured aloud.

In answer to this exhortation came a vision of Gallagher's glittering eyes. They fascinated him. He forgot about a plan. A horde of things crashed together in his brain, making an infernal buzz. He lost control of himself and ran about under the archway, striking out with his hands and feet madly, trying to fight the cargo of things that were jammed together in his brain. It was that insensate rage that overcomes strong men at times, when they have nothing upon which to vent their fury, no physical opponent.

He worked madly at this curious exercise for fully five minutes. Then he stopped, with perspiration streaming from his forehead. He felt better. His head was clear. He was again conscious of a grim determination to escape, to outwit those fellows who were on the Bridge. An idea that he thought amazingly cunning occurred to him, an idea to escape towards the south, by making a wide detour towards the north, up by the North Circular Road to Phoenix Park, then westwards through the Park, then southwards again by Dolphin's Barn. He was toying with the route pleasantly when he was suddenly interrupted by a sound of feet.

Trup, trap, trup, trap ... came the sound of heavy feet coming down the street in front of him. Two policemen on their beat were coming along slowly, rattling door-chains as they came. Gypo's heart began to beat with terror. He thought they were looking for him. In his bewilderment he could not understand that he was now under police protection, an informer. He forgot that he had only to rush up to them and say that the Revolutionary Organisation had condemned him to death and were now tracking him, in order to be taken to a police barracks, into safety. On the contrary, he still regarded them as his enemies. His mentality had not yet accustomed itself to the change that his going into the police-station that evening had wrought in his condition. To his understanding he was still a revolutionary. He was not at all conscious of being an informer, or a friend of law and order, a protégé of the police.

He bolted headlong out of the laneway and clattered away across the street. He wheeled to the right, ran ten yards and then dived into another lane. He continued his flight without stopping. He ran without purpose, without guidance, driven northwards by panic and the impossibility of thought. He ran headlong in all directions, into a street, down its course, then to the left, back again in a parallel line, down once more the street he had left, passing several times the same corner in his mad flight. He ran desperately, as if he were chasing some elusive sprite that delighted in turning on its own tracks. He floundered through pools. He struggled on his hands and knees over waste plots. He crushed violently through holes in torn walls. He climbed over piles of bricks, over walls, jumped into backyards and then climbed back again into another street. He was scratched, covered with mud, dripping wet. His eyes were bloodshot.

Then suddenly a clock struck the half-hour close by him. It was half-past four. He stopped dead, attracted by the tolling of the clock. It was not the sound but the remembrance it brought. He knew that clock. It was near Katie Fox's house where he used to sleep. He stood in the middle of a narrow lane, with his legs wide apart and his chest and shoulders thrust forward listening to it. His lips were opened wide.

He stood, like an uncouth, half-formed thing, alone in the half-grey shadows of the night, wondering at strange things.

'It's two turns from here,' he murmured, 'first to the left, then to the right. She should be in be now. That must be three or four o'clock.'

Now he moved carefully, listening for sounds and planting his feet lightly, close to the side of the lane. He turned to the left, went down fifty yards and then turned to the right. He entered a kind of circular square, a crescent, with a church standing in the middle. He moved around the crescent until he reached the other side of the church. There, at the corner of a little cul-de-sac, was the house in which Katie Fox had a room, about fifteen yards away from the church.

All the houses in the little square were tenement houses, old, dusty and grey, tattered, sordid, with broken panes in their windows. Nearly all the street doors were ajar. There was nothing to steal within.

Gypo deferentially tipped his hat to the church as he passed it. He entered the doorway of Katie Fox's house. The hallway was pitch black. He stood for a few moments peering around in the darkness.

Then he saw a night-light on the first landing. He recognised it as the light placed there every evening by Mrs Delaney, who had become a religious maniac since her son was killed in the revolution of 1916. He had been killed while he was running along the streets, wounded, crying out for shelter.

'If he ever comes home at night,' whispered Mrs Delaney confidentially to everybody, 'he'll see the light burnin' and' he'll know I'm in. God is good to His own people an' He'll look after me Johnny.'

Gypo felt comforted at seeing the night-light. He moved noiselessly up the stairs until he reached it. When he was passing it, rounding the angle of the stairs, he paused, with his hand on the wooden banister, and looked at it. For some reason or other, he tiptoed towards it, leaned out when he was within two feet of it, and blew it out. Then he started and looked about him wildly. It was pitch dark again.

'That's better,' he said with a little sigh.

He mounted the stairs steadily. They remained good until he reached the third floor. Then he had to move up a narrow, rickety, broken stairs to the top floor, where Katie Fox had a room. He made an awful noise, but it disturbed nobody. He heard a child crying when he got near the top of the stairs. The child belonged to Tim Flanagan, an unemployed man, who occupied the opposite room to Katie Fox on the top landing. He lived there with his wife and three children. The baby had the measles and the other two children were awake. One child was laughing. Gypo could distinguish Flanagan's weak, timorous voice, trying to soothe the children.

Gypo stood outside the door to the left, Katie Fox's door. He listened. A shaft of light streamed through the keyhole and through a large, round hole in the bottom of the door. A large piece of the door had been gnawed away by a stray dog that Katie Fox brought home one night. He bit his way out of the room as soon as he got a meal. Gypo listened. Katie Fox was talking within. Gypo knocked.

'Who's that?'

'It's only me, Katie. Open the door.'

'Mother o' Mercy,' she screeched, 'it's his ghost. It's his ghost, Louisa. Louisa, will ye hide me somewhere, for God's sake!'

'Ghost yer gran'mother,' came a cracked, old voice. 'Get up an' open the door, will ye, till we see what he wants.'

'No, no —' began Katie's voice again.

Gypo put his shoulder to the door, burst the piece of string that fastened it on the inside to a nail in the wall, and flung the door open wide. He stalked into the room.

At first the whole room appeared to be a blue bank of fog. Then the blue mist dissipated gradually. The room assumed proportions. Things swam out of the mist towards him gracefully, in the order of their importance. First came the lamp. It was placed on the black, wooden mantelpiece over the fireplace. It was an ordinary, tin, paraffin lamp, painted red. The chimney was three-parts black. Next came the fireplace. There was a huge, open grate, with a turf fire burning in it. The fire was more like the remains of a funeral pyre, because the ashes had accumulated for weeks. The flaming peat sods lay stretched like fallen logs on the top of the great pile of yellow ashes. Next came the bed, with Louisa Cummins lying in one corner of it.

The bed was so huge that it might be mistaken for anything, were it not supported by four thick, wooden posts and had a canopy over it, at the head, after the fashion of those beds that are called in Irish country places 'Archbishops' Beds'. The bed-clothes were indescribable. Everything was pitched on to the bed and everything stayed there. Louisa Cummins lived in the bed most of the day. She had done so for eight years, since she became 'bedridden' as the result of 'injuries' received from the police, one night she was arrested on a charge of trafficking in immorality. She was quite strong and healthy. She did all her work in bed. The blankets were gathered about her bulky person in the far corner, near the wall. In the other corner, Katie Fox's corner, there was a couple or so of tattered blankets. The foot of the bed was heaped with junk of all sorts, from a notched mug, out of which the old lady drank her tea, to a statue of Saint Joseph that hung on the bedpost, suspended from a thick nail by a rough, knotted cord. The cord was around the statue's neck, in a noose. The statue was not suspended there out of crude respect, as might be supposed. It was hung there as a blasphemous protest against the incompetence of the saint. Four years before she had made a Novena to Saint Joseph, requesting a cure for muscular rheumatism, and because her request was not granted she hung up the statue by the neck.

When Gypo's eyes found her through the fog, she was hidden to the chin beneath a pile of blankets and clothes of all sorts, up against the wall. She lay on her side, with her white, shrivelled head ensconced in a grey pillow, that had no case to cover it. The feathers protruded from the pillow. The old woman's white hair was strewn about the pillow and the bed-clothes, like strands of seaweed floating on the surface of a shallow sea at low tide. Her mouth was wide open, in an ogreish fashion, displaying red gums and four yellow teeth, cropping up at unequal distances along her jaws; four crooked, yellow fangs.

Her eyes alone showed life and intelligence. They were small, fierce, blue eyes, blazing with cunning and avarice.

Her body, hidden beneath the clothes, resembled a mountain that had been reduced to a shapeless pulp by concussion.

Gypo surveyed her without any emotion. Then he looked around for Katie. He saw her standing in the corner behind the door. She was still dressed as he had met her in the public-house early in the evening. But her dress had become dishevelled. Her face had changed. It had changed in a strange manner. It had lost the careworn, pinched expression. Her eyes were no longer tired. Her face was flushed and full. The skin was loose. The mouth was firm, with a voluptuous softness in the lips. Her eyes flashed bright. They had the calm aggressiveness of healthy, energetic women, who are passing from one success to another, the calm, aggressive flash of satisfied desire and of vaulting ambition. While, in spite of all that, her hands, clutching her throat, trembled in apparent terror, in contradiction to the repose and vitality of her face. Her feet, too, danced spasmodically.

'What's the matter with ye, Katie?' said Gypo. 'What's that ye were sayin' about me ghost?'

He spoke in a hoarse, morose whisper.

'God!' exclaimed Katie.

She took her hands away from her throat and clasped them behind her back, with the movement of one offered an objectionable thing. Then she fled to the fire at great speed. She leaned her back against the wall to the right of the fireplace and gaped at Gypo. She motioned to him with her head.

'Shut that door,' she said in a whisper. 'Shut the door and come in.'

Gypo turned to the door silently and began to tie the two pieces of broken string to fasten it once more. 'Where have ye ben?' she whispered. 'O Lord! Ye put the heart crosswise in me.'

Gypo tied the door and stalked slowly and quietly to the hearth. He stood still, glanced towards the old woman and then looked with open lips at Katie. 'They're after me, Katie,' he muttered with a shudder.

There was a silence. Gypo shuddered again and sat down in front of the fire. He sat on the floor, with his elbows resting on his knees, stretching out his hands to the blaze.

Katie looked at him with glittering eyes. She stood against the wall, motionless. Her face had become very white beneath her crumpled red hat. Her eyes glittered. Her upper lip was gathered together, frilled.

The old woman in the bed glanced from Gypo to Katie and from Katie to Gypo. Her eyes danced with merriment. She kept cuddling herself, as if in an ecstasy of enjoyment.

'What are ye talkin' about?' said Katie at length.

'Th' Organisation is after me,' he muttered without looking at her. 'Commandant Gallagher is goin' to plug me. I escaped outa the cell in the Bogey Hole.'

'What are they goin' to plug ye for? In the name o' goodness, what are they goin' to plug ye for?'

Katie Fox's voice was cold and passionless, but Gypo did not notice. She had a queer, thin smile on her lips, but Gypo did not look at her face. She had a flashing light in her eyes as she spoke, but Gypo had not seen it. He was staring dreamily into the fire. He was tired out and sleepy. There was no use keeping watch any longer. He was tired, tired, tired. Tired and sleepy. What was the use of keeping watch any longer? Sleep, sleep, sleep. Then he would go straight to the south. He would rush to the south with the wind, through all obstacles. Sleep, sleep, sleep.

'It's doesn't matter what they're after me for,' he muttered.

There was another silence.

Sleep, sleep, sleep.

'They want to get me outa their way,' he mumbled again. 'But they're not goin' to get me. Katie, I'm goin' to flop here for the night. I'll stay till tomorrow night. Then I'll going south. Here's all the money I have.'

He rummaged in his trousers pocket and brought out on his palm four shillings and sixpence. He handed it to her. She approached and held out her right hand for it, with a mincing movement.

'Gimme that money. Gimme that money,' screamed the old woman from the bed. She struggled to sit up.

'You shut up, Louisa,' growled Gypo, half turning towards her across his shoulder. 'Shut up or I'll flatten ye.'

The old woman collapsed, grinning. Then she caught

up a stick that lay beside her in the bed. She shook the stick at Katie Fox.

'She robs me, she robs me,' she wailed, in a thin, cracked voice.

'I'll sleep here on the floor, Katie,' said Gypo. 'Hey, Katie. I'll sleep here in front o' the fire. Katie, what's the matter with ye? Why don't ye talk to me?'

Katie burst into laughter. She had sat down on a low stool to the left of the fire on receiving the money. Now she jumped to her feet and laughed. It was a queer, dry laugh. There was a dreamy look in her eyes. She looked at the floor, wrapped in thought.

'Are ye drunk or what's the matter with ye?' grumbled Gypo.

There's nothin' at all the matter with me,' murmured Katie dreamily, still looking at the floor.

Then she drew in a deep breath and shrugged herself. She became alive and energetic again, wide awake, with piercing eyes. She began to talk at an amazing speed, with her arms crossed on her breasts.

'Sure, Gypo,' she said in a loud, hilarious voice, 'ye can sleep here till the crack o' doom if ye like. Sure enough, Connemara Maggie tole me about Bartly Mulholland comin' lookin' for ye. She came into Biddy Burke's as drunk as a lord, an' she outs with a yarn about Bartly puttin' a gun to ye' head an' drivin' ye up the street in front o' him.'

'Yer a liar, she didn't,' growled Gypo, starting slightly.

'Maybe she didn't say that exactly,' continued Katie, 'but —'

'Did she give ye a quid I gave her to give ye?'

'A quid? Did ye give her a quid for me? Well, of all the

liars! Well, of all the robbers! Of all the dirty sons of pock-faced tailors! She takes the cooked biscuit. Troth then, she only gev me ten bob an' I had to fight her for that. O' course I'm sayin' nothin' about things I might say a lot about, but —'

'Oh! Less o' yer gab,' growled Gypo feeling behind him on the floor with his hand. 'I'm not in humour for yer gab, Katie.'

'Don't lie on the floor,' she cried solicitously. 'Get into the bed. Lie in my corner. Don't mind, Louisa. The corner is mine. I can let who I like int' it. Louisa, if ye don't lie still I'll lave ye for dead as sure as Our Lord was crucified. So I will. Well, what could ye expect? An' I'm sayin' nothin' now, Gypo, seein' the position yer in, but it's the price o' ye all the same. I hope ye don't mind me speakin' me mind out. It's the price o' ye for lavin' them that were kind to ye, an' throwin' yer money away on a strap like that. But sure me poor mother used to say, Lord have mercy on her —'

'Get outa here, get outa here,' screamed the old woman, waving her stick.

Gypo had thrown himself on the bed on his back. The old lady began to beat him feebly about the body with her stick. He took no notice of her. He fumbled with the heap of tattered blankets, arranging them about his legs.

Katie Fox caught up the tongs and approached the bed sideways, making furtive signs to the old woman, urging her secretly to keep quiet.

The old woman subsided, muttering something. Katie went back to the fire and put down the tongs. She continued to talk. She was rapidly becoming more excited. Her eyes now had a look of insanity in them. Her lips were constantly becoming wreathed with smiles, after the manner of a lunatic who is thinking of some demoniac buffoonery in his muddled brain.

'Though few people know it,' she cried arrogantly, looking at the door, while she put a cigarette in her mouth, 'me poor mother was a born lady. Put that in yer pipe, Louisa Cummins, and try an' smoke it. Yev given me dog's abuse since I came into yer rotten pigsty of a room, but still an' all ye know yer not fit to wipe me shoes. So I don't give a damn.'

'Yerra, d'ye hear her, d'ye hear her?' croaked Louisa Cummins.

She began to laugh, making a noise in her throat like a hen, that quaint, cunning, querulous sound that a hen makes at night when disturbed during her roosting hours.

Gypo had arranged the clothes to his satisfaction. The blankets covered his body up to his chest. His eyes began to close. His little, round hat still remained on his head, crushed down over his forehead. There was a continual murmur in his brain. The sounds, the talk, the smells about him no longer had any meaning.

Sleep, sleep, sleep.

Danger, fear, everything was forgotten but his desire to sleep.

Sleep, sleep, sleep.

'Yerrah, is it an informer I'm lyin' beside?' screamed the old woman again, trying to rise with fury. 'Get out, get out. There's blood on yer hands. There's —'

'Lie down or I'll brain ye,' hissed Katie, rushing once more to the bed.

Chapter Sixteen

With a weary sigh Gypo stretched out his left hand and dropped it across the body of the old woman. She subsided under the weight of the massive hand. It lay across her, relaxed and tired. She peered at it curiously, around the edge of her blankets. Maybe she peered at it in terror. Who knows what emotions were concealed behind that hideous skull?

Gypo did not look at her. His eyes were almost closed. His nostrils were expanding and contracting noiselessly.

Sleep, sleep, sleep.

Then a mad rush to the mountains.

Sleep, sleep, sleep.

'Blast it for a story,' cried Katie Fox, stamping on the floor.

She walked to the middle of the floor. Then she folded her arms and stood with her legs wide apart and her chest thrown out, gazing at the dim wall with glittering eyes. She threw back her head and laughed.

'Amn't I the fool?' she cried. 'Oh! Amn't I the fool? Me that could walk with the finest men in the land! Do ye know that me gran'father was the Duke o' Clonliffey? Do ye know that? An' me mother was related to royalty on her father's side. Not to the King of England either, but to me bould King o' Spain, where they grow the oranges an' ye can drink wine out of a well like water from the Shannon. Sure it's there where I was born an' reared, in a palace as big as the County Waterford, with archbishops waitin' at table on me, with red napkins on their arms, an' a rale lady —'

'Yerrah, will ye hould yer whist,' piped the old woman.

She tried to brandish her stick and to disengage herself from the hand that lay on top of her. But the hand stiffened for a moment. She was pressed down beneath it. Then the hand relaxed again.

Sleep, sleep, sleep.

Gypo's eyes opened wide for a moment. Then he closed them. Everything in his mind became a blur. Nightmares stood massed in his brain ready to rush in on the platform of his sleeping mind and carry on their mad acting, as soon as his being soared off, bound in sleep. He had already surrendered to these nightmares.

Sleep, sleep, sleep.

Katie Fox looked at him cunningly for a moment. Her face hardened and her eyes narrowed to points. Then she glanced away again, towards the wall. Her lower lip dropped. Her eyes distended. She puffed twice at her cigarette. She began to talk again.

'I could tell ye stories about them all, Gypo,' she cried, waving her arm wildly in Gypo's direction. 'I could tell ye, so I could, but what's the use of tellin'? Wha'? What's the use of anythin'? An' Fr Conroy refused to give me absolution. Well, he can go to hell. I can get along without his absolution. I'm not afraid o' hell. Oh, Mother o' Mercy!' she cried, suddenly crossing herself; 'what have I said? What —'

'Ha! Cross yersel', cross yersel',' croaked Louisa Cummins. 'But it's no good to ye. Down ye'll go. Down ye'll go. Ha, ha, ha!'

'There's a curse on me family, Louisa, since me second cousin the Duchess of … of … of … where is that place she was Duchess of? … I forget it, although I was there often with me mother. It's somewhere out be Killiney. Well, she put a curse on me family, anyway. She used to have thirteen monkeys sittin' at the breakfast table with her.'

'Yer a liar, yer a liar,' cried the old woman in a sudden fury. 'She couldn't have thirteen monkeys. She couldn't have thirteen. It's them drugs yer takin' that's gone to yer head. Thirteen! Foo!'

Gypo mumbled something in a tremendous whisper. Both women looked at him. His lips were moving, but the words were unintelligible. His massive chest heaved up to an enormous extent and collapsed again slowly, with a great outrush of breath from the nostrils. His tawny face stood out impassively in the glimmer of the firelight. It looked sorrowful and oppressed.

Sleep, sleep, sleep.

He was wafted away by heavy gusts of sleep, to the thunderous music of fantastic nightmares. Primeval memories assumed form in the clouds of sleep that pressed down about him. They assumed form and shape, the shape of the beings that pursued him.

Sleep, sleep, sleep.

His strength was becoming unbound, dissolved in sleep, loosened out and swaying limply on vapours of sleep.

Sleep, sleep, sleep.

'D'ye know what I'm goin' to tell ye, Louisa,' continued Katie in a low, hushed voice. 'When I'm dead they're goin' to canonise me. Then I'll have a Holy Well out on the Malahide Road, an' I'll put a spell on everybody I don't like, an' make them get up in the middle o' the night, an' walk out barefoot to the well, to drink three cupfuls o' the Holy Water. An' never knowin' that I'll have it poisoned. This is a queer world, Louisa, an' ye'll soon be out of it, 'cos yer —'

'Sorra a fear o' me,' croaked the old woman. 'I'll dance on yer grave. Ye little rip o' divilment. Yer not the first nor the fifth that has come into me house this ten years an' gone the same road. No, yer not. An' ye won't be the last. Oho! Ye all got pretty faces. Ye all get the fine strong men to kiss ye. But old, dirty-faced Louisa Cummins 'll dance on yer graves. She dances on yer graves. So she does. Now what are ye doin' with him? Are ye puttin' yer evil spell on him? Informer an' all that he is, I'll not let ye put yer evil spell on him. I'll not let ye do that. Go away from the bed.'

Katie had come to the bed and had bent down with her left ear to Gypo's face, listening to his breathing. She raised her face to look at the old woman.

'He's dead asleep,' she whispered with a smile.

'Well? Is that queer?'

'Don't wake him while I'm gone, Louisa.'

'Where are ye goin'?'

'Mind yer own business, Louisa. I'm givin' ye warnin'.'

'Is it to the polis yer goin'?'

'Don't talk so loud. It's not to the polis I'm goin'. I'm just goin' out.'

'Ha! Yer goin' to inform on him, ye rip o' divilment. Yer goin' to inform on him.'

'It's nothin' o' the kind. Isn't he an informer? Don't make a noise. Don't waken him or they'll fill ye full o' lead when they come. I'm givin' ye this warnin'. Shut up.'

She moved backwards to the door, with her hand held out threateningly towards the old woman. The old woman looked after her. Her mouth was wide open. Her eyes roamed about. Then Katie disappeared out the door. Her shoes went tapping down the stairs. The banisters creaked. The room was still, except for Gypo's heavy breathing.

The old woman remained motionless for several seconds, looking towards the door. Then she groped for her stick and tried to rouse Gypo with it. But Gypo's arm still lay across her body holding it down. In his sleep it stiffened and held her down. She peered at it and frowned. She dropped the stick and smiled.

'Ha!' she gurgled, 'she's gone to inform on ye, me fine boyo. They'll soon be here after ye. Trust a woman, trust a devil. She'll be the ruin o' ye, me bould warrior. An' many's the fine strappin' woman from yer own county would give her two eyes for a night with ye. An' here ye lie, asleep an' weak, with the weariness o' death on ye. Ha! The divil mend the lot o' ye. Ha! There ye are now. Ha! There ye are now, an' be damned to ye. Ha! Ha!'

Sleep, sleep, sleep.

Sleep and strange dreams.

CHAPTER SEVENTEEN

At sixteen minutes to six, Mulholland rushed down the stairs into the Bogey Hole, shouting in a hushed whisper all the way:

'Commandant, Commandant, we have him, we have him!'

Gallagher rushed to the stairway. He found Mulholland grasping the wall with one hand, with his cap in the other hand, panting, with perspiration rolling down his cheeks in drops.

'It was Katie Fox,' he gasped. 'She came runnin' down Mount William Road: Charlie Carrol headed her off. She tole him Gypo was up in her room, in bed. No. 61 Mount William Crescent. Captain Burton has got the house surrounded. He sent me up for orders.'

'Katie Fox?' said Gallagher. 'I thought she was —'

'She's mad with dope.'

'I see. Double back and tell Burton I'll be down immediately. Don't move 'till I arrive.'

'All right, Commandant.'

Mulholland raced up the stairs again. Gallagher rushed back to the witnesses' room. Mary McPhillip had fallen into a doze. He roused her.

'Come on, Mary,' he whispered. 'We are going now. We found him.'

'Who? What? Jesus, Mary and Joseph! Who did you find?'

'The informer. Gypo Nolan. We found him at 61 Mount William Crescent. I am going there now. Come along. Then I'll leave you home.'

She was waking up gradually, frightened and rubbing her eyes. Gallagher fidgeted excitedly, trying to get her to her feet.

'What time is it?' she asked.

'A quarter to six.'

'Heavens above! Mother will be gone to Mass before I get home.'

'What does it matter?'

'Of course it matters. I was to have gone with her this morning. For Frankie.'

'Where does she go to Mass?'

'Mount William Crescent.'

'Well, we're going there too. You can go into the chapel and meet her there.'

'Why? What's at Mount William Crescent?'

She was fully awake now and had got to her feet, wild-eyed.

Gallagher got angry and swore. He stamped his feet.

'Come on quickly. I have no time. I tell you the informer has been found. He is at Mount William Crescent. I'm going down there. Come along.'

'You're going to murder him,' she gasped, with her bosom heaving.

'Murder be damned!' cried Gallagher. 'We're going to wipe him out.'

'You're a beast. You're not going to murder him, not while I can prevent it.'

She rushed from the room. With a fierce oath he rushed after her. He caught her at the foot of the stairs. The sentries rushed up. She kept screaming and striking out with her clawing hands.

'Keep her here,' he hissed. 'Don't let her out on any account for an hour. Then let her off and get home. Goodbye.' He looked fiercely into Mary's eyes. His face was ashen with rage. 'We spare neither man nor woman. Remember that.'

Then he rushed up the stairs.

'Murderer, murderer,' she cried after him, until they stuffed her mouth.

CHAPTER EIGHTEEN

Shapeless figures dancing on tremendous stilts, on the brink of an abyss, to the sound of rocks being tumbled about below, in the darkness, everything immense and dark and resounding, everything without shape or meaning, gloom and preponderance, yawning, yawning abysses full of frozen fog, cliffs gliding away when touched, leaving no foundation, an endless wandering through space, through screeching winds and ... crash.

Gypo awoke with a snort, perspiring with his nightmare, terrified.

The old woman had at last awakened him by squeezing his nostrils between his fingers. He sat up, looked about him and saw her. He saw her weird and pale, with her white hair streaming. He was going to strike her in terror, thinking her an ogre from his dreams, when she spoke.

'They're after ye,' she hissed. 'They're after ye. They're on the stairs.'

He listened. There was nothing. Not a sound. What? Just a whistle of the wind on the roof. Ha! Something creaked. Was it the bed? No. Trup, trip, r-r-rip. Somebody had slipped on the roof.

Gypo bounded from the bed to the floor in one leap. He stood motionless, crouching forward, panting, with dilated nostrils. A sound came on the stairs outside the door. Somebody on the stairs said: 'Hist!' Then utter silence. Gypo stood transfixed, still wet with the perspiration of his nightmare.

Then he moved noiselessly to the fireplace and picked up the tongs. It slipped from his fingers as he rose and rattled to the stone hearth. He whirled about to the door with an oath. Simultaneously the door was flung wide with a bang. Three flashes of light came before his eyes from the doorway. As he rushed headlong towards them there was a deafening roar. Three men had fired together at him. Then there was chaos.

As he dashed across the floor to the landing, he felt a sting like frost-bite in his thigh. Then he saw their terror-stricken, mad faces. He recognised two of them, Mulholland and Hackett. The third man was Curley. When he closed with them and felt his giant hands on the soft warm flesh of their bodies he breathed a sigh of satisfaction.

Somebody fired again, unintentionally, in the struggling mass on the landing. It must have been Curley. For his thin voice screamed querulously after the explosion, 'God have Mercy on my soul!' Gypo smelt burning under his armpit as his head was bent down to mobilise his spine strength.

Then the banister gave way with a crash of breaking wood. The four men went down without a cry. Their fists thudded with dull sounds as they struck blindly at one another in the dark.

They fell on the next landing. Gypo and Mulholland were on top. Mulholland had his right knee on Curley's back. He was cool with the mania of death-terror. He bared his teeth and raised his pistol to fire in Gypo's open mouth. But Gypo rammed him with his monstrous head.

Mulholland was hurled backwards like a gymnast, head over heels, heels over head. He brought up on a black sheepskin carpet outside a tenement door in the far corner. He lay with his knees to his chin, perfectly quiet. The pistol-shot splashed through the whitewashed woodwork of the ceiling. The pistol jingled to the floor.

Gypo scraped around on his hands and knees in the darkness. He groped for the two men who lay beneath him. He felt their rumps, their backs, their thighs, in a wide sweep of his hands. Their bodies were lax and soft, like the carcasses of dead things. One of them sighed and turned over. Gypo rose to his feet. Without looking anywhere he rushed for the stairs and leaped down.

Half-way down the last flight he paused and tried to think. But he drew his hand over his eyes and shook his head.

'It's no use. It's no use,' he said aloud.

There was a great din of disturbed people in the house above him.

He reached the hallway. Through the open door he could see the street outside. The dawn had come. The air was grey, cold, empty and silent. He marched steadily to the door. His body was very cold. And his mind was dead. Cold and dead. Dead and cold.

A stream of red blood trickled down over his right boot from the wound in his thigh. Another stream trickled along his right ribs. He did not know. He was cold and dead. Dead and very cold.

He stopped in the doorway. His eyes expanded. A last passion made his body rigid. He roared. He had seen Gallagher standing against the church railings across the road, with his hands in his raincoat pockets, smiling insolently.

Gypo descended the five steps to the street at one bound. Then as his right foot landed on the pavement there was a rapid succession of shots. They came from all sides. Three of them entered his body. Without bringing his left foot to the pavement he jumped again into the air, with his two hands reaching out and his face turned upwards, in the earnest attitude of a symbolic dancer.

He hurtled out into the street, hopping on staggering feet, writhing and contorting. Then he fell to his knees. He groaned and fell prone.

He struggled up again, looking wildly around him, holding his bowels with his hands. Gallagher was there in front of him, smiling dreamily now, with distant, melancholy eyes.

Gallagher shrugged himself and turned away sharply to the right.

Gypo wanted to go after him. But he no longer knew why he wanted to go after him. His eyes were getting dim. His body was cold. Cold and dead.

Grinding his teeth, he got to his feet. He threw out his chest, shrugged his shoulders and walked ahead like a drunken man. He walked slowly straight ahead, straight, stiff, swinging his limp hands slowly.

He walked through the iron gateway of the church, along the concrete path to the door. He had to crawl up the steps on his knees. Blood was coming up his throat.

Reverently he dipped his hand into the holy water font. He wet his hand to the wrist. He tried to take off his hat in order to cross himself. His hand pawed about his skull, but his fingers were already dead. They could not grip the tattered hat. He tried to cross himself. Impossible. His hand could not reach his forehead. It went up half-way and then fell lifelessly. It was a ton weight. He strode to the left. He staggered through a narrow Roman door. He was in the church.

It was a great high room, curtained with silence. At the altar, away in the lamp-lit dimness of the dawn, a priest was saying Mass. The droning sound of the words came down the silent church, peaceful, laden with the quaint odour of mystery, the mysterious calm of souls groping after infinite things. All round the church the people knelt with bent heads and faces wrapped in prayer for infinite things. Sad, haggard, hungry faces wrapped in the contemplation of infinity, wafted out of the sordidness of their lives by the contemplation of infinite things.

Peace and silence and the quaint odour of mystery and of infinite things.

Deep, long, soft words murmured endlessly in a silent place. Mystery and the phantoms of death breathing faint breaths.

Mercy and pity. Pity and peace. Pity and mercy and

peace, three eternal gems in the tabernacle of life, burnished ceaselessly with human dust.

From dust to dust.

Gypo's eyes roamed around the church. His eyes were very dim. There was a blur before them. He thought he saw somebody whom he knew. He was not sure. Yes. They were looking at him. There, on the left, on the other side of the aisle. It was a long way off. What? Frankie McPhillip's mother!

He set out, with a great sigh, towards her. He fell in a heap in front of her seat. He raised his head to her face. He saw her face, a great, white, sad face, with tears running down the fat cheeks. He struggled to his knees in the aisle before her. People were rushing to him talking. He waved his hands to keep them away. It was very dark. He swallowed the blood in his mouth and he cried out in a thick whisper:

'Mrs McPhillip, 'twas I informed on yer son Frankie. Forgive me. I'm dyin'.'

'I forgive ye,' she sighed in a sad, soft whisper. 'Ye didn't know what ye were doin'.'

He shivered from head to foot and bowed his head.

He felt a great mad rush of blood to his head. A great joy filled him. He became conscious of infinite things.

Pity and mercy and peace and the phantoms of death breathing faint breaths. Mercy and pity and peace.

'Lemme go!' he cried, struggling to his feet.

He stood up straight, in all the majesty of his giant stature, towering over all, erect and majestic, with his limbs like pillars, looking towards the altar.

He cried out in a loud voice:

'Frankie, yer mother has forgiven me.'

Then with a gurgling sound he fell forward on his face. His hat rolled off. Blood gushed from his mouth. He stretched out his limbs in the shape of a cross. He shivered and lay still.

BY THE SAME AUTHOR

Mr. Gilhooley

'Mr. Laurence Gilhooley emerged from The Bailey
restaurant in Duke Street, Dublin. He was slightly drunk,
having eaten a heavy dinner and finished two bottles of
red wine. He stood in front of the door, swaying gently.
His eyes were half closed. His head was thrust
backwards. He looked from side to side, wondering
whither he was going to turn for his night's amusement.'

'*Mr Gilhooley* reads like a Dickens novel written by Sartre.'
Fintan O'Toole

Forty-nine-year-old Mr Gilhooley is living two lives:
the one drinking in the pubs of Dublin, the other
desperate and lonely, longing for love. A chance
encounter with the innocent yet destructive Nelly starts a
chain of compelling, dark and menacing events.

This is the underworld of 1920s Dublin.
Death, violence, sex, religion and love intertwine
in this visually rich and passionate tragi-comedy.

ISBN 0-86327-641-5

A Tourist's Guide to Ireland

From Ireland's master storyteller comes what appears to be a simple tourist guide; but underneath this harmless surface lies a scathing satire on Irish society. No aspect of newly-independent Ireland is safe from his attack.

The Civil War was absurd and futile; the attempt to revive the Irish language is a political gimmick; the politicians, more concerned with Ireland's soul than with its body, are on the verge of turning the country into a 'clerical kingdom'; the priests, concerned only with power, use religion to enslave the people and oppose any writing that questions their blinkered beliefs; and the peasants, Ireland's only hope, must rid themselves of these parasites before they can become 'civilised citizens'.

A vivid, controversial insight into life
in the Ireland of the 1930s — as powerful
and challenging today as it was sixty years ago.

ISBN 0-86327-589-3

Famine

'The author's skill as a storyteller is at times breathtaking.
This is a most rewarding novel.'
Publishers Weekly

Set in the period of the Great Famine of the 1840s,
Famine is the story of three generations
of the Kilmartin family.
It is a masterly historical novel,
rich in language, character and plot,
a panoramic story of passion, tragedy and resilience.

'O'Flaherty is the most heroic of Irish novelists, the one
who has always tackled big themes, and in one case, in
this great novel, succeeded in writing something
imperishable ... Mary Kilmartin has been singled out by
two generations of critics as one of the great creations of
modern literature. And so she is.'
John Broderick, **Irish Times**

'I gladly accept one of the claims on the dustjacket of this
novel: "A major achievement — a masterpiece" ...
It is the kind of truth only a major writer of fiction
is capable of portraying.'
Anthony Burgess, **Irish Press**

ISBN 0-86327-043-3

Short Stories
The Pedlar's Revenge

'The finest Irish writer of his generation.'
John Banville, **Irish Times**

'This collection is a gallery of human emotions,
embracing a clutch of huge eccentrics, sweet and sour
remembrances of distant youth and vivid portraits of
rural Ireland ...
A worthy representation of an unflinching lyric writer.'
The Sunday Times

'This valuable collection displays O'Flaherty's amazing
range, from a love idyll between a wild drake and a
domestic duck to the unspeakable comedy of the
appalling Patsa delivering the contents of his golden belly
under the influence of a cataclysmic purge, from the
burning of young love in that splendid story "The Caress"
to the rheumy old man sitting by the roadside and failing
to recognise, in the old woman who pauses in passing,
the love of his youth.'
Benedict Kiely

ISBN 0-86327-536-2

All books available from:
WOLFHOUND PRESS
68 Mountjoy Square
Dublin 1
Tel: (+353 1) 874 0354   Fax: (+353 1) 872 0207